MADDY MADRIGAL MYSTERIES BOOK 5

TANGLED MAGIC

DEBRA CASTANEDA

SHADOW CANYON
press

ISBN: 979-8-9994829-5-2
Edited by: Lyndsey Smith, Horrorsmith Editing
Cover design by: Jacqueline Sweet

To the members of my family who lived in Chavez Ravine.

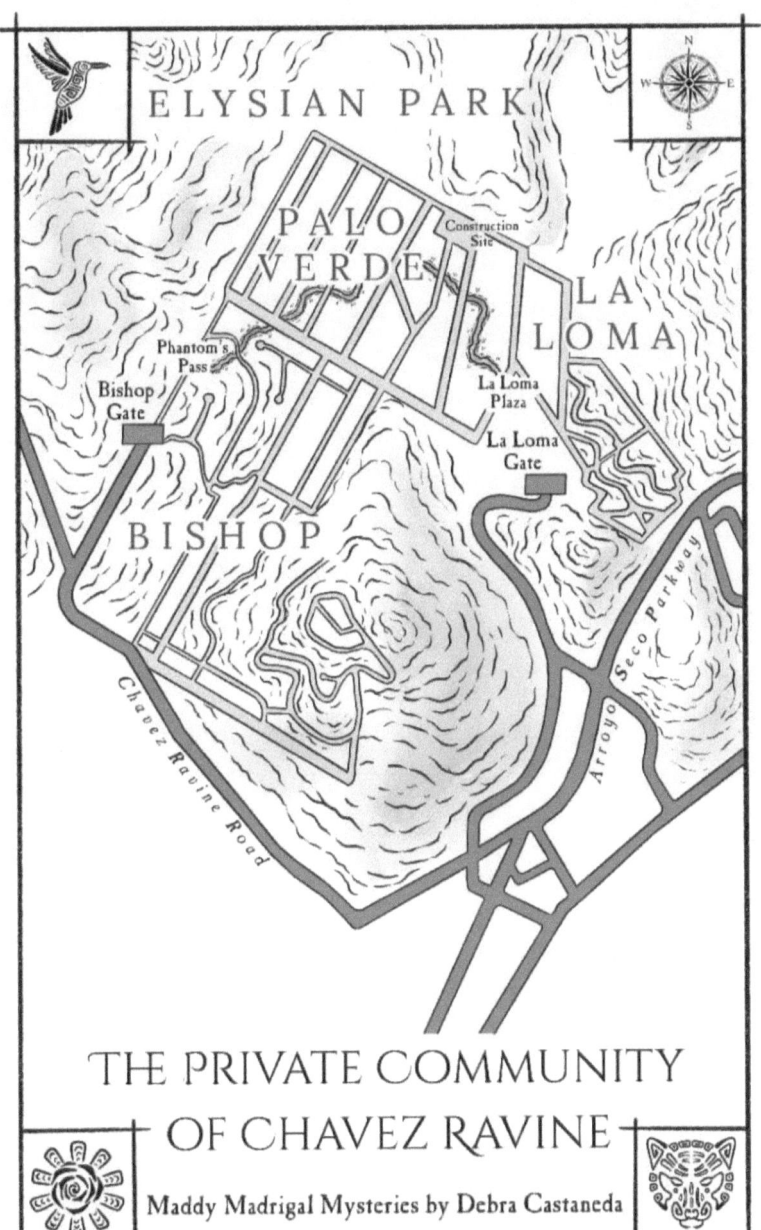

ELYSIAN PARK

PALO VERDE

Construction Site

LA LOMA

Phantom's Pass

Bishop Gate

La Loma Plaza

La Loma Gate

BISHOP

Arroyo Seco Parkway

Chavez Ravine Road

THE PRIVATE COMMUNITY
OF CHAVEZ RAVINE

Maddy Madrigal Mysteries by Debra Castaneda

Chapter 1

In the months I had been head of security for Chavez Ravine, I had seen some scary things. Chupacabras, for starters, along with murderous ghouls, giant vampire birds, and El Cucuy. But none of them compared with what greeted me Friday morning.

It was an email with the subject line "HOA Budget Meeting – Your Attendance is Required," and I knew exactly what that meant.

In the security business, peace had its price. When the Cucuy was lurking in the gully and giant birds were on the attack, our residents were willing to spend whatever it took to restore order. But after a few peaceful months, they had turned their attention to the monthly dues and were beginning to ask whether we still needed such a large security force.

I had assembled a team to protect the residents of our gated community, and they had done an incredible job. Cutting costs would only leave us vulnerable to the next supernatural assault, and besides, I had become quite attached to my group.

No one had said anything to my staff, but I could tell they were nervous. Each one was smart and had been around the block. They knew full security staffing was tough to defend when residents were grumbling about their HOA dues.

Of course, I had repeatedly made the argument to the board that anything could happen at any time, especially considering the unique history of Chavez Ravine. Even when they agreed—well, some of them agreed anyway—the board answered to the membership, and the membership wasn't happy about seeing a bigger number on their monthly statements.

If we did have to lay people off, they would land on their feet. LAPD's Occult Affairs Division had a turnover problem, and they would be thrilled to hire any of my folks. But then my team members would lose their housing in Chavez Ravine, and finding an entity-free place to live in Los Angeles was impossible. Especially on a crappy OA salary.

While I read the fateful email, my lungs seemed to shrink inside my ribcage, and my mind unleashed a stream of worst-case scenarios. How much staff could I lose? Who would I cut?

I had to burn off my nervous energy, so I grabbed a bucket, filled it with hot soapy water, and attacked the kitchen floor. My cat, Sam, lounged on the ottoman, watching with half-closed eyes. If I had started my cleaning frenzy in the sunroom, with its magical wooden workbench, he would have been right there beside me. But baseboards were unworthy of his feline attention.

It was Friday, and I had taken the day off. I planned to spend the morning reading a new British thriller outside on my patio, enjoying the rare cool weather that had settled over Los Angeles, but that email had made me too restless.

Stu, my "boyfriend"—which was a ridiculous term to use for a man closing in on fifty—and his teenage daughter, Clare, were coming over for dinner, so I decided I might as well burn off some energy. I went into my weight room—the guest bedroom—and did a thorough lifting session, focusing on my lower body and finishing off with a hundred kettlebell swings because I am crazy like that. Then I showered and got dressed to hit the grocery store.

Outside, I spotted my neighbor Leo heading to his car in a pinstriped suit, which suggested he was an attorney for the mob and not the prosecutor's office.

"I heard a rumor," he said in a sing-song voice over the begonias.

I tossed my tote into the passenger seat of my Jeep. The vehicle needed a wash, but grime had its uses, like camouflaging the rust spots along the wheel wells.

"Good morning to you too. What category of rumor are we talking about?"

Leo was in his forties, with black hair and a silver streak so perfect people thought it was fake. "It has to do with your mamacita."

I closed the passenger door and folded my arms across my chest. "What has she done now?"

"You don't know?" Leo raised his eyebrows. "You have to know. You're her only child."

I laughed. It sounded forced. "Seriously, it could be anything when your mother is Malena B. Can you be more specific?"

"It's kind of bad, actually. Just warning you." Leo grimaced. "Toby didn't want me to say anything."

I sighed. "I'm sure I'll find out anyway, so I might as well hear from you, especially if I'm gonna need legal advice."

"Personally, I think it's kind of funny." Leo grinned. "And it's going to be hilarious to see this play out. But some people are really freaking. Of course, *I'm* fine with it because we have the head of security living right next door and *you* wouldn't be okay with it if you were worried."

Ah. Got it. "Are you talking about my mom moving in with Hernan Frias and the rock she's wearing on her left hand?"

"Bingo! It was the talk at Muertos Café this morning. But some people are really pissed off. They say the famous *Entity*

3

Whisperer has no business living here, that she'll attract entities to Chavez Ravine and then there goes the neighborhood."

There had been a time I would have been worried about my mother attracting entities to Chavez Ravine, but that was before I cast a protection spell around the community. That spell had been tested, and while we had experienced a couple of supernatural breakthroughs, those invaders weren't entities. I was fairly confident my spell would keep us entity-free, despite my mother's tendency to draw them to her.

My gaze drifted beyond Leo, up the street to where Rory Tuck's McMansions loomed at the edge of Elysian Park. The developer would have a fit when he found out about my mother's new living arrangements. He was good at having fits. I would have to come up with a response that would calm him down when he called.

"There's something else," Leo added.

Oh, good. I was hoping for a little more drama on my day off. "What's that, Leo?"

Leo leaned in closer, the edge of his tie disappearing into the begonias. "I overheard some people talking at Muertos. They were collecting signatures for a petition to recall Hernan Frias from the board. Something about conflict of interest."

My relationship with my mother's fiancé had started off awkwardly. He had tried to stab me when I caught him conjuring creatures to terrorize residents of Chavez Ravine, but we had moved on from that unfortunate beginning. Though he sometimes annoyed me, I had come to appreciate the retired professor's knowledge of the supernatural and the area's history.

"They'd recall him for what, exactly?"

Leo flicked a small leaf from his tie. "In California, there doesn't have to be a specific reason. An association can hold a recall election with or without cause. But those people at Muertos had done their research because they were talking about breach of fiduciary duty, which is a fancy way of saying Hernan wasn't acting in the best interests of the community when he sneaked your mother into Bishop, knowing she might attract entities. And now who knows what will happen?"

I swallowed. "Do they have a case?"

"It's a recall, not a lawsuit. If they get enough signatures, they can do it, and then it'll come up for a membership vote."

It was a lot to take in. My mother had sold her house in Beverly Hills, and her furniture would arrive soon. There might not be anything anyone could do to force her out of Chavez Ravine, but losing his spot on the board would devastate Hernan. I also had a personal stake in having him there—I had found him to be persuadable on most important security issues.

"Any idea who's organizing the recall?" I asked.

Leo shook his head. "I don't know their names. Some older ladies, though. They might have been from Bishop?"

I could ask around, but I didn't want to stir the pot. Besides, I was head of security. If residents were pissed off enough to organize a recall, I couldn't stop them.

There *was* one thing I could do: warn Hernan to get ahead of this mess and inform the board about my mother before they received that recall petition.

But first, I had to go shopping.

At the market in Palo Verde, I ordered skirt steak and pork al pastor. Usually, I preferred to make my own marinades, but Jose was behind the butcher counter. He assured me he had used an authentic family recipe for the al pastor, so I decided to try it.

I was checking out when my phone chimed, alerting me to a new message in my work portal.

An item had been added to the agenda: "Pending Recall Notice of Board Member Hernan Frias."

I sighed. Too late.

Fun times.

Chapter 2

The groceries had just been unpacked when my phone rang. I dug my cell out of a deep pocket in my trench coat, fully expecting Hernan's name to be displayed on the screen.

But it wasn't Hernan calling to vent about the recall petition. It was Occult Affairs researcher Steve Zhou.

I accepted the call, my heart picking up its pace. "What's up?"

"There's something you need to see," Steve replied, his voice breathless.

"What is it? Where are you?"

"I'm in the gully between Palo Verde and Bishop. Can you meet me? It'll take too long to explain, and I want you to see it for yourself. See if I'm missing something."

I hung up, my stomach knotting. Steve rarely called me for help—usually, it was the other way around. He was awkward and could spend hours talking about entities, but he was brilliant. Occult Affairs' best researcher by far.

That was why he and I had a simple arrangement: Steve and his colleagues received unrestricted access to Chavez Ravine for their research, and I got a heads-up if they discovered anything unusual. Given all his expertise, Steve asking me for help was a bad sign.

"All right, I'll come find you. Are you still driving the same generic silver car?" I asked.

"No, I'm driving a Charger now." It was very un-Steve-like to drive a muscle car. He was too young for male menopause, so something odd must have been going on behind those glasses of his.

I quickly put the groceries away and traded my cute linen pants for a pair of worn jeans. No sense in ruining new clothes. From the Jeep's cargo area, I retrieved my hiking boots and laced them up. Ten minutes later, I pulled up at the far end of Palo Verde, where Steve was pacing next to his very red, very shiny car.

"Are you going to quit being all mysterious and tell me what's going on?" I asked, locking up my Jeep.

Steve pinched his lips together and made his way down the gully. I was wearing a sweatshirt, which was just thick enough to cut the chill in the air. If it got any cooler, I might have to bust out some jackets from the back of my spare closet. Some years, the fall and winter in Los Angeles barely reached sweater weather, so the brisk fifty-five degrees was glorious. Energizing.

I picked my way around rocks, brush, and scraggly scrub oaks, brushing up against a sage bush. Its soft, feathery leaves released a sweet, musty scent.

Steve had his hands stuffed in his pockets. Possibly not the best strategy for walking on uneven terrain. It made me nervous, watching him lurch his way down the rocky slope, but he was a grown man with health insurance, so I kept my mouth shut.

After a couple of minutes, he stopped and pointed. "There."

"There" was a hole in the ground, several feet across and surrounded by dirt, as if something had come out of it. A classic entity emergence point.

Shit.

I looked around, a little wildly, scanning the trees for something lurking in them. The gully offered plenty of hiding places, winding its way through Chavez Ravine up to the wild, overgrown area known as Phantom's Pass.

"Our heatmap didn't detect it. My phone would have gone off. Someone would have called me." What the hell had happened to my protection spell?

Steve rubbed the back of his neck. "Our heatmap didn't catch it either, according to Jo."

Jo being my friend and head of the command center at Occult Affairs.

"There's no sign of an entity. I looked," he continued, then resumed walking, gesturing for me to follow. We went another few yards, and he stopped again. "See under that tree behind that rock? There's another hole right there. And over there"—he paused long enough to swing around and point in the opposite direction—"we've got another one. It's more recent."

I squinted at the hole. "It's bigger than the normal entity hole, isn't it?"

"A *lot* bigger." Steve sighed. "About twice the usual size."

Intrigued, I stepped around a jagged boulder and lowered myself into a crouch. I leaned forward, narrowing my eyes to get a better look into the shadowy depths of the hole.

"Weird," I said.

"It is, right?" Steve sounded relieved.

Unlike the other Occult Affairs researchers, who had big egos, Steve could have done with a little more confidence. "What do you make of it?"

"I don't know."

That was what I liked about Steve. Any other Occult Affairs nerd would have made up some theory on the spot, then mansplained it to me for the next fifteen minutes.

Steve began pacing. "The obvious explanation is that whatever came out of it is large, maybe even super-sized, but if that was the case, even if it emerged hours ago, it would still be hanging around. Larger entities like trolls and ogres suffer from more severe disorientation. But there could be other reasons to explain the size of the hole. I just don't know what they are yet."

"Is it possible whatever made these holes is not an entity? Still a creature of some sort, but not, strictly speaking, an entity?"

Steve shuddered. "Like those vampire birds and that Cucuy monster? I wondered that too. I don't know, but I don't like it."

"We'll check the video feeds." I wasn't the least bit optimistic that the surveillance cameras had captured anything worthwhile. It was protocol for my staff to monitor our cameras in real time and review the recordings at the end of each shift. If anyone had seen anything unusual, I would have known.

"Jo's nervous," Steve said. "She asked if there was any way you could monitor this area to catch an emergence in real time. I told her I'd mention it. I agree…That would be very helpful."

Helpful…yes, but also a manpower challenge. Impossible if my budget got whacked. But maybe this was exactly what I needed.

I knew why Steve and Jo had been so worried, but I wanted to hear him say it out loud. "Why is Jo concerned?"

Steve's gaze flitted between the emergence holes. "Oh, come on. What else? Entities 2.0. If these are really entities—and it sure looks that way from these holes—they're not behaving the way we'd expect. Entities don't run and hide. Well, except for gnomes, but they're a little weird. And no entities evade heatmap detection. So, what else could these be?"

My legs were cramping, so I stood up. "Yeah, that's what I was afraid of. In that case, I'd guess these three headed up to Phantom's Pass. It's a straight shot up the gully and into the woodland. There are plenty of caves and ravines to hide in. Let me get a couple of my folks up there to take a look around."

I was already working out which of my team members would be best suited for a reconnaissance mission.

Steve nodded. "By the way, we've developed a new Smoke Bomb for larger, more aggressive entities. Your folks should have those. I'll ask Jo to send some. Just in case."

"Finally!" Occult Affairs officers had been asking for a stronger sedative to knock out bigger and meaner entities for just about forever. "Yeah, I'd really appreciate that."

Occult Affairs had spent years developing tools to contain the entities that began emerging after massive earthquakes created a passage between our world and theirs. One of the original OA researchers had been an anthropologist and a chemist. He invented the Smoke Bombs OA used every day to keep entities in check. The researcher had also speculated that the first round of entities would eventually be followed by a second wave of more complex, possibly more dangerous varieties.

It was suggested that these "Entity 2.0" creatures might be immune to Smoke Bombs. Of course, the researcher had no way to prove his theory, but a lot of people in OA were inclined to believe him.

He had died not long after coming up with his concept, but by then, his Entity 2.0 theory had taken on a life of its own. Even reasonable, smart people like Steve Zhou had bought into it.

It was anyone's guess what an Entity 2.0 might look like. For all we knew, they could be werewolves, leviathans, or weird skeletal angels. Unlike the normal, disoriented entities we had encountered, the 2.0 variety might pop out of emergence holes as alert as a soldier on patrol. They might be immune to Smoke Bombs and refuse to stay inside the entity preserve near Palm Springs. And then where would we be?

Starting all over again, facing a next-level nightmare.

Obviously, it didn't take much imagination to come up with a pretty dire scenario.

I didn't know if these holes were caused by Entities 2.0 or not, but one thing for certain: we were facing a new, unknown threat, and I would need every available body on it.

Chapter 3

Monday morning, in the Palo Verde Plaza parking lot, I watched while Hernan Frias struggled to park his car. He made one attempt after another to back into a spot.

"Why don't you just pull straight in?" I asked. "It's much easier."

Hernan finally succeeded, got out, and shook his keys in my direction. "If you hadn't been standing there, judging me and making me all nervous, I would have done it quicker."

I nearly made a crack about performance anxiety, but I decided against it. Instead, I patted his arm and said, "How you feeling about that recall?"

Hernan's bushy eyebrows shot up. "What kind of question is that? How do you *think* I'm feeling? There's nothing in the HOA disclosures or in the rules anywhere that prohibits Malena from moving into Chavez Ravine. Not a darn tootin' single word."

Hernan was the only person I knew who busted out old-timey phrases on a regular basis. "So, what are you going to do?"

He pointed his key fob at his car like he was setting off a bomb. "There's not a thing I *can* do. The board can't stop it, even if they wanted to. And I'm not sure they want to. Eileen Simpson has been making a real fuss about Malena moving in. Not that it's any of their business, mind you."

I noticed my reflection in the community center's glass doors when we approached. My lavender trench coat and navy pants looked professional enough, but I still second-guessed my choice. A bolder outfit might have projected more authority. After all, I was headed into battle to keep my security team intact.

"The rules may not say anything, but it's more of an optics thing, you know. Maybe you should have given the board a heads-up before the word got out."

"Baloney," Hernan said hotly. "It's better to ask for forgiveness than permission, which, I believe, has been your motto since you started working here." He paused. "Which reminds me. You're the one in the hot seat today. Eileen's been gunning to reduce the security staff. You don't have to worry about me—I'll support you. But you know Dan goes along with whatever Eileen wants. And I'm worried about Cora, truth be told. She's under a lot of pressure about the dues going up."

Before I could answer, Eileen Simpson went clicking past us on her high heels. Minutes later, all six of us had settled into the second-floor conference room, where autumn light filtered in through the high windows.

Dan Berman drummed his fingers on the table. "I'd like to propose we discuss the recall issue and other items first, before getting to the budget."

All eyes turned toward me. I shrugged.

Cora Bernal appeared a little surprised at my nonchalance. She hadn't expected me to show up looking so relaxed. If the meeting had taken place just a few days ago, I would have been a wreck, but my hike with Steven Zhou had strengthened my hand.

As I suspected, Eileen was eager to give Hernan a public spanking for his transgression, but beneath her outrage, I caught the slight tremor in her voice when she mentioned my mother's name.

"Hernan, you should be ashamed," Eileen said. "I know the board can't keep Malena B. out, but where she goes, entities follow. You said so yourself when we were interviewing Maddy! Her ability to attract entities was the entire premise of her last tour! She's on stage, then some newly emerged entities appear, and she has a chat with them. Aren't you in the least bit concerned about what that means for our community? After everything we've gone through, you've opened the door to who knows what!" Her voice was high and shrill.

Well, crap. Why hadn't I made the connection? Just Friday, Steve Zhou had shown me unusual entity emergence holes, and guess who was new to Chavez Ravine? My mother. Why hadn't I thought of that before?

Eileen would certainly put that together when I shared my news, but it was the only thing I had which might save my team.

I felt a flicker of sympathy for Hernan. He was going to be darn tootin' mad when he heard what I had to say. But at the moment, his anger was focused on Eileen.

"Since when does anyone in our community need to send out an alert that someone new is moving in? Who I choose to live with and who I choose to marry is no one's business!"

Cora and Charlie exchanged looks. Charlie, sitting next to Hernan, patted the older man on the back.

"This one's a little tricky, Hernan. Malena's not just *anyone*. She's a celebrity, and she poses a serious entity risk. But she's here now, and all we can and should do is offer you our congratulations." Charlie turned his deep-set eyes and jowly cheeks on Eileen and Dan.

Charlie was an easygoing guy, but when he talked, people listened.

Dan cleared his throat. The retired music executive wore a faded tie-dye hoodie. "Congratulations, Hernan."

Eileen mumbled something, then nodded. "Are you getting married in the Santo Nino Church?"

"We haven't decided yet." Hernan sounded as sullen as a child still recovering from a scolding.

Cora decided she had been silent long enough. "Well, I think we've covered what there is to be said about the matter." She paused and shot Eileen a chilly smile. "Now, as for the recall petition. We received it this morning. You each have a copy in your inbox. We need to verify all the signatures, which will take time."

Hernan crossed his arms in front of his chest. "And then what?"

Cora glanced at him with a look of thinly veiled sympathy. They had served together on the board for decades, and while they sometimes butted heads, there was enough common ground between them to smooth over any rough spots. "And then we have twenty days to schedule a meeting to review the recall petition. After that, it will go to a vote of the entire membership. Depending on the turnout, it's possible to recall a board member if as few as twenty-six percent of the owners vote yes."

Dan twisted the end of his ponytail between long fingers, studying the frayed gray strands. "If Hernan loses his position, then what?"

"The ballot will include a list of candidates to replace him," Cora said. "But first things first. Let's verify the signatures, and we'll go from there."

Cora moved on to the next item on the agenda: Julia's proposal for a Day of the Dead celebration. The last fair had been a wild success until some nasty chupacabras ruined things, so I was a little surprised by the overwhelming enthusiasm and quick approval for the Day of the Dead festival. Apparently, the lure of outside visitors spending money at our restaurants and shops was too much to resist. And, lucky for me, I would need my full staff to secure the event.

The other items were so boring I tuned them out until Cora cleared her throat.

"I will be completely honest about my feelings on this next matter. We have Maddy and her wonderful team to thank for keeping us safe from all the threats our community has faced. And if we don't maintain our security team, we risk being caught off guard. But since we've entered a protracted period of...quiet...some board members believe we should re-evaluate the staffing level to save money."

Eileen clicked a nail against her water glass. "In my mind, those were emergency measures only and were never meant to continue permanently."

"Funny, Eileen. I don't remember you complaining about the staffing level when those vampire birds were chasing you," Charlie replied, rubbing his wide, square jaw.

Eileen rolled her eyes but said nothing.

"I agree with Eileen." Dan leaned forward, his upper arms pressing onto the table. "While I greatly appreciate everything our security team has done, we can't support the current staffing level without raising dues again, and they are already high enough. Some of us are up for reelection early next year, and if we vote to raise the dues—"

"Exactly." Eileen ran a manicured finger across her throat. "We'll be out. Believe me, I'm out and about in the community all the time, and I'm getting an earful."

"Yes, Eileen. We all are," Cora said briskly. "But we need to remember it's our responsibility to focus on the bigger picture, and that is safety. Which, may I remind everyone, is directly connected to property values."

Hernan pounded a fist on the table, and we all jumped. "Let's stop this right now! Take resources from Maddy's team and there will be hell to pay the first time something happens. You may survive the election, but look how easy it is for a few unhappy homeowners to put together a recall petition!"

Even I was caught off guard by Hernan's enthusiastic show of support.

Eileen flashed Hernan a fake smile. "That's so sweet. Considering Maddy will soon be your daughter-in-law." She turned to Cora with raised eyebrows. "Isn't there a conflict of interest once Hernan is Maddy's father-in-law?"

Cora pressed her lips together. "Let's stick with the budget. It's time we heard from Maddy. I understand she has a few things to say on the matter."

"I'll just bet she does," Eileen muttered.

Cora shot her a scowl while I took a deep breath, opened my laptop, and clicked on a tab.

I cleared my throat and began. "Well, as Hernan pointed out, reducing our security team puts us at a disadvantage when the next threat occurs. And it occurred yesterday." I paused long enough to register the expressions of alarm around the table. "We've identified entity emergence holes in the gully leading to Phantom's Pass. But there's no sign of any entities, which is a serious concern. And the holes are so unusual that I've asked Occult Affairs to take a look at them."

Eileen and Dan opened their mouths to say something, but I continued.

"Occult Affairs has long feared a new kind of entity would appear, Entities 2.0. That may be what's happening."

I pulled up the photos I had taken with my phone and turned the laptop around so everyone could see them.

Dan scowled. "What are we looking at?"

"The holes are extra-large," I explained. "We've never seen that size before. And there are no tracks or other indications of what came out of them. Also unprecedented. Which leads us to believe these are different than anything we've seen so far." I cleared my throat. "Since yesterday afternoon, I've had my team out searching for clues. Every person who isn't monitoring the command center is trying to figure out what came out of those eruptions."

"How convenient," Eileen whispered to Dan, just loud enough for me to catch it.

Cora was staring at me. I wished I had told her in advance. Blindsiding the HOA president who had hired you was never a good idea.

"This is terrible," she said. "If they are the next wave of entities, why would they appear here, of all places?"

"They might not be entities at all," Hernan said gloomily. "They might be of a supernatural origin. Like the vampire birds from Mexico."

Charlie crossed himself. "Oh, please, no."

Eileen and Dan exchanged dark looks. I took a deep breath, preparing for what would come next.

"This is all very interesting," Eileen said through gritted teeth. "Malena B. shows up at Hernan's place, and suddenly, we have mysterious holes not too far away. It doesn't take a genius to figure that out."

Ouch. Hernan winced and turned toward me, his dark eyes pleading.

I shook my head. "I considered that, of course. My mother's psychic abilities allow her to connect with entities. They're attracted to her, but she doesn't bring them into our world. The earthquakes did that. She only works with them once they're here. And believe me, if Occult Affairs believed my mother caused entities to emerge, they'd have found a way to neutralize her years ago. Instead, they hire her to help with difficult cases."

Eileen tipped her head back and stared at the ceiling.

"Well," Cora said briskly, "it sounds like today is not the day to discuss cutting our security budget. Unless anyone has any additional business, this meeting is adjourned."

I closed my laptop and walked quickly out of the conference room. The last thing I wanted was to get into a conversation with anybody.

My staff had lived to fight another day, but while I climbed into my Jeep, I knew the budget battle was not over.

Chapter 4

My phone chimed before I was out of the parking lot. Cora and Charlie wanted to see me right away.

I turned around and parked under a large Jacaranda tree. A wave of uncertainty rolled down my spine.

Cora couldn't be blamed for being miffed I had not told her about the new emergence holes, and I really should have thanked them both for their support in the board meeting. But when they put me into Charlie's gigantic Mercedes and drove toward La Loma, I figured it was something else entirely.

"Close your eyes," Cora instructed from the front seat.

I was too old and too suspicious for that, but I decided to play along. After putting my hand over my eyes, I peered through an opening between two fingers. "It's not my birthday, you know."

"It's better than a birthday," Charlie said.

The car turned right. "Is it a tamale party? I love tamales. Especially Cora's."

Cora chuckled. "It's even better than that. You'll see."

The car stopped, and we all got out. I took my hand from my eyes. Charlie and Cora were standing on the sidewalk, beaming.

I knew where we were—I had been there before, once with Ben Tomas and once with some special visitors. We were in front of the property in La Loma that had once belonged to my great-aunt Lencha Bantacorte, the lot with the sturdy palm tree standing guard.

Charlie reached into his pocket and pulled out a set of keys, grinning. Cora produced a plastic document folder from her voluminous leather bag. With great ceremony, both were handed to me.

"Lencha's property is now officially yours!" Cora announced.

Ever the businessman, Charlie said, "Now, don't worry. You won't have to pay dues. That's part of the legacy rules. But you will if you decide to build on it. Then the dues will be calculated on the square footage."

Tears filled my eyes.

I was now the owner of not one but two properties in Chavez Ravine: my home, which once belonged to my grandmother, Liliana Bantacorte, and now, the property that had belonged to Chavez Ravine's most famous bruja and my great-aunt, the one whose magic I had inherited and who had mentored me from the grave.

I was beyond grateful. In fact, I was blown away. "I can't believe it." I wiped my eyes with the back of my hand and sniffed.

"It's rightfully yours." Cora patted my arm.

Charlie smiled so hard his eyes seemed to disappear into the folds of his cheeks. "We have another surprise for you." He punched in the gate code, and the tall wooden door swung open. Charlie stepped aside. "After you."

The long yard stretched out before me. The original house was long gone. All that remained was the shed where Lencha used to dole out remedies and sometimes practice Mexican witchcraft, depending on the situation.

Cora took my hand. "Your great-aunt Lencha died without leaving a will. Eventually, the HOA took possession of this lot to hold it for her heirs. And, in the meantime, Ben Tomas has been using the yard as a nursery."

Potted orange marigolds lined the space from fence to fence, their pungent scent hanging in the air. I immediately thought of Julia, who had pushed for a Day of the Dead Festival, where the flowers would play a central role. The timing and sheer number of them could not have been a coincidence.

A figure stepped out of the shed, and I did a double take. Ben Tomas smiled and gestured toward the structure. It had been completely transformed. The last time I saw it, it had been so dilapidated I half expected it to collapse on my head. Someone had repaired it, filling in the gaps with new slats, and the roof had been replaced as well, now taller and peaked. New paint and paver stones surrounded it.

My heart bumped in my chest. "Did you do this?"

Ben flashed a big smile, showing off lots of white teeth. "Sure did." His chin came up. "What do you think?"

"I think I'm gonna cry." I squeezed his arm and practically danced into the shed. It was nice and cool inside, and with the high ceiling, it was also surprisingly airy. The counter where Lencha had worked was still there, but it was usable now, the wood sanded and polished.

Ben poked his head in. "I tried to keep as much of the original wood and hardware as possible to maintain its character." He smiled shyly. "You can actually use it now, if you want."

I turned toward him, wiping away fresh tears. "It's beautiful, Ben. Thank you. Thank you so much." I lowered my voice and leaned a little closer. "How about the clay?"

"Are you kidding me? It's still there. I wouldn't dare mess with it. I even did a little something to protect it." He motioned for me to follow him.

The stretch of red clay, which my great-aunt had used to fuel her magic, still extended to the rear of the property, but it was now covered by a low wooden trellis.

Ben came up to stand beside me. "I know that clay has been here for a long time, but I started to worry what might happen if we had a bad rainstorm or even a windstorm. I'm going to tack some plastic sheeting on the sides to keep the worst of the weather out."

"That's incredibly thoughtful of you." The lump in my throat made it hard to get the words out.

"It was Julia's idea, actually," he said. "I think she's hoping you might let her use the clay for some of her sculptures. Your mother's commissioned her to make a statuette of your Grandma Liliana."

I nodded. "Of course."

My mother. She wasn't going to be happy when she learned I had inherited my great-aunt's house. In fact, she would probably be resentful and furious to have been passed over once again.

"Cora, this is amazing of you, but my mother will be pretty unhappy when she finds out this property didn't go to her."

"She already knows. Charlie and I met with her. There might not be anything specific in our rules to prevent her from living here, but we do have the authority to prevent her from owning property. She's made a name for herself as a psychic with a connection to entities, and we've made a name for Chavez Ravine as the one place in all of Los Angeles that is free of them. Mostly. With your continued help, of course." She winked.

"How did she take it?"

Cora gave a little shrug. "She was…disappointed…but eventually she understood."

I winced, picturing my mother's face turning white with rage while she unleashed her fury. But if anyone could weather a

Category Five Malena B., it was Cora, the no-nonsense HOA president and founder of a tamale empire with a steely gaze all her own.

Cora looked past me at Ben and Charlie, who were deep in conversation next to an enormous prickly pear cactus. "Hernan's really stirred things up by allowing Malena to move in, but that's his affair."

"Do you think he really might lose his seat on the board?"

"It's hard to predict these things, but yes. There's a good chance it will happen. At least he'll have your mother to console him." She winked again.

I gave a shudder. "Thanks. One more image I need to wipe from my mind."

Cora laughed. She could afford to. She didn't have to deal with those two like I did.

Cora and Charlie soon left, and I returned to the expansive yard, walking among the rows of potted plants and admiring the refurbished shed.

Ben followed along beside me. "I'll give you a ride back to Palo Verde Plaza when you're ready. But no rush."

I could tell by the tone of his voice he had something on his mind.

"Everything all right?" I asked.

Ben scraped a hand through his hair. "Yeah, but now that this property is yours, I need to get busy and move this stuff out of here."

There was a lot to rearrange. Hundreds of pots of marigolds and other flowers and plants, plus all the landscaping equipment stored in the yard.

"There's no hurry, Ben. I already have a house. To be honest, I don't even know what I'm going to do with this place. Besides using the clay and Lencha's shed."

Ben raised his eyebrows. "You could build a bigger house here. It's a nice, quiet street. The lot is deep enough that you can have a house and a pool and still have a decent yard. You'd be closer to the clay and your shed that way."

I snorted. "And where would I get the money to pay for all that?"

"I don't know. Maybe sell the other house?" He shrugged. "Maybe Stu can sell his place, and you can build something really nice that's perfect for the both of you."

I laughed. "Did you think of that all on your own?"

Ben threw up his hands and smiled sheepishly. "No. That was Julia's idea. She said you don't like Stu's house and that you two should move in together, but your house is too small. And Stu's daughter will need her own bedroom."

"Sounds like Julia's thought of everything." I gave him a little shove toward the gate to show I wasn't offended, then walked around, inspecting the shed and the clay.

What was I going to do with the property I had just inherited?

I closed my eyes. Felt the cool autumn air on my face. Wriggled my toes.

With a sigh, I grabbed a kneeling pad from a bench and sat cross-legged on it near the mound of clay. The red earth had an energy all its own. It hummed with a power I couldn't quite grasp. Maybe it wasn't necessary that I understand it. Perhaps all I had to do was feel and accept it. Trust it, like I had finally come to trust my own magical abilities.

I suspected its power was tied to the land itself. Maybe my great-aunt had even chosen this house deliberately, but she had been a single woman of very limited means. It was probably all she could afford.

Magic wasn't rational or logical. And neither were entities. But hopefully the red clay could help combat whatever was coming out of those holes in the gully.

If we ever found them.

Chapter 5

In retrospect, the next day was when things started going wrong. The signs were there, but I wouldn't connect the dots until much later.

Late morning, Julia called in a panic. "Maddy! Something's wrong with me, and I'm scared. Can you come over? Please?"

I was just wrapping up a meeting with my security team. We had hammered out a plan for tracking down whatever had popped up in the gully.

"Are you sick? Should I call an ambulance?"

"No, it's not like that!" she cried. "Can you come to my house? It'll be easier if I just show you."

Julia sounded panicked, and she didn't frighten easily. Once, I had watched her take out a naked, hairy golem with a rolling pin, so it took a lot to fluster her.

I jumped into my Jeep and drove as fast as I dared toward La Loma, imagining all sorts of horrible things. Within minutes, I pulled up to Julia's property—two small houses she had inherited and joined by a breezeway. She stood in the doorway, paint-splattered overalls hanging from her bare shoulders, her auburn hair held back by a green bandanna.

Julia waved me into the house, through the living area with its riot of color, and into the room that served as her studio. Clay-spattered tools covered her worktable. Wooden shelves displayed half-finished sculptures and pieces of pottery. Julia's art was in high demand, and the price tags would make most people wince.

She plucked a figurine from the table and held it in the air. "This! Just look at it!"

The lopsided, neckless clay figure stared back at me with bulging eyes, its stubby appendages jutting at odd angles. Nothing like Julia's usual, elegant work. It looked like something a kindergartener would make in class.

"I'm looking at it, but what am I supposed to be seeing here?"

Julia burst into tears. "I made it. *Me*! This is supposed to be a figurine of your grandmother. Your mother commissioned it, and I started on it this morning. But look at it! It keeps coming out all wrong!" She gestured at a pile of sketches on the table. "I did those last week. That's what she's supposed to look like. No matter how many times I start over, I can't even get the clay into the right shape."

I stared at the deformed figurine, at a total loss. Though I could handle supernatural threats, I was ill-prepared for artistic meltdowns. But Julia hadn't called the head of security. She had called her friend.

"That's weird. How frustrating!" I said in my best soothing voice. "Maybe you just need to step away and take a break?"

Julia shook her head. "I already tried that. I got up early to start on it. I was really excited about it, yeah? And then it came out all...blobby...so I thought maybe I was just having a bad morning and my fingers were stiff or something, so I took a walk, and then I started again. And it was still no good."

Her brown eyes were pleading. I felt helpless—I was way out of my comfort zone.

"Has this ever happened before?"

"Not like this!" she wailed. "I've had some off days, yeah, but something is seriously, *seriously* wrong with me."

Julia flopped into a lumpy chair, tears welling in her eyes. Not knowing what else to do, I started pacing. Could there be an explanation for what Julia was experiencing? Some sort of neurological issue? It didn't seem likely. She was young and healthy. Wouldn't symptoms come on gradually? I glanced at Julia, lying sideways in the chair, her legs over an armrest, staring blankly at the ceiling.

When I was working in Occult Affairs, an officer had come down with Bell's Palsy. He had been in his mid-thirties, and it hit him suddenly. His face drooped on one side, and his jaw and head ached, but he was otherwise fine and made a full recovery in a few months. Julia was obviously upset, but her face wasn't drooping.

Still, there might have been something medical going on. "I think we should go to urgent care. Just in case."

Julia swiveled her head toward me, her eyebrows lowering. "I feel fine. Honest."

Rushing Julia to a clinic because she'd had a bad creative morning did seem like an overreaction, but it was something to do. A box to check.

"All right. How about we go to lunch? And then you take a nap, and maybe when you wake up, you'll be back to normal."

Julia sniffed and nodded. "Okay. Yeah. Can we go to Olga's? It's Taco Tuesday."

She didn't have to ask me twice. I loved tacos, and Olga made some of the best.

We climbed into the Jeep and headed toward Palo Verde Plaza. I tried distracting Julia from her artistic crisis with food talk. "So, what are you going to order? The regular tacos or the street tacos?"

"Street tacos, of course," Julia said. "I like the shrimp and the carnitas, and I'll probably get one al pastor too."

"The shrimp is really good. I love the chipotle sauce they use."

My phone rang.

Julia picked it up from the dash, checked the screen, and said, "It's Ben."

Ben was her boyfriend and not mine, so I said, "Go ahead and answer it."

She did, and from her tone, it was immediately obvious something was wrong. "We'll meet you there, yeah." She hung up. "Ben wants us to come to Lencha's old place. He has something to show you."

My heart sank. "Did he say what it was?"

"No. He said you needed to see it." Julia's face lit up. "And congratulations, by the way! I've been so into my own problems I completely forgot to mention your new inheritance! It's amazing you have two properties with family ties, yeah?"

"Yeah, it is pretty amazing," I agreed, but my mind was racing. Maybe Ben had discovered entity holes on the property. In which case, my great aunt's magical red clay hadn't been much of a deterrent.

Lencha's place—correction, *my* new place—was just a few blocks away, and we arrived in no time. Ben was waiting on the sidewalk, pacing alongside his work truck. Unlike my Jeep, it was spotless. Julia jumped out before I pulled up the parking brake and ran over to Ben, who gave her a distracted peck on the cheek.

"Please tell me it's not another Camazotz," I said. We'd had a bad experience with one of the enormous vampire bats in his equipment yard a few months before.

Moments later, we were standing in the yard, surrounded by a sea of dead marigolds. The vibrant orange flowers had turned brown, petals shriveled, stems nearly black.

"Oh no!" Julia cried. "What happened? Did something go wrong with the irrigation?"

Ben lifted one of the pots, then dug his fingers into the soil and extracted a crumbling handful. It was slightly moist. "The irrigation's fine. To tell you the truth, I don't know what happened." He set the pot down and bit his lip. "But I'm beginning to think I'm bad luck."

"What's that supposed to mean?" Julia asked, her voice rising.

"I'll show you." Ben motioned for us to wait. He hurried toward a tent and, moments later, returned holding a plastic pot with a profusion of purple flowers. "These are chrysanthemums. Grown from seeds. Carefully tended. No sign of disease. Perfectly healthy. Now watch."

Ben reached for the plant. His index finger brushed a petal and traced down to the stem. For several seconds, nothing. Then a brown spot appeared where he had made contact. It spread like a stain seeping through fabric, the purple darkening to the color of an old bruise. The leaves curled inward. In less than a minute, the healthy plant had withered and died.

Ben's forehead was shiny with perspiration.

"What the hell?" Julia whispered.

Ben set the pot on the ground and crossed his arms across his chest. "All the plants I touched today have died. Every single one of them." He grimaced. "Talk about a black thumb."

Ben had the greenest thumb I knew. If my mother was the entity whisperer, he was the plant whisperer. It was because of his skills—and his vision—that Chavez Ravine had been transformed from dusty hillsides to the lush oasis it had become. The HOA board's annual surveys consistently showed one thing: residents would gladly pay higher dues to fund Ben's landscaping projects while nickel-and-diming almost everything else.

I walked up and down the rows of dead plants, thinking. While I wasn't sure what was going on, it sure didn't feel like a coincidence that Julia had lost her ability to sculpt and Ben had started killing plants on the same morning.

A hex might account for it. Which meant a witch, somewhere, had it out for Julia and Ben.

When I had first taken the job in Chavez Ravine, Hernan had used some hex bags against me. The ingredients were common enough. Salt, cumin, and ground glass—basic household ingredients. But in the hands of a bruja or brujo, even a tiny amount could cause great harm, from physically injuring someone to ruining their reputation or even sending them into bankruptcy. A hex bag wasn't anything to mess with.

Luckily, I had found Hernan's and disposed of them before they could get me fired from my new job, which had been his original intent. I didn't think he had something against either Julia or Ben, but that didn't mean there wasn't another witch behind the attacks.

I turned to Ben, who stood with Julia tucked against his side, a protective arm around her shoulders.

"What happens if you wear gloves?"

"Let's find out." Ben dug through a storage bin, pulled out a pair of gardening gloves, and tugged them on. He retrieved another pot of mums and gently brushed the top of the bright red blooms with a gloved finger.

The flowers shriveled up and died.

Julia gasped. In the distance, a dog barked. Birds chirped in the trees. Somewhere nearby, a door slammed shut.

I thought for a moment. A hex bag could be anywhere. We needed help. As much as I hated the idea of pulling my folks off their entity search, it was important we find whatever was behind Ben and Julia's troubles.

"You two wait in Ben's truck. I'll get some people over here, and we'll see what we can find."

I tapped out messages to Ron Mendez and Justin Torres. When they arrived, they looked around at all the dead flowers, shifted on their feet, and exchanged uneasy glances.

Ron spoke first. "Something bad is going on here. But at least a chupa isn't going to jump out from behind a bush and rip out our throats."

Justin punched his arm. "Don't get too comfortable. We don't know what we're dealing with yet."

"You're right, Justin. We don't know for sure, but I suspect someone may be leaving hex bags for Julia and Ben."

"What's a hex bag look like?" Justin asked.

"You're looking for a pouch, but it could also be a plastic or paper bag," I said. "If you see anything unusual, something that doesn't look right, don't touch it. Take a picture, then call me and let me deal with it."

I told them to search the yard and asked Julia and Ben if my team could go through their houses too.

"Look under the beds," I instructed. "Under chairs, under rugs, or any place someone might spend some time and be exposed. Don't forget their vehicles. When you're done, we'll check Julia's shop and Ben's office."

My team got to work, and I walked over to the truck.

"Now what?" Julia's voice was subdued.

"Now, we're going to Olga's Cantina, and I'm going to ask both of you a bunch of questions. I need to know who might want to hex you."

Chapter 6

Julia, Ben, and I pushed through the crowded plaza toward Olga's Cantina, only to find the patio packed with people who clearly weren't eating.

"What's going on?" Ben asked. "Looks like they're closed for some kind of private event."

Julia frowned. "On Taco Tuesday? No chance."

I approached a well-dressed couple in their seventies. "Do you happen to know what's going on? Are they open?"

"No, I don't think they are," the woman said. "Mel and I had just placed our orders, and we were waiting for our food when the server came over and said there was a problem in the kitchen and they were suspending the lunch service."

Mel held up a white plastic card stamped across the front. "They gave us a gift card and said to come back another time, but we're waiting around to see if they reopen because Sharon had her heart set on the street tacos. Didn't you, dear?"

Sharon nodded sadly. I felt for her. Nobody should be denied street tacos from Olga's.

Mel took a long look at me, and his furry white eyebrows shot up. "You're that security gal, aren't you?"

I gave him my most disarming smile and nodded toward the group. "Yes. Madeline Madrigal. Do you have any idea what's happening in the kitchen? A fire, maybe? I didn't get an alert about a fire."

"No, I don't think they had a fire," Sharon said. "We would have smelled smoke. Wouldn't we, Mel?"

"No smoke," Mel agreed.

They were pretty adorable and seemed delighted to have an audience. Sharon cleared her throat. Her face was tanned and lined, and her tennis skirt and visor suggested she had just come off the courts.

"We did hear some yelling from the kitchen. Didn't we, Mel?" she said.

Mel nodded eagerly. "We certainly did. It sounded like a couple of the cooks were arguing, and then Olga stepped in, and she started yelling too." Mel cleared his throat. "To be honest, she sounded a little—"

"Hysterical," Sharon finished for him.

I had met Olga Sanchez. She was a shrewd businesswoman, and she could be intense, but hysterical? Never. Whatever had happened in the kitchen had to be serious. Time to find out.

I returned to Julia and Ben. "Olga's is closed. I'm not sure what's going on, but I'm going to go talk to her. Why don't you two head to Muertos Café? I'll meet you there."

Julia pressed a hand against her throat. "I can't believe I'm going to say this, but I think I've lost my appetite. I really had my heart set on Olga's tacos."

"You didn't eat breakfast. You need to eat something," Ben said firmly. He took her by the elbow and led her away.

Ben was a solid guy with his feet planted firmly on the ground. He was a perfect fit for my happy-go-lucky friend.

I circled around the plaza and slipped in through the kitchen door. The argument that had started earlier seemed to have reached the point where everything had already been said.

Olga stood in the center of the kitchen, her cheeks flushed, brandishing a spatula like a weapon. "I just don't understand how all the meat that was delivered this morning could have gone bad."

A short man with a shaved head and a neck tattoo leaned against the steel counter, arms folded tightly across his chest. "I don't know, Olga. Maybe the refrigeration wasn't working right in the delivery truck."

A petite woman with a purple crew cut rolled her eyes. "The meat was fine when it got here. I keep telling you, everything was fine. I checked the meat and accepted the delivery, like I always do."

Half a dozen other employees in white aprons over black T-shirts stood around, their faces registering everything from confusion to a wary defensiveness.

Olga noticed me and drew her arched eyebrows together. "Madeline! Did someone call you?"

"Should they have?"

Olga was about fifty. Her salt-and-pepper hair was pulled back into a thick ponytail. She wore a red T-shirt with La Virgen de Guadalupe on the front, black jeans, and a slash of bright red lipstick. Olga gestured with her spatula, waving it for emphasis. "Maybe…because I'm beginning to have my suspicions!" She cast a dark look at the bald guy.

Bald Guy lifted his chin. "Hey. That's not fair, Olga. You can't pin all these pendejadas on me. No way, no how."

Olga pressed a hand against her chest and took a few deep breaths. "All right, all right. Why don't you guys throw everything away, clean up…and we'll start over."

The woman with the purple hair raised her hand. "I'll go to the market in Palo Verde and buy whatever I can."

"I'll go with you," Bald Guy said. "You'll need help."

Olga motioned for me to follow her into her office. The room barely fit a desk and two chairs.

She kicked the door closed and dropped into the chair behind the desk. "What a fucking day. I don't think this is a security matter, but I can tell you what happened if you want to hear it."

Olga definitely had my attention.

"Sure. Go ahead."

"The two who just left? Martina has been with me since I opened. She's my right hand. Nico used to be executive chef at Muertos Café, but he and Bernie Mora had a falling out over something or another. So, he gave Bernie his notice and came here, and now he's second-in-command." She frowned.

"And?" I prompted.

Olga sighed. "Bernie and I have a history. We started out together at a restaurant in Pasadena, and we became friends. We talked about opening a restaurant together, and then both of us learned we were eligible to claim properties in Bishop, so we moved to Chavez Ravine around the same time. Then this space came up for lease, and we decided to go for it. Except Bernie was dead set on naming the place Muertos Café. Pardon the pun. He thought it was cool. You know, edgy. And then he started talking about making pan dulce, and I said, 'No way. That's a bakery, not a taqueria. A totally different concept.' And he said, 'Screw you. Go ahead and open a boring old Mexican restaurant.' Then we really got into it." She bit her lip.

"Olga, do you think Bernie had something to do with whatever happened in your kitchen?"

She pressed her tongue into her cheek. "I had my doubts about hiring Nico. Sure, he's got a great reputation, and it's hard to find good people. But it always felt a little funny, having someone who was so close with Bernie working in my kitchen. My husband thinks I'm being paranoid. But when everything went to hell this morning—and on Taco Tuesday—I don't know. It just feels like I'm being sabotaged."

A prickle ran along my scalp. "So, what happened? Exactly? And do me a favor…Start from the moment you got here."

Olga leaned toward me. "I got in early, as usual. I put on the beans and made the masa for the tortillas. Martina accepted the meat delivery, and Nico started on the salsas. Everything was going just fine until Nico took out the meat and we discovered it had gone off. All of it. Including the chicken and fish. The rice came out mushy, and the beans wouldn't soften, no matter what we did. And the masa turned hard as stone. We didn't have a damn single thing we could serve."

Her story was starting to sound familiar. "All right, Olga. This might be a strange question, but out of all the food you just mentioned, what did you actually touch?"

Olga tucked a strand of silver hair behind an ear. "All of it. I double-checked the meat delivery, made the masa, started the beans, and added spices to the rice. Honestly, it drives Martina and Nico crazy that I'm always messing with the dishes, but it's *my* reputation on the line."

A pattern was starting to come into focus, but I needed to be sure. "Can we go back into the kitchen and do a little experiment?" I asked.

Olga cocked her head and narrowed her eyes. "What kind of experiment?"

"One with masa," I said, standing up.

In the kitchen, the staff was staying busy by giving the kitchen a deep clean.

"Can you mix up a little masa?" I asked. "Not too much. Just enough for a few tortillas?"

"With my eyes closed." Olga laughed, then set to work. "Lard or olive oil?"

I shrugged. "You pick."

"Lard, then."

A few minutes later, we were staring at a glass bowl filled with half a dozen dough balls.

"Now what?" Olga asked.

"Whatever you'd do next."

Olga grabbed a roll of parchment paper from the counter, tore off a sheet, and laid it over the open tortilla press. But when she went to close the lid, it bounced upward, and Olga cried out in surprise.

I picked up the ball of dough. It was as hard as a rock.

My suspicions were confirmed.

I patted Olga's arm. "If you want to have dinner service tonight, you need to leave this kitchen and stay out of it until I figure out what's going on. And please keep this to yourself."

Chapter 7

Julia, Ben, *and* Olga.

Three cases that looked a lot like hexings. But why? I couldn't find a single thread connecting them. Julia and Ben hadn't been together long enough to share friends, much less enemies. Olga's Cantina was a favorite haunt for both, but they had never actually met Olga herself. She almost never left the kitchen.

I asked Olga if there was any chance Bernie Mora, the owner of Muertos Café, or Nico, her chef, might dabble in brujeria. She just laughed.

"Those two? No way. Bernie is old-school Catholic, and Nico calls himself a naturalist."

"Naturalist?" I had heard of atheism before, and I had met people who called themselves "irreligious"—my friend Jo at Occult Affairs, for one. But "naturalist" was a new one. "Does that mean someone who studies nature?"

Olga nodded. "It can, but Nico says it means he doesn't believe in the supernatural or the spiritual. But how is that possible, with the entities and monsters we've had around here? He and Martina argue about that stuff all the time. Nico loves it. He's as stubborn as they come."

I thought for a moment. "How about Martina? Or anyone else on your staff?"

"Martina can't even watch a scary movie!" She paused, then slowly shook her head. "No one else comes to mind."

Ron and Justin had swept Lencha's old property for hex bags, but after coming up empty, they moved on to Ben and Julia's houses. I took Olga's kitchen and restaurant, which turned out to be an hours-long ordeal. So many hiding places in commercial kitchens.

Julia and Ben helped, but nothing turned up for them either.

When Hernan had planted hex bags in my Jeep, office, and bedroom, I only felt their effects when I was nearby. So, I focused my search on the places where my friends had first noticed something was wrong. But what if *I* was wrong? What if these hexes were different?

I called Hernan and asked if we could use his house for a little experiment.

"Of course, mija. You are always welcome here. Whatever you need!"

Um, that was way too easy. Maybe it was the recall election. Perhaps it was the expectation he would be my stepdad someday soon. But I didn't care. I could get used to this new, docile Hernan Frias.

I sent Julia, Ben, and Olga to his house in Bishop. It was far from Julia's house, Lencha's garden, and Olga's restaurant—a perfect place to see whether the hexes worked at a distance.

"Isn't it wonderful Hernan could offer you his home for your little experiment?" my mother said, greeting us at the door.

"Yes, Mom. It is wonderful. We won't be long." I was in no mood for Mom games.

I took Julia through the house and into the backyard and the shed, where I knew Hernan had a supply of clay. Julia picked up a lump and started to form a figurine.

"I've done this one a million times," she said, working the clay into the shape of a child. But the longer she worked with the gray mass, the worse it looked. We gave up, and Julia carried the sad blob back into the house.

My mother was waiting. "Oh my. That looks even worse than the horse thing Maddy made for Mother's Day when she was in the first grade!"

Lovely. It took all my strength to keep my mouth shut.

"Olga, why don't you go into the kitchen and see if you can whip up a snack?" I suggested. "Ben, let's take a look at the roses in the front yard."

Ben and I went out the door and found a small rose bush along the side of the house. He gently touched a delicate stem with three buds. In seconds, the entire bush had withered and collapsed into a brown heap.

A loud string of swear words came from the house. Ben and I ran back inside in time to watch Olga emptying the contents of a small molcajete into the trash with a dramatic flourish.

"I can't even grind some pinche spices!" she wailed.

We all gathered in the sunny living room. For all her faults—and there were many—my mother had good taste. The room was beautiful and comfortable, with pillows and throws softening the heavy, dark furniture. An area rug added a splash of color and pulled the room together.

"Obviously, we still don't know what's going on or who is behind it," I said. "At least, not yet. But we do know that if you keep trying to go about your work as usual, you'll just get frustrated. So, until this mystery is solved, I think it's best for you to take a step back from your usual activities. Think of it as a little vacation!"

Ben stared at the floor, and Olga mumbled something about not having taken a vacation since she had opened her restaurant.

Julia was cheerful and positive, as usual. "Well, I have plenty of inventory in the shop, so it won't kill me to take a little break. I'm sure Maddy will have this fixed in a jiffy!"

I didn't share her confidence. But there was still dinner to make for Stu and Clare, so I went home, showered, and fed the cat.

The menu was simple, and since I needed something to keep my hands busy while I tried to untangle my thoughts, I decided to make corn tortillas. I mixed the masa and rolled the dough into balls, wondering if maybe I had been too quick to blame a hex for what was happening to Julia, Ben, and Olga. But what else could it be?

If it wasn't a hex, it was something so close to one the difference hardly mattered. The result was the same: they couldn't work; they couldn't do the things they loved. If I couldn't solve the mystery, it could ruin them. All three of them needed their talents to keep living the lives they had made for themselves.

My phone rang. It was Bailey Nixon. She sounded breathless.

"We found two more holes. I'm going to send you some pictures."

I smoothed out a piece of parchment paper on my tortilla press while I waited for the photos to arrive. When my phone chimed, I wiped my hands on a dish towel and stared at the screen.

"Where are you?" I asked.

"About a quarter mile into Phantom's Pass," Bailey replied. "They're big."

"How big?"

"Plus-sized. Hold on a sec." Bailey covered the mic, and I could hear a low mumble of voices. "Jason says he guesses maybe three yards by two. He paced it off. We've checked the immediate area for entities but haven't found anything. And we're moving more people over to help expand the search. Is there anything specific you want us to do?"

I loved having Bailey on my team. She was smart, brave, and always a step ahead. "Yeah. Send me your location. I'm going to forward your pics to Steve Zhao, and he might want to come out and take a look for himself."

We hung up. Ten minutes later, Steve called. He was headed to Phantom's Pass with two of his colleagues and a set of new probing tools they wanted to test. Not that I had much hope these would work any better than the other gadgets the Occult Affairs researchers had already thrown at the problem. Sticking long, sharp poles into the ground where entities had just emerged had always sounded risky to me, but the nerds couldn't help themselves. Where there were holes, they had to poke. It was a miracle nothing had ever grabbed the other end and yanked one of them into the void.

I had everything simmering on the stove, ready to be served, when Stu and Clare arrived. Clare, who was usually fairly cheerful for a teenager, walked in wearing her soccer uniform, muttering under her breath. She pecked my cheek, then flung herself onto the couch beside my cat.

Something was off.

Stu set a bottle of red wine down on the entryway table and let out a heavy sigh. He wrapped his arms around me and squeezed. "It's so good to see you," he said quietly into my hair. "Just be nice to me tonight. We've had a rough couple of hours."

That set off a few alarm bells. "Did something happen?"

Stu kissed my temple and pulled away. "Clare's in a bad mood. I mean, we're talking *foul*."

I glanced at Clare, who was taking off her shin guards. "Soccer?"

Stu grimaced. "Yeah. She just switched soccer clubs, and she's really been stressing about it." His voice was barely above a whisper. "Today was their first game, and I don't know how to put it…It was a disaster. An epic disaster."

"Everyone has a bad day now and then," I said, matching his low tone.

Stu shook his head. "Oh, no. It was way more than that. She played like a rookie. She fell, she fumbled, she mistimed her runs, she blew opportunities…She didn't even seem to know where to stand. It's like she was starring in her own blooper reel." He paused, frowning. "She's been playing since she was four. I can't even remember how many times she's been voted MVP. I swear, it's like she was jinxed or something."

It took just a moment to slot that bit of news into place. Clare was number four.

Chapter 8

Dinner was ready, and Stu's stomach was rumbling.

Clare perked up when I said we were having nopales. Stu poured the wine and mixed Clare a club soda with grenadine.

Clare asked if she could press some tortillas, so I showed her how. Then we cooked them on the dry skillet, turning them over when they started to bubble.

With the tortillas in the warmer, we set out bowls of beans, rice, and cheeses. I spooned the pork al pastor with nopales and the grilled carne asada onto platters, then brought those to the table. Since I didn't have a proper dining room, we ate in the kitchen, windows open to let in the cool evening air.

Clare speared a cube of cactus, chewed thoughtfully, then grinned. "Oh, it's really good! I wasn't sure I'd like the texture, but I do. And the pork is delicious." She held out another forkful of cactus, waving it in front of her father. "Dad! You *have* to try this."

Stu pinched his lips together. "No, thank you. I'll stick to the steak."

"You always stick to the steak!" Clare rolled her eyes. "You are the most boring eater ever. Isn't he, Maddy?"

I cleared my throat, for once choosing diplomacy. "He knows what he likes."

Stu snorted and wagged a fork in my direction. "Hey, you have me eating all sorts of things I never used to eat. Guacamole, rice, beans…and that sauce with the chili and chocolate your mom made. Which was fantastic, by the way."

"Mole," I said automatically.

"That's it! See? I'm not so boring, right?"

Clare turned to me with a snort. "Oh, my god. Did you just hear that? I swear, Maddy. You deserve a medal for getting him to eat something other than meat and potatoes. It's sad."

"Steak and potatoes were the two things my mother cooked," Stu said, a little stiffly. "Besides hamburgers, hot dogs, and macaroni and cheese. And, once in a while, spaghetti. So, yes, I may have developed a limited palette."

"That's no excuse for a man your age," Clare replied.

I laughed, and Stu faked a pout.

"Hey! You're supposed to be on my team."

"There are teams in food?" I sipped my wine and batted my eyelashes.

Stu opened his mouth to say something but was interrupted by Clare falling back in her chair and clapping her hands over her eyes. "Uh! *Team!* Uh! Dad! Did you have to say that?"

I glanced at Stu. He put down his fork and stared helplessly at his daughter.

"Did I say something?" I asked.

"*Team*," he said. "It's a soccer thing."

"Oh." I didn't know what else to say.

He reached across the table and squeezed Clare's hand. "It was just a fluke, honey. A freaky bad day. Lots of people seem to be having a bad day. Look at Pete."

Clare's hands slid off her face. Her eyes were red with tears. "Yeah. Poor Bad Pete."

Pete Drury, international pop star and part-time Chavez Ravine resident, was a nice guy, and I liked him.

"What happened to Pete?" I asked.

48

"Talk about bad days. He lost his voice. Not completely. He can still talk but barely, and he can't sing at all. He's cancelling his Vegas shows this weekend."

I set my tortilla aside. "Has that happened to him before? Losing his voice?"

"No. He said it was the first time."

Clare pushed a cactus cube around her plate. "That's what he said. It seems like everyone is having a bad day. What's the name of that woman who was visiting Pete, Dad?"

"Becca," replied Stu. "Becca Tey."

Becca Tey was an actress who lived not far from me in La Loma.

"I know Becca," I said. "What was wrong with her?"

Stu topped off my wine. "She's in a new series, and rehearsals started today. During the table read, she said she couldn't remember a single line. Not one. It got so bad she thought she was having a stroke and went to the ER."

I put down my wine glass. Six people suddenly unable to do what they did best. A pop star who couldn't sing. An actress who couldn't remember lines. A chef who turned out meals fit for the trash. A landscaper who killed plants. A sculptor who couldn't sculpt. Plus a soccer player who seemed jinxed. All in a single day.

Definitely not a coincidence. My spine tingled. Something unnatural was at work.

Clare smashed a slice of avocado onto her corn tortilla, sprinkled it with salt, then rolled it up, just the way I had shown her. "It's so sweet," she said. "Pete and Becca are really good friends. He totally fanboys over her because she used to be in his favorite vampire show. He even put her in his music video. That's where I first met her. She was hilarious, and she was so nice to me. Right, Dad?"

49

"If you say so," Stu said. "I just dropped you off at the studio, remember?"

I froze with my fork halfway to my mouth, a piece of carne asada dangling from the tines. "Wait. What studio? Pete made a music video, and Becca was in it? What were you doing there, Clare?" My voice came out sharper than I had intended.

Clare blushed. "Oh, that was my dad. He knows I'm a big Bad Pete fan, so he asked him if he needed any extras for his video. Pete was so nice. He said yes. It was really fun. I play a saloon girl. We're filming at Western Studios just outside Bishop. They have all the old Western sets and props he needs."

Clare seemed a little young to be playing a saloon girl, even as an extra, but I filed that away for later.

"They're still filming the video, then?"

Stu helped himself to another scoop of rice. "Yeah. They only started shooting yesterday. Pete's been tapping into the local talent in Chavez Ravine. Olga's Cantina is handling the catering, your friend Julia's pitching in with set design, and he even brought in Ben Tomas as the greensman for the outdoor scenes."

"So, Olga was on the set?" I asked Clare.

Clare nodded. "Yeah. She's a Bad Pete fan too, so she wanted to be there herself. She even served the food! It was really good."

I felt breathless. There it was. The connecting thread.

The hex—or whatever it was—was targeting people involved in Bad Pete's video. Julia, Ben, Olga, Becca, Clare, and Pete of course, had all lost their talents when production began.

Chapter 9

The day ended better than expected. Clare left for a sleepover at a friend's, so Stu was free to spend the night at my place. We sat around, talking about the hex and making out, while Sam glared at us from the ottoman. Which was a big improvement—glaring didn't draw blood or require bandages.

I planned on visiting Becca Tey in the morning to find out more about Bad Pete's music video. The actress seemed the most logical place to start.

Stu got up to start the coffee while I drifted in and out of sleep. We had left a window open, and I tucked the blanket under my chin, relishing the cool morning air. Stu let Sam outside to do his business—he was still above using his litter box—and my cat immediately began chittering at something. Probably a bird or a squirrel, I assumed.

"Maddy," Stu called, his voice loud with alarm.

My legs kicked free of the blanket. I lurched upright, grabbed my robe off the floor, and hurried down the hallway, half expecting to hear Sam screech while he attacked whatever was outside. But there were no sounds of a struggle.

Soft morning light pooled against the far wall of the sunroom.

Stu stood frozen in front of the sliding glass door, sweatpants slung low, his bare skin covered in goosebumps. He was staring outside, as if hypnotized.

I followed his gaze, and my mouth went dry.

Sam was perched quietly on the patio table. The object of his attention wasn't a bird.

It was Beady, his gnome buddy from Beverly Hills.

Beady wasn't alone. Three other gnomes were poking around my garden, their stubby fingers busy in the pots of herbs I used for my magic.

"Aren't these the same things you dealt with in Beverly Hills? Did they follow your mother here?" Stu asked.

I felt lightheaded. "They're gnomes, and yeah, they're hers."

Stu's arm went around my waist. "What are you going to do?"

Find my slingshot and take them out. Tackle them with a magic-boosted Smoke Bomb, then throw them in a crate and haul them back to Beverly Hills.

My fingers itched to do something, anything. But it was useless.

My throat was closing. I recognized that feeling. Panic.

"I don't know what to do. The gnomes must have bypassed my protection spell somehow. The trouble with gnomes is, even if I managed to round them up and ditch them somewhere far away, they'd find a way back. Once they've settled in a place, it's nearly impossible to get rid of them."

"You've got rid of far worse before," Stu said. "Like the Cucuy and those vampire birds. And they were way more dangerous. You'll figure something out."

I should have felt reassured by Stu's faith in me, but instead, my chest tightened. El Cucuy and the vampiric creatures had supernatural origins. The gnomes were something else entirely. They had appeared in the first wave of entities, but they were different. They could evade capture. The usual tools, like Smoke Bombs, didn't always take them out. And apparently, they were impervious to my protection spell.

They were pesky little buggers, and now they were loose in my community.

Stu cleared his throat. "You *will* figure something out," he repeated, "right?" He sounded nervous, and I could guess what he was anxious about.

"No pressure," I said, my voice tight. "Either I fix this or Chavez Ravine is no longer entity-free, and property values will tank."

Stu gave me a one-armed hug. "Is there anything I can do to help?"

"If I think of something, I'll let you know." I sighed. "You better get ready, or you'll be late."

Sam and Beady glanced in our direction and began talking in a language all their own. I had made psychic contact with the gnome leader before, but it was still difficult to understand him. Why were he and his friends here, and how long did they intend to stay? I needed my mother's help.

Somewhere in the house, my phone rang.

"I'll get it for you," Stu said, disappearing inside.

"What the hell are you doing here, Beady?" My voice was loud and sharp. I hadn't had my coffee, and I was cranky.

The gnome ignored me. Rude. One of Beady's friends picked up a pot of spearmint and gave it a tentative sniff.

"Hey!" I yelled. "Put that down. You're not in Beverly Hills anymore. This is *my* property."

Stu came running back with my phone. "It's your mom." He handed me the phone and hurried back inside.

"Mother?"

"Don't speak to me in that tone," she snapped. "I'm already going through enough as it is without your attitude." She cleared her throat. "We have a problem."

"Oh, we do, do we?" Sarcasm dripped from my voice. "Let me guess. You created a problem, and now you're expecting *me* to clean it up?"

"Are you psychic all of a sudden? How do you even know what I'm talking about?"

In the background, Hernan shouted, "Leave my roses alone!"

"Because I have three of your gnomes in my backyard and I know *I* didn't invite them here. Care to explain?"

My mother cleared her throat again. "They aren't *my* gnomes. They were in Beverly Hills before I got there. But I'm guessing they sneaked into the van that delivered my furniture. We discovered them this morning. Hernan tried to run them off with the hose, so they disappeared for a while, but now they're back. At least, most of them are. A few seem to be missing." My mother didn't sound half as upset as she should have been.

I pressed a finger between my eyes. It was possible I'd had one glass of wine too many and I was a tiny bit hungover.

The aroma of fresh coffee drifted outside. I needed a mug…badly.

"You need to come over and translate. Sam's talking to your head gnome, and I have no idea what's happening. Sam could be granting them squatter's rights to La Loma for all I know."

Stu reappeared, pressed a mug of steaming coffee into my hand, and disappeared again.

I took a sip of coffee. "Can you drive Hernan's car?"

"I have a driver's license, Madeline," my mother replied. "Of course, I can drive."

That was questionable. "While I've got you, would you hand the phone to Hernan? I need to talk to him."

54

My mother clucked her tongue. "I didn't hear you say 'please,' but I'll get him." She yelled his name so loudly my ear hurt.

A few moments later, Hernan answered, muttering. "What a terrible morning. Your mother and I woke up to gnomes! And I don't know what she plans to do about them."

Welcome to my world. "Listen, Hernan. The gnomes complicate things. A lot. For you *and* for me. You're already facing a recall petition. Even if we manage to contain the gnomes and they're not running all over the place, people are going to connect your fiancé to the creatures that ruined Beverly Hills, and guess who's going to get the blame? You. And because she's my mother, also me. We need to get in front of this and fast."

"What are we supposed to do?" Hernan shouted.

I put him on speaker before I lost my hearing. "I'm not sure yet. But you need to call Cora and let her know what's going on. She can decide how to proceed."

Hernan sighed dramatically. "Why can't we wait? See how things go? What if Malena talks them into leaving, and I get Cora all riled up for nothing?"

I glanced over at Beady and his gnome posse. They strutted around my garden with the smug satisfaction of new homeowners touring a their property.

"My mother couldn't talk the gnomes into leaving Beverly Hills, and believe me, she tried. They aren't going anywhere."

"You don't know that!" Hernan sputtered. "You need to try!"

The poor guy sounded desperate. There was a lot on the line, including his reputation and his position on the board.

"I will," I said firmly. "But I'm just being realistic."

A scream blasted through the speaker. The connection dropped.

Chapter 10

I wouldn't say he planned it, but a good way to get the attention of the head of security is to scream into the phone, then hang up.

The gnomes would have to wait. I threw on some clothes, gave Stu a quick explanation, and jumped into the Jeep, headed for Hernan's.

When I pulled up to his house in Bishop, the front door was wide open. No Hernan. No Mother. No gnomes. I tore through the house, calling his name, checking every room, and bursting into the backyard.

Nothing but flowers, an empty shed, and a hammock swaying slightly in the breeze.

I ran along the side yard, sprinted into the street, and pivoted in place, eyes darting up and down the block. Cora lived just a couple of doors down. No sign of unusual activity there. It was quiet, but that wasn't unusual. Many of the residents had already left for work. Kids were back in school.

Angry voices drifted toward me. I pinpointed the commotion—*across the street*—and took off running. My footsteps matched the hammering in my chest.

The racket was coming from the Mendez family compound. I followed the shouting down the long driveway, where three houses formed a horseshoe around a shared garden.

Three gnomes were kneeling in the dirt, patting soil around thorny rose bushes. There was Hernan, flinching while two older women berated him, jabbing fingers in his face. Ron Mendez, my off-duty command center supervisor, stood off to the side, wearing nothing but boxer shorts. He looked on, arms folded across his chest, his face frozen.

I ran up, breathless. Ron turned toward me. His eyes widened, and he let out a huge breath. "I was just going to call you! We've got gnomes!"

Yes, we did, and two residents of Chavez Ravine had seen them and were blaming Hernan. It was going to be impossible to contain the story.

"This is all your fault, viejo!" Ron's grandmother yelled. "If you hadn't brought that woman here, we wouldn't have these things here, ruining our yard."

The younger woman, who had to have been Ron's mother, clapped her hands at the gnomes like they were pesky birds. "Go on! Get! Váyase!"

The gnomes, of course, ignored her. Ron's mother pulled a flip-flop off her foot.

"Mom," Ron said through clenched teeth. "Please don't throw your chanclas."

Ron's mother shot him a dismissive look, then hurled her leather flip-flop at the closest gnome. She had impressive aim. It smacked the back of his head with such force it nearly dislodged his pointy hat.

The gnome whipped around, its eyes narrowing. It snatched up the sandal and hurled it back. Ron's mother leapt aside just in time.

Time to intervene before a full-blown chancla war broke out.

I stepped between Hernan and the Mendez ladies. "All right, all right. Everyone, please…" I was about to say, "Calm down," but the venomous look the women cast in my direction made me stop. Instead, I nodded politely at Ron's grandmother, whom I had met before. "I know we have an unusual situation on our hands, but—"

"Unusual situation, baloney!" Ron's grandmother interrupted. "No disrespect to you, Madeline. I'm grateful for what you've done for my grandson. But these horrible things are here because Hernan Frias couldn't keep it in his pants and he brought your mother into our neighborhood. And now look what's happened!"

My sentiments exactly. "I understand. I really do—"

"You don't know the half of it, Madeline!" Hernan thundered. "That woman, my so-called friend and neighbor, has done me dirty. She's the one behind the recall petition! She's the one organizing everyone against me! And how long have we known each other, Carmen? Our entire lives, that's how long! We even babysat Barbara when she was little!"

"It's a miracle I survived," Ron's mother muttered.

Carmen wagged a finger at Hernan. "You got what you deserve! If your poor wife knew what you were up to with that woman, she'd be rolling in her grave."

I laid a hand on Hernan's arm, but he shook me off.

"My wife has been dead for more than ten years, Carmen! And my personal life is none of your darn tootin' business."

Everyone seemed to have forgotten the gnomes. Not that the gnomes were paying any attention to us. They were too busy trying to get the rose bushes into the ground.

Ron leaned in, his voice low. "My grandma and Hernan's wife were best friends."

Interesting, but it didn't solve our problems in pointy hats. "Okay, everyone. Why don't the ladies go inside and leave Ron and I to deal with the gnomes?"

"That's probably best. Come on, Mama. Let's go." Barbara turned and began walking toward her house, then added over her shoulder, "We started the recall because of the danger Malena Bantacorte presents to our community, not because Hernan's unfaithful to his wife's memory." She shoved her hands into the pockets of her fuzzy pink robe.

Carmen stood still, her angry eyes shooting daggers at Hernan.

Hernan pressed his hands to his head as if trying to keep it from exploding. "Do you see what I'm dealing with, Madeline? It's insanity. Sheer insanity!"

Barbara paused and turned my way. "What I'd like to know is why you haven't sent out an alert to the community telling everyone we have a gnome outbreak? I nearly had a heart attack when I came outside and found them. I yelled so loud I woke up poor mijo."

That explained Ron's stubble and tousled hair; she had ruined his sleep-in.

Arguing with three mothers hadn't been on my agenda, and my nerves were fraying. "I didn't have time for an alert. I came straight here."

Barbara exhaled loudly. "Well, you're not sending one now, are you?"

"Mom!" Ron's face turned bright red. "You can't talk to my boss like that!"

Barbara's shoulders slumped, the fight visibly draining from her body. Her pink robe sagged around her frame, and she rubbed at a deep crease between her eyebrows. "I'm sorry, Madeline," she said, her voice softening. "It's just been a very upsetting morning. Mama, let's go inside."

The women headed toward the main house, with Carmen muttering all the way. Lips pressed tightly together, Hernan stomped off.

Ron scratched at his stubble. "So, what's the plan, boss?" he asked, eyeing the gnomes warily.

"I'll try and get these back to Hernan's place," I said. "If I need your help, I'll let you know."

Ron's eyes widened. "Really? You don't want me to help now? I can go get changed real quick."

With gnomes, sometimes fewer people were better—gnomes tended to disappear when confronted.

I scanned the yard. It was filled with fruit trees, cacti, and other succulents, but there were a few healthy-looking begonia bushes growing along the main house. Those would be enough of an enticement.

"Ron, I just need one favor. Can you bring me a shovel?"

Ron eyed me nervously. "You're not going to hit them, are you?"

I laughed. "They wouldn't let me close enough to try. Don't worry. I've got something else in mind."

Minutes later, shovel in hand, I marched over to the begonias and began digging them up as awkwardly and clumsily as I could manage. My award-winning performance brought the gnomes dashing to my side. I handed my shovel to the closest one.

"Oh, thank you! These need to be planted across the street. Can you help me?" I batted my eyelashes.

Playing the part of the hapless gardener paid off better than I expected. They trotted obediently behind me, carrying the begonias, all the way across the street and into Hernan's backyard, where I pointed to the back fence. I found a large bag of potting soil and another of mulch and dragged them out. A gnome came over and hauled them away.

I sank into a patio chair, exhausted.

Something, probably a gnome, was moving around in Hernan's shed. I got to my feet, approached the door, and nearly ran into my mother.

"What are you doing here?" we asked at the same time.

"You first," I quickly added.

My mother sat down on the hammock. "Well, when those horrible women started yelling at Hernan, I thought it best I stay out of the way, so I came out here to wait until things calmed down." She huddled into her sweater. "Your turn."

"I heard screaming when I was talking on the phone with Hernan, so I came over as quickly as I could to see if you two were in trouble. I didn't quite expect to sail directly into Hurricane Carmen. But here we are now, so let's talk. We need to find a way to get rid of those things."

My mother rocked back and forth a little on the hammock, avoiding my gaze. "Madeline, I have good news and bad news."

I sighed. Might as well get it over with. "Bad news first."

"The gnomes like it here, better than Beverly Hills."

Not a complete surprise, but my heart sank anyway. "And the good news?"

"We've come to an understanding. It took some negotiating, so I'm hoping you can agree to it, and—"

I jumped to my feet, panicked. "Mother. Whatever it is, you shouldn't have done anything without talking to me first."

"Beggars can't be choosy, Madeline, and you need a solution. If you will allow me to finish what I was saying, I think even you will be pleased." She paused, probably for dramatic effect. "Actually, I didn't negotiate with them. Your cat did."

It took me a moment to realize what she had just said. "Sam? *My* Sam? Sam did a deal with the…gnomes?"

"It's not a bad one either. Honestly, Madeline, it's time you figure out where the heck he came from because he's no ordinary cat. At any rate, here's the plan: the gnomes will be allowed to stay in exchange for working *with* Ben Tomas as part of his landscaping crew, supervised by Sam and his cat appointees."

I was stunned. It was impossible to get rid of the gnomes once they arrived, but I hadn't thought about turning them into free labor. I hated to think what the entity rights people might have to say about that. At a minimum, they would accuse us of exploiting the gnomes.

Gnomes weren't scary like ghouls or mermaids with teeth. Personally, I found them slightly creepy, but they were small and kind of cute. Crystal De Lucca, the most vocal entity advocate, and her well-funded entity rights group in Santa Monica would definitely be knocking down the guard gates to express their outrage. After contacting all the TV news stations, of course.

"Well, Madeline. That's the good news. What do you think?"

"I think this is going to bite us in the ass, but what's done is done. I can actually see how it might work. But the next part is going to be tricky."

Would Ben even want the extra help? And what was I going to say to Cora and the board about a resident entity workforce?

Chapter 11

Cora arranged an emergency board session for that evening. Everyone arrived dressed more casually than usual, except for Dan Berman. He wore his uniform of jeans and a tie-dye shirt, his gray hair scraped back from his long face into a thin ponytail.

Even in a black vintage-washed sweatshirt, Eileen managed to look like a woman about to talk you into buying a luxury property you couldn't afford.

Cora had come straight from babysitting her grandson, silver hair tousled, sneakers on her feet. She had briefed Charlie Perez about the gnome situation, and he was uncharacteristically grim. No surprise there. He was in real estate and knew what gnomes could do to property values.

Hernan sat beside me, fidgeting. As well he should, considering he was the cause of it all.

"Madeline has some information she'd like to share with us." Cora nodded in my direction.

Wrong. I had information I preferred to keep all to myself, but Cora had other ideas.

Eileen gasped. "Is it the new entities? Have you found them?"

I cleared my throat. Folded my hands on the table. "No. I'm going to tell you something, but before I do, I would like you to know there is nothing to worry about. The situation has been handled, and it will be monitored with all the attention it deserves."

Dan Berman lifted his eyebrows. "That sounds serious."

Charlie snorted, quickly masking it with a cough. He raised his water glass, his eyes meeting mine in apology while he took a slow sip.

I took a deep breath and continued. "A small group of gnomes has infiltrated Chavez Ravine—"

Eileen gasped. Dan Berman gripped the edge of the table, his eyes bulging.

"As you know," I went on as if the two people across from me weren't in the process of having fits, "they are impossible to displace once they've moved in, so our strategy is to contain them and minimize their impact." My words sounded as cold and matter-of-fact as an Occult Affairs training video.

Eileen's voice appeared to have stopped working. Her jaw was opening and closing soundlessly.

Thankful for the silence, I continued. "My mother's psychic abilities allowed her to communicate with the gnomes in Beverly Hills. There, she harnessed their gardening skills and came up with a plan to redistribute them across the city. We decided a different approach was needed here. Rather than a costly eradication plan, which would cause disruption for our residents and which would ultimately fail, we have taken a more cooperative approach. We are going to put the gnomes to work under the direction of our master landscaper, Ben Tomas."

Eileen shifted in her seat to glare at Hernan. "This is your doing! Those gnomes followed Malena here, didn't they? If you hadn't invited that woman to move in with you, this would never have happened."

Charlie drummed his fingers on the table. "New clusters of gnomes pop up all over Los Angeles, Eileen. We're surrounded by them—they're in the valley, in Pasadena, in Altadena. We've been lucky they haven't found their way here before now. There's no way to prove Malena brought them here. It may be a coincidence, and I would think very seriously about making accusations you can't prove. We don't want to find ourselves on the wrong end of a lawsuit, do we?"

Eileen blinked, clearly taken off guard. "But…but…" she sputtered. "Ben has enough to do without having to wrangle those awful things."

The next part would be tricky, but there was no avoiding it. I took a deep breath and made eye contact with each board member. "Ben won't be supervising them alone. When Beverly Hills had a new influx of gnomes, my cat helped control them. Gnomes seem to be willing to work with cats, and they bring out their feline herding instincts. Or they did in my cat, at least. So, he'll be assembling a team of cats, and they'll act as"—I paused, searching for the right term—"gnome guardians."

Dan joined Eileen in a fresh burst of outraged sputtering.

I held up a hand. "I know, I know. It sounds a little crazy, but believe me, it's effective and—"

"And more importantly," Charlie interrupted, "it won't cost us a thing. Also, whatever we can say about gnomes, they have green thumbs and work hard. And they work for free. Which means we can tick off Ben's request for additional staffing. And that is a savings to our community."

Charlie made it sound like the gnomes were doing us a favor.

"Cats!" Dan nearly shouted while he glared at me. "You're going to rely on cats to keep the gnomes in line? That's ridiculous. That's *your* responsibility. Your security staff's responsibility."

I pressed my palms into my thighs and counted to five before responding. "It is. But animals have worked alongside humans for centuries. Do you think a rancher is shirking their responsibility when they use dogs to guide their herd? Or a police department is being lazy because they use dogs in their investigations? We're doing the same thing. Gnomes respond better to cats than to people, and my staff has its hands full monitoring entity emergence holes and searching for missing entities. That's a much better use of their time than chasing gnomes. That said, we have a backup plan. We've installed trackers on the gnomes, so we'll know where they are at all times. We can monitor them in the command center."

Dan's hand flew to his heart. "You didn't chip them, did you? Like cattle or something?"

"My dog's chipped," Charlie said. "It's no big deal."

Dan shook his head. "We can't treat gnomes like we treat the family pet! If this were to get out, we'll have entity rights groups breathing down our necks and threatening litigation."

I held up a hand. "We didn't microchip them. We attached trackers to their hats. They never take them off." I paused, frowning. "As a matter of fact, I'm not sure they *can* take them off. Anyway, don't worry. It's all very humane."

Eileen sat back in her seat, with a hand placed against the side of her face. "What are we supposed to tell residents? Or buyers? This is just too much."

I pulled my laptop closer and tapped a few keys. "I've drafted a message. Cora's approved it, and it's now in your inbox."

Everyone except for Cora checked their phones. When they were done, Dan gave a long exhale.

"Okay. It's good."

"Let's just see what residents have to say about this," Eileen muttered, dropping her phone into her red leather tote. "One vocal group in particular," she stared at Hernan.

I got to my feet, relieved to have the conversation behind me, though my day was nowhere near finished. Ben was not happy about the plan and needed some handholding. And there were logistics to figure out. Where would the gnomes stay at night? How would they get to wherever Ben needed them to go? And where would Sam find cats to help keep the gnomes in line?

When I got home, I was surprised to find that, between my mother, Sam, and Ben, they had managed to work everything out. The gnomes would stay in the equipment yard in Palo Verde. In fact, they were there already. Sam had hopped into the bed of Ben's truck, and the gnomes had climbed in after him.

And, according to Ben, Sam had already managed to recruit his staff. "It was the weirdest thing. Ten minutes after Sam walked into the equipment yard, cats started showing up. I saw some of them coming down the hill from Elysian Park. They looked feral. There were about a dozen of them. It was like Sam called a meeting or something."

"What do you say about that cat of yours now, Madeline?" my mother asked smugly.

"What I always say," I replied. "He's a mystery."

My mother, striking a regal pose in a high-backed chair, smoothed her purple caftan over her knees. "And mysteries are meant to be solved. If you ask me, I think you need to find out where he came from."

I *hadn't* asked her, but when did that stop my mother?

Rory Tuck had mentioned paying big bucks for Sam. Presumably, that meant he had bought him from a reputable breeder.

If I had been a nicer daughter, I would have offered my mother a wine spritzer, but I wanted her out of my house before she started rearranging the furniture. She had already hit my workbench. Julia's handcrafted bowls now sat empty, while my herbs, seeds, and ritual ingredients had been imprisoned in kitchen jars with lids—"rescued" from the evils of dust and cat hair.

My mother got to her feet with a sigh. "I better get on home. Hernan will be wanting his dinner. It's a good thing we have plenty of leftovers."

My mother's leftovers were better than most people's special occasion meals. Hernan was a lucky guy. In some respects, anyway.

I pecked her cheek. It was warm and dry. She smelled faintly of jasmine. "Thank you, Mom. For everything you did today. I really mean it."

My mother sniffed. "See? Did that little bit of appreciation hurt you? No." She pulled me toward her and pressed her lips against my temple. "Aren't things better when we work together, hija? Because who else has your best interests at heart? Your mother, that's who. All you need to do is trust me a little."

We were miles from trust, but I had to admit, we'd had a pretty good day. I had needed her expertise, and my mother had come through with minimal fuss. Not bad.

I wanted nothing more than to change into sweatpants and curl up on the couch with a book, but I had one more thing to do. After touching up my makeup, I changed into black pants and a cream-colored sweater and drove to Olga's Cantina. It was time to meet Becca Tey and pump her for information about Bad Pete's music video.

Chapter 12

Olga Sanchez stood at the host station just inside the door, her salt and pepper hair braided and coiled atop her head, Frida Kahlo style, with small red flowers tucked into the plaits. The cheerful flowers contrasted with the tight line of her crimson-painted mouth and the cool assessment in her eyes while she watched me approach.

I scanned the restaurant. It was busy. The bar was packed, but there didn't seem to be quite as many people in the dining rooms as usual.

"Hi, Olga. I've never seen you out here before."

Her nostrils twitched. "No. Because it's never been necessary before. My place is in the kitchen and not out here. But Martine and Nico think it's best if I stay out of the kitchen. They don't even want me to *watch* them cook the food." She sounded outraged.

Her chefs had a point. I gave a noncommittal "Mmm" and cleared my throat. "I'm meeting Becca Tey. Is she here?"

Olga jerked her head in the direction of the bar. "Becca's where she usually is. As close to the booze as possible. I put you at a quiet table in one of the alcoves." She scowled. "Are you doing anything? To solve this pinche hex…or whatever it is? I don't know how much more I can take."

I took a deep breath. Olga's bad mood seemed unfairly focused on me. Twenty-four hours was hardly enough time to solve the mystery, especially when I had dealt with a gnome infestation and an angry board at the same time. But Olga was not only a resident of Chavez Ravine; she also ran a business in La Loma and paid dues there. I owed her a reassuring professional response.

"I totally understand, Olga. What I'm about to tell you is very preliminary, but I'm following a lead, which is why I'm meeting with Becca. You and several others seem to have been affected by a curse or a hex or something that targets your talents, and all of you were on the set of Bad Pete's music video."

Olga's eyes snapped open. Six customers filed in, and she flagged down a passing server. "Take them to table sixteen." She pointed toward a window with a view of the lush gardens. When they were out of earshot, Olga leaned over the podium. "Who else was hexed?"

Was there confidentiality when it came to hexes? If word somehow made it to the tabloids…I didn't want to think about what that might mean for Pete.

"Look, Olga. This is a sensitive situation. I'd need their permission to talk about it. I haven't told anyone about you either. I suspect you wouldn't like it if your customers knew. Did you tell your staff?"

Olga sighed. "Yes. I was so upset I just blurted it out. And I may have suggested that Bernie Mora was behind it all. Nico got pretty mad and told Bernie, and Bernie called me and told me off. So, it's fair to say it's not exactly a secret."

Well, I had advised her to stay quiet until I found out more.

She frowned. "Maddy, there were a lot of people at that music video. And if you're talking to Becca, I'm guessing something happened to her too?"

I ignored that and continued in as strong and confident a voice as I could muster. "I'm just gathering as much information as possible about that music video, and Becca knows a lot of people. Hopefully, she'll be able to give me the background I need for my investigation."

Olga looked at me through narrowed eyes. "You're nowhere near solving this, are you?"

"No." I sighed. "I'm just getting started. But I'm taking this very seriously. You can count on that." I raised my right hand and held up three fingers. "Scout's honor."

Her mouth twisted. "That's funny. You, a Girl Scout. Haha."

"Hey! I was a member of the Los Angeles Police Department."

"Well, just Occult Affairs, but okay." Olga's voice had softened.

It was a bit much dealing with Olga right after my mother, so by the time I was sitting across from Becca Tey, I was more than ready for a glass of pinot noir. Becca had ordered a bottle from a nice winery in Monterrey County and poured two glasses. I grabbed mine and took a big, thirsty gulp.

"Wow," she said. "Bad day, huh? I heard about the gnomes." She shrugged. "I mean, really, who cares? It's not like they're scary. They're gnomes. Kinda cute. Kinda useful. And you've got the cats to make sure they stay in line! How adorable is that? Honestly, it's practically a novelty act. Chavez Ravine should charge admission to see the show."

Like Becca herself, the idea was a little over-the-top. She wore a purple blouse, her long black hair hanging loose around her shoulders. Due to the miracle of an aggressive anti-aging regimen, she looked both younger for her age and, at certain angles, somehow older too. Early fifties, I guessed.

"Hey, Stu told me about the trouble you had at the table read."

Becca moved the red glass jar holding a burning candle from one side of the table to the other, a faraway look in her eyes.

"Yeah, that freaked me out. And it didn't help that I was the oldest person in the room, getting carted off to the ER. Not sure how I'll live that down. I went to a neurologist, and she's ordered a bunch of tests." She bit her lip.

Poor Becca. She was obviously worried. I owed it to her to reveal my suspicions, so I took a sip of wine—a normal, non-gluttonous sip—and put down my glass.

"Becca, there may not be anything wrong with you. Pete lost his voice. And there are others. So far, I know of three more people having trouble after working on the music video. I think it's possible you may all have been hexed. Or something."

Becca's artificially plumped lips fell open. "Hexed!" She frowned. "Is that even a thing?"

In a world with gnomes and supervising cats, it was a wonder she even had to ask.

"Yes. Long story, but I've been the victim of hexes too. If I can find the source, it's possible I can figure out how to reverse it."

Becca stared into the candlelight, her face scrunched. "So, there are at least five other people who can't function, and they all worked on the video?"

I nodded.

"Then I believe you. What can I do to help?"

"I need to know more about Pete's music video. It's being shot at Western Studios, right?"

Becca nodded. "Yes. The location was Pete's idea. He'd read about the old Western set at the back of the property. It hasn't been used since the 1950s. It's amazing because all the old facades are still standing. There's a saloon, a general store, a little church with a steeple, a hotel, and even a jail. Pete's agent got the studios to open it back up and rent it to him. It's really quite something."

I didn't want to reveal the names of Becca's cursed cohorts, so I chose my words carefully. "How many people are involved in the video?"

Becca knitted her eyebrows together. "Around sixty, I'd guess. Pete's a superstar, so they've got a big budget. It's basically a mini movie. There's a production team with a director and producer, then there's a director of photography, the camera and lighting crews, the set design people, wardrobe, makeup, all the talent, like dancers and extras, and all the postproduction folks too. Oh, and I almost forgot. The choreographer, who is the second-biggest piece of work on the set."

"Second biggest? Who's the biggest piece of work?"

"The director. If there was an award for Best Entitled Asshole, he'd win."

"Not well liked, I take it?"

Becca's lips thinned into a grim line. "Universally despised but tolerated because he's Hollywood royalty. His great-grandfather was a famous director of Western films. That's pretty much all I know. The creep has been chatting up Clare Wells. Such a pretty girl. I told her to be on her guard, and you should have seen her expression. I get the impression Stu's ex has been overprotective with that girl. She has no street smarts."

Alarm bells began to sound. "Has she been alone with him?"

"Not as far as I know. Some of us older gals have been looking out for her. Honestly, I'm less concerned about the director than I am about one of the dancers." Becca pursed her lips.

"She's almost eighteen," I pointed out. "She's starting college next year."

Becca sniffed. "Ask me how old this dancer is."

My heart sank. "How old?"

"Twenty-four. A very, *very* experienced twenty-four. Rumor is he's already hooked up with half the dancers and one of the backup singers, and she's got to be thirty."

"And you think he's going after Clare?"

Becca rolled her eyes. "He doesn't have to 'go after' anyone. They just seem to line up and throw themselves at him, including Clare." She grimaced. "I was going to mention it to Stu, and then I had the whole memory lapse thing to deal with, and I forgot."

I remembered when Clare had met Malik, a young Occult Affairs officer. She had made it no secret she found him "hot," and when I pointed out he was too old for her, she called the age gap "no big deal."

Clare was not my daughter, but my stomach churned at the thought of her getting involved with someone like that.

"What's this guy's name?" I asked through gritted teeth.

"I thought you'd never ask," Becca said. "Theo Patridis. There are pictures, you know."

I didn't know, and I wasn't sure I wanted to see them, but I owed it to Stu to get to the bottom of this. "Show me."

Chapter 13

Becca rummaged through her purse. A moment later, I was staring at a photo on her phone. Clare and a good-looking guy, their heads together, in a selfie. Clare appeared older in the photo and deliriously happy. And no wonder. Her companion wasn't just good-looking; he was in Greek God territory, with curly dark hair, a strong jaw, high cheekbones, and a straight nose. With that name, he might actually have been Greek. His heavy black eyelashes were an insult to mascaraed women everywhere.

Becca leaned across the table and swiped to the next photo. Another image of Clare and Theo, mouths open, scream-smiling at the camera. I never got the appeal of that pose. It made people look unhinged.

"Oh, boy. I wonder if Stu knows about this kid. He looks dangerous."

Becca put her phone back in her purse. "He's no kid," she said with a sniff. "He's twenty-four. Stu knows if he follows his daughter's Instagram account. That's where those pictures are."

I didn't dare follow Clare's account. As her father's girlfriend, that would have been weird. But that didn't mean I couldn't stalk her. The age difference between nearly twenty-four and eighteen was significant. A sheltered nearly eighteen-year-old at that. Talk about a power imbalance.

My talk with Becca had spun me off in a completely new direction, but the Clare-Theo situation would have to wait.

"Becca, I know this is an odd question, but is there anyone involved in the production who might possibly be a witch?"

Becca blinked in surprise. "A witch? Really?"

I glanced around. It wouldn't do for people to overhear the head of security talking about witches. But the room was loud, with people talking and laughing over the clinking of glasses, and our conversation was lost in the noise.

"A witch is the most likely kind of person to issue a hex," I said, keeping my voice low. "Or a practitioner of folk magic. Does any of that sort ring any bells?"

Becca topped up our wineglasses. "Not one. Everyone on the production seems to be under thirty, except for me and the director, and they're very serious about what they're doing. And for whatever I can say about Theo—like the guy's a *total* player— he's a talented dancer. None of that seems like witch behavior to me."

I didn't quite see how young, talented people couldn't also be witches, but I decided not to belabor the point. "Who's the director? You said he's an asshole. Tell me about him."

"Not much to tell. Jason Wood is the original nepo baby. I told you about his grandfather, and his father was a producer who churned out some popular sci-fi series."

Becca named a few titles. I had heard of some but never watched them myself.

"Jason went to film school at USC and got his MFA. His first movie did well enough, so he kept working. He mostly does outdoor adventures. His last project was a Western set in Arizona, which is why Pete hired him…because he was going for a similar aesthetic. Jason is a brilliant director, but he's a control freak and really intense. And when actors push back, he can get very confrontational."

"I'm surprised Pete hired him," I said.

Becca shrugged. "Well, Jason thinks Pete has what it takes to make the leap to acting. Personally, I agree. Pete's one of those people you can't take your eyes off of. But just thinking about acting makes Pete nervous. I think he's testing the waters with someone he trusts, and that's Jason."

All of that was very interesting, but it didn't help me solve the problem of the hex bags or whatever they were. My team really needed to search the set. I could ask Pete for permission. He might look at me sideways, but he would probably arrange it.

When I got home, I messaged Pete. He called me immediately and listened without interruption to what I had to say. When I finished, he exhaled loudly.

"Wow. Okay. Yeah, not a problem. If this helps me get my voice back, I'm down. One hundred percent. We're not shooting tomorrow, so that would be ideal…if your team can be ready."

"We'll be ready. How about eight thirty tomorrow morning? And is there any chance I can visit the set later during production?"

"No problem. We're back at it again the day after tomorrow."

"How does that work?" I asked, curious. "Given that you can't sing?"

Pete barked out a laugh. "We recorded the song ages ago. Now it's all lip-synch. But it kills me to cancel concert dates."

Minutes after we hung up, the doorbell rang. It was Ben escorting Sam home. The cat darted past Ben's legs and raced into the kitchen, where he began meowing loudly. It was after eight o'clock, a couple of hours past his usual dinnertime. He must have been starving.

I pulled Ben inside, closed the door on the dark, chilly evening, and hurried into the kitchen, where I opened a can of Salmon Delite. Noting how fast Sam was gobbling it down, I cracked open a second one. After I refreshed his water, I placed some treats in a small ceramic bowl, retrieved a Negro Modelo from the refrigerator, and handed it to an exhausted-looking Ben.

"Thank you for taking care of Sam, Ben. How did things go?"

"Better than I expected," he said grudgingly. "It's a little crazy, but we're figuring things out. The gnomes don't understand me, or they pretend they don't, so I tell Sam what I want them to do. He makes these weird noises, and Beady talks to the other gnomes, and then they get to work. I had them plant periwinkle on some steep slopes, and that went really well because they're practically goats, so the hill was no big deal at all..." His voice drifted off, and he frowned.

"Yes?"

Ben took a swig of beer. "Well, I didn't want to leave Sam out there alone. I wanted to make sure the gnomes didn't run off. And it all went fine, except some people running the path along the top of the ravine saw them and stopped to watch and take pictures. They must have let their friends know because other people started showing up with their kids, and suddenly, it felt like we were an exhibit at the zoo."

"Did the people seem upset?"

Ben shook his head. "No. That's the weird thing. I was going to call you and ask if you wanted to come and do some damage control, but Julia was there and started talking to people. They thought the gnomes were really cool and fun to watch."

A lightness came over me. I couldn't believe it. Gnomes had a terrible reputation in Los Angeles. But people seemed to like the sight of the little creatures hard at work in Chavez Ravine. I could work with that.

"If I remember right, you needed the extra staff to plant on all the hillsides to prevent mudslides, right?"

Ben drank more of his beer and nodded. "That's right. It's a huge project. I was a little nervous about putting the gnomes in such a visible spot, but it really paid off. They can move twice as fast as my regular crew on those steep slopes."

Sam strode into the living room, jumped onto his favorite piece of furniture—a colorful ottoman—and fixed his green eyes on us.

"Great job, Sam," I said before turning my attention back to Ben. "It would be a big help if you could keep the gnomes on Project Hillside for as long as possible. The more people see them helping to prevent a possible disaster, the better off we'll all be."

"Let's just hope they continue to cooperate," Ben said gloomily.

I rapped my knuckles on an end table. "Knock on wood."

Ben walked into the kitchen, rinsed out his empty beer bottle, and dropped it into the recycling bin in the pantry. Julia had said he kept a spotless house and had a cleaning routine that put hers to shame.

I leaned against the kitchen door. "So, the gnomes are back in the equipment yard for the night?"

Ben picked up Sam's empty food bowls and washed them in the sink. "Yeah, I'm pretty sure. Some new cats arrived just before Sam and I left." Ben paused. "Maybe we shouldn't be parading them around in public? It might be a bad look, with the entity rights groups and all."

It was a risk, but one worth taking.

"No. We need to take advantage of the goodwill the gnomes seem to be generating. If we need to switch gears, we'll do that."

Ben ripped off several sheets of paper towels and wiped the cat bowls dry. "Sounds like a plan." He scraped a hand through his hair. "One more thing. It's Julia. She's feeling really low, not being able to sculpt or paint. She's got the shop, and there's plenty to sell, but she needs a creative outlet. Any ideas?"

I thought for a moment. "Doesn't she have that freelance gig on Bad Pete's music video?"

"She helped work on the set, but her part is done," Ben replied.

Julia's name had been mentioned at a board meeting recently, but it took a few moments for my tired brain to recall exactly why. And then I had it. "How about the Day of the Dead Festival? The board approved it. It's not that far off. Shouldn't she be working on it?"

Ben wrinkled his nose. "She should, but Eileen Simpson said she wanted to take the lead organizing it. You know how she is."

Oh yeah. I knew how she was.

"Well, that's not okay. It was Julia's idea," I protested. "And it needs to be run by someone who understands the Day of the Dead and knows its history. I can't think of anyone more qualified than Julia."

"That's what *I* thought," Ben said on his way out.

I flopped on the couch and pulled out my phone. Sam jumped into my lap in a rare show of affection, pressed his big head against my chest, and purred. It was so loud it made my bones vibrate. I scratched the top of his head, starting slowly, watching for signs of an incoming swipe of his dagger-like claws.

"Let's check and make sure our gnomes are behaving."

Sam straightened and peered at the screen expectantly. I loaded my heatmap app and waited while it connected. In a few seconds, green dots appeared in Ben's storage yard, exactly where they should have been.

One less thing to worry about.

But there were plenty of other worries to take its place. Like the strange hex bag lurking somewhere on Bad Pete's set, causing people to lose their ability to work. And the entity emergence holes that were missing their entities.

But those were tomorrow's problems.

Sam and I walked to the bedroom. I really needed a good night's sleep.

Chapter 14

Sam, being a cat, was nocturnal. No matter how busy his day had been, he prowled around all night, doing whatever cats do.

Not me. I had hit the sack hard, so I ended up being the first one awake, making coffee and checking the overnight security reports while Sam snoozed away in the bedroom.

Until seven o'clock. Since my cat had been appointed Chief Gnome Officer, he had to be ready for Ben's pickup at 7:30 a.m. Which was why I found myself shaking a grumpy cat awake, coaxing him through breakfast, and standing guard at the sliding glass door while he groggily took care of business in the backyard.

By the time Ben's truck rumbled up the drive, Sam was pacing in the entryway, fully alert, tail twitching, like he couldn't wait for someone to open the door and let him loose on the day.

Sam hopped into the front seat of Ben's truck and didn't even spare me a backward glance while they drove away.

"I'll miss you too," I muttered.

I was driving toward Western Studios to meet my team when my phone went off. A glance at the screen told me it was Rory Tuck. The developer rarely called, and when he did, it was usually bad news. I picked up immediately.

"We've got a problem," he said.

"Good morning to you too." What was it with people skipping the niceties all of a sudden?

"Well, you won't think so when you see what I'm looking at."

My fingers spasmed on the steering wheel. "Please don't tell me it's gnomes."

"Actually, Maddy, now that Hugo's got them in line, I wouldn't mind a few gnomes to help out. No, what we've got here is a lot more serious. When can you get here?"

I made a U-turn and headed back toward La Loma. "In a few minutes. And his name is Sam, not Hugo."

"He'll always be Hugo to me, you cat thief."

I smiled. The real estate developer and I had come a long way since we first met.

Five minutes later, we were walking to the farthest end of the development, past rows of charming new houses. They were smaller than the typical Chavez Ravine property, but with high-end finishes and fancy features, buyers had snapped them up while the foundations were still wet.

Rory refused to say why he had wanted me to see so badly. He walked fast, hands stuck in his pockets, head down. At the back of the development, near the pond and under the shade of a willow tree, he came to an abrupt stop and pointed.

My eyes followed his index finger. Another entity emergence hole. A very big one.

"I've never seen one like that before," Rory said.

I sighed. "No. But I have. I need to tell you something, but you need to keep it to yourself. Can you do that?"

Rory swiped a hand across his bald head. "Sure, but here's the deal. I can't have that thing sitting here. Take some pictures or whatever you need to do, and then I need to get my guys to fill it in. I can't—and I repeat, *can't*—have the owners seeing that here because if they do, they'll be asking for refunds. Though, of course, their disclosures clearly state there's no guarantee Chavez Ravine will remain entity-free."

"Yes, I'm sure they do. Just give me a few minutes before your guys fill it in."

I explained the other unusual entity emergence holes we had discovered in the gully, then called Steve Zhou. He picked up on the third ring.

"Where are you?" I asked.

In the background, sirens blared over a news reporter's chipper voice announcing an entity eruption outside the La Brea Tar Pits.

"I'm having a spa day," he said.

Aw, Steven's first attempt at irony. My little nerd was growing up.

"We've got another hole, and I need you to see it. I'm in La Loma. How soon can you get here?"

"Minutes. I'm actually headed into La Loma now. Send me your address."

I forwarded him a pin with our location and turned to Rory. "We're in luck. One of the researchers at OA will be here soon." I scanned the area. Luckily, there weren't any houses with a direct view of the area. But three walking paths led from the neighborhood down to the pond. "How about blocking off access? That should keep the looky-loos away until we're finished."

Rory scrunched up his face. "I can do that, but what am I supposed to say if anyone asks?"

I rolled my eyes. "I don't know. Make something up. The pump in the pond broke, and it's overflowing. Whatever."

The real estate developer with questionable scruples appeared scandalized. "I can't say that! People just moved in. They'll be none too happy if they hear stuff is breaking already."

"I'm sure you'll figure something out." I gave him a little shove.

Rory dipped his head and stomped off.

Moments later, Steven Zhou came sauntering down one of the paths. When he saw the hole, he gave a low whistle. "Now, that's really something."

The Occult Affairs researcher had undergone a transformation since I had last seen him. Instead of his usual nerd uniform, he wore a cream shirt tucked into charcoal pants, topped with a sharp brown corduroy jacket. His hair was different too— tousled on top. The style suited him. Complimented his high cheekbones and strong jawline.

The new clothes seemed to have given him a confidence boost. He was standing straighter, feet planted wide apart, hands shoved in his pockets.

Normally, I avoided making personal remarks about a colleague's appearance, but it just burst out of my mouth. "Are you having a photo shoot with GQ later?"

Steve swiveled his head toward me, a slow grin coming to his face. He smoothed the front of his jacket. "Oh, these old things? It was just something I threw together this morning." Noting my expression, he laughed. "I decided it was time for a change. Got a stylist and everything." He paused, now serious. "What do you think?"

"A stylist!" I echoed. "You?"

He shrugged. "My sister talked me into it. Did I tell you she's a career coach? She's always going on about dressing for the job you want, not the job you have. And since I was passed over for another promotion, I decided it was time to take her more seriously." He grimaced. "Is it too much?"

I shook my head. "No. You look great. Good for you. Now, can you look at the hole?"

"With pleasure." He slid his backpack off his shoulders and rested it on the ground.

This new Steve was a bit hard to take on just two cups of coffee. I stepped back and let him get to work.

Few things in the world were more boring than watching an OA researcher do their thing, so I called Bailey Nixon to let her know about the new hole and that I would be late joining her and the rest of the team at Western Studios.

Then I had a look around for our missing entity, with two magic-boosted Smoke Bombs dangling from clips secured to my belt. I didn't expect to find whatever had come out of the hole—the heatmap hadn't detected anything—but it was part of the protocol.

Nothing hiding in the bushes. Nothing in the trees. I stared at the pond for a long time, keeping a safe distance between me and the sandy edge, watching for ripples or bubbles that could suggest an aquatic creature, but the water was still.

I broadened my search beyond the caution tape Rory had put up and ventured along the paths, scanning the yards for any signs of disturbance, walking between the houses, and finally, scaling the hill leading to Elysian Park. It was possible the entity had made its way over the tall stone wall separating Chavez Ravine from the parkland and was hiding out over there. It had happened before.

Elysian Park was enormous. Way too large for one person to cover. But I hesitated to call in backup and pull my crew from their assignment at Western Studios. Who knew when we would have another chance to search for hex bags without the entire music video crew as an audience? Besides, if someone on the production was the culprit, we didn't want to tip them off.

When I wound my way back to the hole, Steve was kneeling on a plastic tarp, holding one end of a sleek metal pole. It hummed and beeped.

"Is that your new toy?" I asked.

Steve glanced up. "Yes. It's a spectral sampler. It's supposed to extract trace energies from the hole. Whatever it records is uploaded to an app on my phone. Cool, right?"

"You're not talking about ectoplasm, are you, Dr. Venkman?" I wondered if Steven would catch the *Ghostbusters* reference.

"It's more complicated than that," Steve said huffily.

So, no to the reference.

He pulled out the pole, unscrewed the end, and affixed another attachment, one with a long, thick needle about the length of my forearm.

"Please don't tell me you're going to poke the Yeti." That was what we used to say back in my Occult Affairs days, when some new, overzealous officer decided to provoke an entity. It always ended badly.

Steve's eyebrows smashed together. Had they always been that nicely arched? No, they had not. He had definitely plucked them.

"Well, in a way, I suppose I *am* poking something. This is an entity mapper. The theory is, if there are any more of them down there, they'll project images of their shapes based on their residual artifacts. Again, it'll go straight to the app on my phone. Of course, I'll need to analyze whatever it captures with our new equipment later, back at the farm."

"Yes, of course." It came out a little more sarcastic than I had intended.

Either Steve didn't notice or he chose to ignore it. "The history of this sort of thing is fascinating. Did you know that people used to draw maps of spiritual realms? You've heard of ley lines, right?"

I pressed a finger between my eyes. "Yes. My mother told me about them."

What I didn't say was that when she started talking about those kinds of things, I did my best to tune her out. All that science-meets-supernatural stuff had done was make my mother a nice living. It did nothing to help our understanding of entities or how we might send them back to wherever they had come from.

When OA figured out how to do that, I would be the first to jump up and down with joy. Until then, I was more than happy to leave the details to the nerds.

Steven removed the probe, squinted at the tip, and then shoved it back down into the hole.

"I think whatever was down there is long gone." Steve pulled his probe out of the hole. "But wouldn't it be cool if this thing actually caught something? Like, actually provoked a reaction from an entity in the process of emerging?"

OA nerds didn't think like normal people.

"No, Steven. I do *not* think that would be cool. And if you'd spent less time in the lab and more time in the field, you wouldn't think so either. Speaking of which, I'd like you to go with me next door, into Elysian Park, and help me look for our missing entity."

He shot to his feet, his mouth opening and closing. "Me? But...but...you have an entire team that handles entities."

"They're out on another assignment. An important one. Don't worry. You can bring your toys."

I called Bailey and let her know my plans had changed. She was now in charge of the hex search. I needed to prioritize finding the new entity, and Steven was the perfect assistant.

Chapter 15

Steve grumbled the entire drive to Elysian Park. Luckily, we didn't have far to go. The OA researcher sat in the passenger seat of my Jeep, hanging onto the grab handle and making hissing noises at every turn. He was nearly as dramatic as Hernan Frias, and it was getting on my nerves.

"Calm down over there," I said, turning into the park. "I'm not going that fast."

Steve gasped when I took another turn. "Yes, you are. These things are top-heavy, with a short wheelbase. They're bad at cornering at high speeds, so they have a higher-than-average rollover rate."

I didn't bother to argue. While I loved my Jeep Wrangler, I had heard it all before. But out of respect for his nerves, I slowed down. No reason to antagonize the guy, who was already jumpy about accompanying me to search for the entity—or entities—that had emerged from the double-wide hole in La Loma.

I parked in a small lot. Since it was a weekday and we were far from the playground and picnic areas where families usually gathered, it was deserted.

With a martyred sigh, Steve unbuckled his seatbelt. "I can't believe you talked me into this."

I went around to the back of the Jeep, opened the hatch, and began rummaging around. "There's nothing we can't handle on our own." I paused, frowning. "Well, there was that time a ghoul showed up at Muertos Café. That was definitely an all-hands-on-deck situation. And it did take a few of us to subdue a Mayan vampire bat, but—"

Steve adjusted a strap on his backpack. "You're forgetting the chupacabras."

I glanced up. "Okay. The chupacabras were challenging, but there are two of us, which is the standard response team. I'm an old pro at this, and you are the premier entity researcher. We've got this."

Steve looked far from convinced. "Elysian Park is an entity hotspot."

"Yes, that's what makes it perfect..." I turned.

He was shifting from foot to foot and scanning the trees in the distance.

"Wait. You aren't afraid of entities, are you?" I raised my voice in disbelief.

Steve's face contorted like he had just bitten into something sour. "Remember when the chief decided researchers needed 'field experience' and made us tag along on entity calls? I wasn't too happy about it, but what could I do? The officers I was paired with treated it like hazing. They thought it would be hilarious to leave me on Santa Monica Beach with what they called 'a little mermaid situation.' We're talking the scary kind with teeth, and she did *not* respond to smoke bombs. I had no idea they could move that fast on the sand. She almost got me...when the officers decided they'd tortured me long enough and threw a net over her." He shuddered at the memory.

For once, the chief had it right. Nothing like a close encounter with rows of teeth to remind researchers that entities weren't just theoretical. But hazing was out of line. Poor Steve.

I walked around to the back of the Jeep and reached into the cargo area for a utility belt.

"There's no excuse for that kind of behavior," I said lightly. "But it's good to be aware of what entities can do. I've worked with some people who think it's all fun and games...until something goes wrong."

He managed a half-hearted smile and took the belt from my outstretched hand.

"You don't happen to have some of those new super-powered anti-entity sprayers, do you?" I asked.

"Yeah, actually." Steve reached into his backpack and pulled out what looked like a child's water gun on steroids—army green with orange accents. It resembled the pump-action squirt gun a neighbor kid had used to ambush me in the fourth grade. Once.

"You're kidding me," I said.

"No, it's really cool. The new deterrent is liquid, so we needed a better, more efficient delivery system. I helped with the design." Steve puffed out his chest.

I snorted. "It looks like a kid's toy. But fine. If you say it works, I believe you." I examined the gun. It had a trigger and a small nozzle at the end of a long, fat barrel. The reservoir was made of clear plastic, so I could see a greenish, murky liquid sloshing around inside.

Steve tapped a square white box at the center of the gun. "Those are the batteries. It's motorized, so there's no need to pump. All you need to do is point and fire."

I flipped open the battery box and peered inside. The chambers were empty. "Tell me you brought batteries."

Steve flushed. "I did, I did," he said hurriedly.

A few moments later, we were locked and loaded, striding down a tree-lined path in the part of the park closest to La Loma. If a new type of entity had made its way into Elysian Park, there was no telling where it would be, but it was the most logical place to start. Maybe we would get lucky and it would be disoriented and hanging around near the new stone wall.

We walked in silence, leaves rustling in the breeze, me looking for anything hiding among the branches, Steven scanning both sides of the path. He was obviously nervous. Lots of throat clearing and ragged breathing. Once, his shoulder collided with mine, sending me stumbling sideways into the bushes. Maybe carting along a jumpy researcher hadn't been such a great idea after all.

It was cool, but his forehead was shiny with perspiration. I hated to think how he would react if something jumped out at us. Fainting was a distinct possibility.

"You okay over there?" I asked, even though he was practically glued to my hip.

"Yeah, fine," he said faintly.

A scent hit my nostrils. Unpleasant. I couldn't quite place it, so I automatically gave a big sniff and immediately regretted it.

Steve breathed in too and wrinkled his nose. "Do you smell that?"

"Yeah, it's like wet, dirty dog and fish past its sell-by date."

"You forgot rotting eggs." Steve gagged. "What is it?"

"Maybe some picnickers left their lunch behind." Now that I'd had another whiff, I didn't think it was food. It smelled more like an animal.

The gentle breeze turned into a gust that enveloped us in the full force of the stench. My hair flew around my face, reminding me I hadn't tied it back. Sloppy. I slipped an elastic band from a pocket, pulled my hair into a low ponytail, and tucked it down into my shirt.

"What's with the wind?" Steve asked.

I was wondering the same thing myself.

Chapter 16

The wind had come out of nowhere, lifting dry leaves from the ground and sending them swirling through the air. Unlike normal gusts, which blew in one direction, this one seemed to push at us from all sides.

"Something's not right," I said.

Several yards ahead and just to the right of the path was a hole. It was normal-sized, with piles of dry dirt around its edges.

Steve's eyes were fixed on the sky, so I poked his arm and pointed. "Emergence hole."

He came to an abrupt stop, a hand cupping his nose and mouth. "Is that where the smell is coming from?" he asked through his fingers.

"Maybe." I had no desire to stand over the hole and sniff. That was what Steve was for. "Why don't you go check it out?"

Steve looked past me and gave a strangled cry.

Another blast of wind so strong it nearly knocked me over.

I struggled to turn my head as fast as Steve's expression demanded, but I managed it, raising my plastic gun in anticipation of whatever was behind me.

My alarm turned to horror. A creature hovered in the air, long light hair whipping in the wind. It had an old woman's face, the body of a bird, and pendulous bare breasts. Her talons were outstretched toward me. It was like something from a nightmare.

I stumbled backward, raised my gun, and fired. A stream of blue liquid shot through the air and hit her in the face. Behind me, Steve whooped. Prematurely.

The thing didn't drop to the ground but teetered in the air. The expression on its wizened face relaxed, and I had a brief impression that, once, it had been beautiful. This was not a creature I had ever encountered before, and for about a second, I wondered what it was. I pulled the trigger again.

Its eyes bulged, its body jerked violently, and then it fell to the ground, a heap of dark feathers.

We had just found the source of the stench. She reeked.

I took a deep breath and turned to Steve, who was doubled over, hands on his knees.

"What is it?" I sounded a little unsteady myself. My body gave an involuntary shudder.

"Harpy," he gasped. "I think."

Harpy. I remembered hearing another Occult Affairs researcher talking about harpies. Not singular. Plural. Because they always emerged in groups. Gnomes were like that. The same with Chaneques and chupacabras too.

I glanced at the clear plastic reservoir on my gun. Nearly empty.

"Hand me your gun." I turned toward Steven.

He stared at me as if he suddenly didn't understand English.

I was just about to snatch it from his hand when a new blast of wind sent clouds of dirt, pebbles, and leaves into my face. Instinctively, I threw up my hands to protect my eyes, but it was too late. Temporarily blinded, I lurched toward Steve, and when I managed to open my eyes, he was cowering against a tree, his mouth agape.

I was just inches from the gun dangling from Steve's hand when something hard and sharp cut into my shoulders and I was lifted into the air, arms and legs flailing.

Steve's horrified expression told me everything I needed to know. Another harpy had me in its grip. And if there was any doubt, its breath, which stank of rotten fish and death, confirmed the awful truth. It was flying around in circles, its movements erratic, taking me along for the ride.

It was nauseating, but it gave me hope. The harpy appeared to be in the throes of new entity disorientation.

We were low enough that I probably wouldn't break anything if I could get free. Or so I hoped.

Something hard pressed into the top of my skull, and damn, it hurt.

"Let me go, you ugly pinche harpy," I yelled.

The monster whipped me around. My vision blurred. Blood trickled down my forehead and into my eyes. The harpy lurched to the left, nearly slamming me against a tree, before abruptly swinging around in midair and dropping low. My feet came dangerously close to Steven's head. And something else too.

His gun. Which was now pointing straight at me.

"Wait!" I shouted.

Too late. I was hit with a blast of anti-entity elixir. The stuff found my open mouth and nose, and I coughed and sputtered. Steve fired again, but that time, the spray went over my head and hit the harpy.

I crashed to the ground. A moment later, a heavy mass slammed to earth in a foul-smelling tangle of wings and talons that missed me by inches. I rolled over on my back and stared up at Steve.

"Got her," he said triumphantly.

My head throbbed. I wiped blood from my eyes and blinked up at him. "You got both of us." I slurred my words like a drunk.

Steve dropped to his knees, staring anxiously into my face. "Are you okay? I'm so sorry I panicked. And then it was a little hard getting a clear shot. She wouldn't stay still."

"Entities rarely cooperate," I said, struggling to sit up.

Steve produced a plastic bag from his backpack, tore it open, and began to wipe the stuff off my face with a cloth. I sputtered and tried to pull away, but he kept at it, like a parent dealing with an ice-cream-covered child.

"Lie still. I know what I'm doing." He tugged on latex gloves, pulled out a first aid kit from his backpack, lined up a half dozen foil packets on the ground, and ripped one open.

Steve dabbed a damp square against the top of my head. The sting was enough to make me yelp.

"Ow, that hurts!"

Steve made a clucking noise. "Calm down. It's just an antiseptic. Head wounds are the worst."

It hurt, but it was also somehow comforting. Steve was a lousy shot, but he made a decent nurse. He squeezed a tube of something on my head, pressed a thick square of gauze on the wound, and taped it into place.

I turned to stare at the harpy. It was hideous. And I had thought the vampire birds from Mexico were bad. Compared to these monsters, they were regal.

The wind had faded. Steve seemed to guess what I was thinking.

"Yeah. Harpies are personifications of storm winds. Between the wind and the smell, I should have guessed it would be harpies, but I wasn't thinking straight." Steve looked around, his eyes landing on the other harpy several yards away. "Well, one good thing. The new stuff worked well, and so did the guns. I'm actually glad I got to see them in action."

"Yeah, well, they didn't go after you," I said with a wince, then sighed. "I guess I shouldn't take it personally. There doesn't appear to be any rhyme nor reason whom entities attack."

Steven nodded. "Well, in a way, it's lucky it was one of us and not some poor jogger." He paused, squinting at me. "Hey, that wound on your head is going to need stitches. We need to get you to the clinic and have an entity doc look you over."

I sat up slowly, trying to ignore the gashes in my shoulders where the harpy's talons had dug into my flesh. A trip to the clinic would take more time than I had. I needed to join my team at Western Studios. They didn't need my help, but I wanted a chance to snoop around while the production crew was away.

Steve pulled me to my feet, and I whimpered a little.

He ignored me and consulted his phone, tapping at the screen. "All right. The harpies registered on the heatmap, of course, and a crew is on the way. I messaged Jo to tell her we dealt with them, so they're just sending cleanup. Since these are the first harpies to emerge in a while, I'm asking another researcher to meet me at the Dump. Have a good look at them before they're processed and carted off to the preserve."

Steve glanced at the downed creatures and straightened his shoulders.

"Cool. Harpies." Then he turned toward me again, biting his lip. "I think harpies are the ones that contaminate people they touch, so we need to get you to that clinic ASAP."

The harpy had done a lot of touching. On my shoulders and the top of my head. I shuddered.

"They *contaminate*? In what way, exactly?"

Steve shrugged. "I'm not sure. The documentation at OA is a little iffy. We just don't see that many of these things. But the entity docs probably have more information."

I struggled to my feet and put my arm around his shoulder. Together, we lurched back to the SUV.

"Hey, Steve?"

"Yeah?"

"A bit of advice?"

"Sure, of course."

"Words like 'iffy' and 'probably'? Not the best choice for someone who was just attacked by a harpy."

Chapter 17

Dr. Timothy Chen sat hunched at his computer, utterly absorbed in whatever he was reading, tapping at keys, his gaze fixed on the screen.

Meanwhile, I sat on the exam table in the chilly little room, stripped to my bra and covered by a thin, blue smock.

I cleared my throat a few times to remind him I was there.

When he failed to take the hint, I said, "Any idea how long I'll be here? I need to get back to work."

The young doctor swiveled toward me with a frown. "You won't be going anywhere today. But if you're lucky, you should be back at work tomorrow."

"*Tomorrow?*" I felt like screaming.

"Tomorrow. *If* you're lucky," he repeated firmly. "Which you weren't today. You are the first person ever to be attacked by a harpy, at least in this century, which means there's not a lot of information about treatment. I've got a researcher at Occult Affairs sending me as much as she can about their history, and we'll proceed accordingly. But the first thing we're going to do is clean up those wounds and start you on antibiotics."

I sighed. "Fine."

I had been in Occult Affairs long enough to know arguing was useless. Some entities were nasty, and their bites, stings, and scratches were venomous or poisonous. Either way, the medical precautions weren't fun, but the alternatives were even less so.

I tapped out a message to my team and explained the situation. Bailey promptly replied with an update. They had just finished an extensive search of the music video set and had found nothing resembling a hex bag. Did I want them to look for something else while they were there, or did I want them to resume their search for the missing entities? I chose the latter.

Dr. Chen, a tall, thin man who managed to look elegant in a lab coat, began poking around my head, making little hissing noises. "All right. You've got a nasty head wound here. Given everything I've seen from the photos Steve Zhou sent and from the odor he described, I'm going to do a little irrigating, clean up the edges, and stitch you up. But first, let's give you something to make you a little more comfortable."

That "little something" turned out to be a few sharp jabs around the wound.

While the anesthetic took effect, a nurse came bustling in. The middle-aged woman—Sandra, according to her name tag— had a cute turned-up nose and frizzy blond hair. She tucked a warm blanket around me.

"You poor thing," she said. "Flying entities are the worst, aren't they? I've only seen one—some sort of fairy, I think—and it was so mean. That was enough for me. I know fliers are rare, and thank goodness for that. When you came in, it was Code Double E around here. Dr. Chen came running down from the third floor, where he was doing his rounds. Dr. Ackerman was ready to treat you, but Dr. Chen is our designated Double E specialist, and while Dr. Ackerman is perfectly capable, Dr. Chen insisted on seeing you himself."

Dr. Chen made "Mmm" noises near my head.

I was feeling a little woozy and was having trouble following the woman. She talked fast.

"Double E? What's that?"

"Entity extra," the nurse said. "That's what we call the next wave of entities we keep hearing about. I don't know who came up with it, but we all knew exactly what it was when the alerts on our phones went off. There are lots of emergency color codes, but we have letters for entity-related emergencies."

"But it was just an ordinary entity," I said faintly.

"There was some confusion when Steve Zhou called it in," Dr. Chen explained. "I know Steve. We went to school together. He said there were some unusual emergence holes found next door in Chavez Ravine that suggested a new type of entity, and he wasn't sure where the harpies had come from."

"Well, I saw the hole in Elysian Park, and I'm sure."

Sandra made a disapproving face. "Let's leave that to the experts at Occult Affairs," she said briskly. She seemed offended that I had dared to question the "experts."

"I'm a former OA officer," I replied, hoping to clear up any misunderstanding. "I was working with Steve when the harpy showed up."

Sandra's broad face loomed over me for a moment before she stepped out of view, making room for Dr. Chen to make another pass at my head wound.

"I see." Her tone suggested she *didn't* see. Not at all.

"Madeline is head of security for Chavez Ravine," Dr. Chen said.

"Are you!" Sandra gasped, still out of sight. "Do you live there? In Chavez Ravine?"

The tugging on my scalp didn't hurt, but the sensation was weird, and I hoped Dr. Chen would hurry up. "I do. In La Loma. I inherited my grandmother's house."

Sandra gasped again. "Aren't you a lucky girl! I'd give anything to live there. Although…my husband says it's not the same as it used to be, with all the troubles they're having up there lately. He's heard all about it on the news. And you have gnomes now! Good luck with those!"

She patted my arm.

"I do think it's unfair that it's become so exclusive. You either need to be rich or you need to have family connections, and then everything is practically paid for. There's nothing wrong with inheriting property, of course, but I've never understood why some people continue to get special perks. My husband and I watched a documentary about the history of Chavez Ravine. The evictions that almost happened and all that. It was awful, but it was so long ago. Why should the descendants of those original residents get such special treatment when they didn't have to leave after all? It's ridiculous, if you ask me."

I hadn't asked her, but Sandra was going to unleash her opinions whether I wanted to hear them or not. Dr. Chen muttered something. A drawer opened and closed somewhere behind me.

"Pardon me, Dr. Chen?" Sandra asked.

"We're out of mesh caps. Can you please hunt one down?"

After Sandra hurried away, Dr. Chen cleared his throat. "Sorry about that. My great-grandfather was a doctor. He lived and worked in Chinatown and used to make house calls up at Chavez Ravine. He told my grandfather quite a few stories, and he passed them on to me. Most people don't understand what the residents went through to save their homes, not to mention the systematic discrimination Mexicans experienced at the time."

"Tax-paying Mexican Americans," I said automatically.

"Exactly," Dr. Chen replied. I couldn't see his face, but he sounded like he was smiling. "I'm almost finished. Twelve stitches did the trick. I've ordered a whole-body MRI. They're squeezing you in as soon as we're done here. That'll take an hour. We want to make sure none of your organs have undergone any changes after that harpy bite. Then you'll go to the lab for a blood draw. Once all that's done, we're going to check you in and get you hooked up to an IV and start you on broad-spectrum anti-entity therapy. We also want to monitor you in case there are any delayed reactions."

Dr. Chen came around the table.

"All right. You can sit up now. Let's take a look at your shoulders and see what's going on there."

Just some nasty scrapes, as it turned out, which required cleaning but not stitches, thankfully. I wasn't happy about staying overnight in the hospital, but I decided to be a good patient and do what I was told. It would have been just my luck to get home and start frothing at the mouth or something.

I made a mental note to text Julia and ask if she could feed Sam. I could have asked Stu or even Ben, but Sam loved Julia. After a hard day's work with the gnomes, he deserved a treat. I also needed to tell Stu what had happened and update my staff.

Sandra finally returned, holding something that resembled one of those white nets placed around pears to protect them from bruising. She looked like she was trying hard not to laugh while it dangled from a finger.

"Here you go, doctor. We only have extra-large in stock, but I'm sure you'll be able to make it work."

Dr. Chen took it and began fussing over my head, stretching the cap this way and that, grunting softly while he moved my hair around. When he was finally done, he said, "That should do it."

The nurse clapped a hand over her mouth, turned her head, and giggled.

"It's not that bad," Dr. Chen said sternly.

Sandra looked back, took one glance at me, and giggled again. "You're not the one who has to wear it." She gestured dramatically to a mirror above the sink.

Reluctantly, I walked over and peered into the mirror to see how bad it was.

It was much, much worse than I had expected.

Sandra burst out laughing. Dr. Chen gave a wan smile.

"Okay, that's enough. Sorry, Maddy, sorry. It's not pretty, but it'll keep the dressing in place. I don't want to bandage it yet because the nurses need to monitor the wound overnight. Just in case."

I stared at my reflection. A white mesh cap covered the top of my forehead, stretching all the way to the base of my skull. Dr. Chen had pulled the excess material into a knot at the top and secured it with medical tape. I looked like some kind of sleepy cartoon character.

There was no way in hell anyone was going to see me looking so ridiculous.

Come hell or more harpies, I planned on visiting Western Studios the next day, when filming of Pete's music video resumed.

Without the stupid cap.

Chapter 18

When I told Stu about the harpy attack, he was horrified and said he would swing by the hospital on his way home from work. But the nurse told me to keep the beanie on for another twenty-four hours, plus I smelled bad and needed a shower, so I decided to spare Stu with a white lie.

"I'd love to see you, but I'm stuck in the hospital overnight. Just for observation. But no visitors allowed. Can I get a rain check?"

"Of course. Let's plan for tomorrow evening. Take care of yourself tonight. It sounds like you had a rough day."

"I'd say that describes it pretty well. Say hi to Clare for me."

I'd lost the better part of a day, so after I moved into my room, with help from the weirdly passive-aggressive Sandra, I got busy.

Julia happily agreed to stay with Sam, and Ben reported all was going well with the gnomes. They had managed to cover an entire hillside with periwinkle. Bailey reported another large entity hole at the end of the gully by Phantom's Pass, and, with my approval, the team planned to scour the area for as long as there was enough light, then resume in the morning.

On a whim, I checked Clare's social media. She had posted new photos of her and Theo, taken on a beach. Also, a video of him showing her some complicated dance moves on the sand and Clare laughing hysterically when she couldn't pull them off. At least she had a sense of humor about her dancing skills, which could best be described as stiff and awkward.

Theo had the grace to encourage her, but I still couldn't bring myself to like him. Stu said Clare had gone out with a few guys but had never been serious about a boyfriend. She was certainly old enough to date—she was starting college the following year, after all—but Theo sounded like trouble. And with all the older, more experienced dancers throwing themselves at him, why bother with a high school girl?

It sounded off. *He* sounded off.

It was a weird position to be in. I wasn't Clare's mother, but she sometimes treated me as though I were. And I was protective of her. She was a good kid, and she had dealt with some ugly stuff, thanks to her mother, so I could relate.

With luck, I would see them at the studios the next day. I didn't know what I would do, if anything, but I would need to tread carefully. Clare's prickly side had come out when I first started dating her father. If she thought I was meddling in her personal life, there was no telling how she would react. I could find myself tossed out of our happy trio.

Dr. Chen stopped by, clipboard in hand, while I was pecking at my boring hospital dinner, pushing a rubbery green bean around my plate.

"Good news," he said. "Your full body scan was clear, and your blood work looks perfectly normal."

Dr. Chen lifted the bandage on my head wound. He smelled of mouthwash and antiseptic.

"Good containment," he murmured, then checked under the gauze on my shoulders. "Talon marks aren't extending either. Looks like you're on the mend."

"Great! I'll see you around, then." I pushed my tray back and stood up.

He laughed. "Not so fast. We're still going to keep you overnight. We can't let our first harpy victim go without making sure we don't have any latent symptoms.

I did my best to get a good night's sleep, but that was impossible. Nurses came and went, and there was a constant assault of noise: carts wheeling down hallways, monitors beeping, and the murmur of voices filtering in through the door.

When morning finally came, I didn't wake up as much as I stopped trying to sleep.

As soon as breakfast arrived, I began pestering the nurses about getting discharged, but they all said I needed to wait until Dr. Chen could see me. Luckily, he arrived at the hospital early— seven thirty—and after some more pestering, I was home an hour later.

Sam was with Julia, but she had made cheese scones and left them on a plate in the kitchen, along with a nice note.

I started a pot of coffee, went into the bathroom, and stared, horrified, into the mirror.

Dr. Chen had said to wait forty-eight hours before attempting to wash my hair, but it was disgusting with the anti-entity stuff Steve had shot at me during the harpy attack. I decided a little compromise was in order.

I leaned over the sink and pulled off the embarrassing mesh cap. Careful to keep my bandaged scalp dry, I ran the warm water and scrubbed at the sections of hair that had hardened into stiff clumps. The gray residue finally loosened, swirling down the drain like dirty cement.

Then I ran hot water into the tub, adding several cups of lavender-scented Epsom salts. I eased myself in slowly, wincing when the heat stung my talon-damaged shoulders, then sighing while the tension in my muscles began to ease.

Since I was going to be spending my morning on a film set, I took extra care with my makeup and clothes, choosing black pants and an emerald-green trench coat. I couldn't very well show up with a giant bandage on my head, so I grabbed Stu's faded USC cap from a hook in my closet and tugged it on. It settled against the tender spots, making me wince. I headed out the door.

My neighbor Leo gave a friendly wave while he hurried to his car. "I saw the gnomes on my way home yesterday! They're so cute! Way to go, Maddy!"

I stared at him in surprise. "Aren't you worried about your property values?"

Leo's dramatic salt and pepper hair popped against his electric blue suit. "No way!" He laughed. "We have the distinction of being the only neighborhood in L.A. that's been able to tame the gnomes, thanks to Sam and his cat cadets. And it livens things up, you know? I'm going to come home early so Toby and I can go watch them. Our friends have a view of the hillside, and we're going to sit out on the patio and have a little watch party with G&Ts. Doesn't that sound like fun?"

It actually sounded terrible. I'd had enough run-ins with gnomes to make me forever suspicious of them. Also, I didn't want to step on Sam's toes. Or paws.

Western Studios was just on the other side of Phantom's Pass, so I drove down the hill and up the other side. Soon, I arrived at the security gate and gave my name to the guard.

"Just follow the main road down the middle of the lot all the way to the back." He handed me a lanyard with a temporary security badge. "When you see a wagon wheel on the side of a low wooden building, that's the best place to park."

Western Studios was a lot busier than the last time I was there. I drove slowly to the parking lot, past two women struggling to push a rack of long, frilly dresses along the sidewalk.

Every few feet, they stopped to kick a misbehaving wheel. A half dozen or so casually dressed people waited in line at a coffee cart outside a white, two-story building with oversized columns. Production offices, I guessed.

I parked in the last available spot, directly in front of the wagon wheel. After checking my makeup in the mirror—my expensive new eyeliner hadn't smudged, which I was happy about—I slid out of the Jeep, bumping the top of my head on the doorframe. My vision went all blurry.

It took a second for my brain to register the pain coming from the fresh stitches. I stood there, breathing heavily, waiting for the throbbing to subside. The scrapes on my shoulders must have decided they weren't getting enough attention because they began to ache. I dug out two ibuprofen from my tote bag and choked them down dry.

My stomach rumbled. I had skipped breakfast. Maybe the coffee cart sold food. I could spare a few minutes before the crew arrived at eight o'clock.

As I headed toward the coffee cart, I passed a narrow walkway between two buildings, with an old gate that was partially open. Voices drifted from somewhere behind it. On a whim, I pushed the gate open, and there, under the shade of an overhang, was a couple.

Even though I could only see dark, curly hair, I recognized one of them immediately. Theo. For a moment, I thought I had caught him and Clare in an intense make-out session, and my stomach did a little flip. But the girl had red hair, not brown.

Well, well, well.

I banged through the gate, making such a racket that the couple sprang apart. The redhead, who I guessed was in her mid-twenties, turned the color of a cherry tomato, while Theo looked annoyed at the interruption.

"Excuse me," I said. "Is this the Pete Drury production?"

Theo took in the temporary security pass hanging from a lanyard around my neck. He narrowed his eyes. "Yeah. Are you the schoolmarm?"

"Um, no."

Theo turned to his…friend. "Aren't we shooting with the schoolmarm today?"

Red shrugged. "I don't know. No one ever tells me anything."

I pointed at the end of the walkway. "Will I find Pete over there?" Which was my way of saying "Please move."

The couple pressed their backs to the wall. The young woman's expression turned sheepish, but Theo had the nerve to smirk. He was medium height, with a tight, compact build. Shorter than he appeared in Clare's photos and even better-looking. To Clare's credit, he also appeared younger than twenty-four. I would have guessed nineteen.

The little shit. Clare might be shocked to learn he was locking lips with someone else. And there was something defiant and dismissive in his attitude. I had to resist the urge to kick his shins when I strode past.

At the end of the walkway, I found myself on a street lined with weathered facades. I had stepped from modern Los Angeles straight into a frontier town. It was disorienting. Wooden buildings lined both sides of a crooked, dusty street. Carved double doors led to a saloon. A red sign advertising a bathhouse was next door, and a hotel was just down the street. A handful of people sat in camp chairs near the bank.

An older man with silver hair waved me down. "Are you the schoolmarm?"

That was twice, and it was a little concerning. Did I look like a schoolmarm? "No. I'm a friend of Pete's."

"Everyone's behind the schoolhouse," he said, pointing at a building with a bell tower in the distance. "They're finishing up a scene there. After that, we'll break for lunch and then do a few pickups at the saloon."

I thanked him and headed toward the schoolhouse, a single-story whitewashed building with a peaked roof. A man's strident voice drifted toward me. When I rounded the building, the owner of the voice was waving his arms around and yelling at a sweaty-looking guy with a movie camera rigged to his torso. It looked like a highly uncomfortable setup.

Yet the cameraman didn't seem the least bit bothered by the tirade.

"Go fuck yourself, Jason," he said calmly. "I'm right, and you know it."

Jason didn't look at all inclined to follow the cameraman's advice. "No, *you* go fuck *your*self. Just do what I'm telling you to do."

The cameraman tipped his head back and groaned loudly. "Fine. I'll do it, you fucking prick. And then you'll see I'm right."

The rest of the crew stood around, watching the action. Nobody appeared surprised by the outburst.

I kept to the wall of the schoolhouse and surveyed the area. The back of Phantom's Pass wasn't far off, maybe the equivalent of a block away, and all the trees made a nice background for the sets.

Standing in the dusty street were Pete Drury, nearly unrecognizable as a scruffy cowboy, and two actors dressed in costumes which suggested they were lawmen.

Jason Wood glanced around, threw up his hands, and yelled, "What the fuck! Where's my schoolmarm?"

Here we go, I thought when he looked in my direction, but then the back door of the schoolhouse flew open and a figure appeared, all decked out in a calico dress and a bonnet.

"Here!" the girl cried. "I'm sorry! I'm here!"

The schoolmarm was none other than Clare Wells.

Chapter 19

A woman in a low-cut dress, with a huge pile of dark hair hurried toward me. It was quite the outfit. Red and black, poofy with flounces. Was that...

"Becca?"

She was hardly recognizable in that getup. Also, her mouth was weird, like someone had painted over the lines to give her Cupid's bow lips. A single, large curl dangled over her forehead.

"Of course, I'm Becca," she snapped, taking my elbow and steering me back around to the side of the schoolhouse, where we were out of sight from the crew.

I looked her up and down. "What are you supposed to be? A madam?"

Becca tugged at her waist, which appeared even smaller than usual. "This corset is going to kill me, I swear. And no, I am *not* a madam. I'm an opera singer turned dance hall proprietress. Very respectable."

I snorted. "Then why are you dressed like a madam?"

Becca pressed the heel of her palm against her forehead and sighed. "I am not. Although...no thanks to Jason. You should have seen the outfit he originally wanted me to wear." She paused. "Did you see Clare?"

I nodded. "Yeah. So, what's the deal? I thought she was supposed to be a saloon girl?"

"Oh, that." Becca grinned. "I made a bit of a stink about it. Took Jason aside and told him how inappropriate it was to have a high school kid playing a saloon girl, especially in those costumes, with their boobs falling out. And then he went on and on about Britney Spears videos, and I was like, "Yeah, that was a long time ago." But he wouldn't do anything about it, so I talked to Pete. He got it immediately. The schoolmarm is a teeny tiny part that doesn't require any dancing, so Pete told Jason to give it to Clare. Jason hates being told what to do, but because it's Bad Pete, he did it, and he's been in a bad mood ever since."

A whole lot of drama, and it wasn't even lunch yet. Which reminded me.

"I saw Theo on my way in," I said. "He was making out with a redhead."

Becca's eyebrows shot up. "That sounds like Mia. I thought she was seeing one of the production assistants. Oh well. Typical Theo. Such a fuckboy. That's what the kids call them these days. Back in my day, it was *womanizer*. Fuckboy has a better ring to it, don't you think?"

"I think Clare has no business with him."

"Good luck with that," Becca said. "Clare's a sweet girl, but I don't think she'll like it if you interfere."

"She won't like it when she finds out what he's really like."

"True, but she may have to find out the hard way about guys like him. Just like the rest of us idiots. That's how we learned, right?"

Becca had a point. But I wasn't ready to just let it all go. Clare didn't have a lot of experience with guys, let alone one like him. I might not have been related to Clare, but I was a responsible adult in her life.

I caught myself. Once again, I was thinking about Theo instead of hexes. And Clare wasn't even my kid. How did working mothers balance it all?

I shook my head, trying to clear my thoughts, but that only made the wound on my scalp throb.

"What's with the hat?" Becca asked, frowning. "You never wear hats."

I popped it off and tipped my head. "I was never bitten by a harpy before. Ran into one at Elysian Park yesterday. Long story."

"Ouch! And I thought *my* job was rough."

"So, now that I'm here, what should I be looking for?"

Becca winced and gave her corset another tug. "I have no idea. At lunch, I'll introduce you to people. This afternoon, we're shooting some saloon scenes again. Something about dancers jumping over the bar. But it didn't turn out how the choreographer wanted, so he's gonna try a new move. Which is another reason Jason is in such a bad mood. The choreographer is even more of a perfectionist than he is."

I was getting stressed out just hearing about all the conflict. It put our HOA politics into perspective.

A thought struck me. "I have a question. Who else was in the original saloon scene besides you? Clare? Pete?"

Becca nodded. "That's right." Her eyes widened. "Are you thinking the saloon is related to the hex?"

"I don't know. Just trying to connect the dots at this point."

A short burst of music blared over a speaker, and Becca whirled around. "Gotta go. See you at lunch." She hurried off as quickly as her flouncy skirt and lace-up boots would allow.

Pete spotted me and gave a friendly wave. A moment later, a young woman trotted toward me carrying a camp chair, her high ponytail swinging.

"Hi! You're Pete's friend! Nice! Okay, so, he said you're his guest today and you'll be watching. Cool, cool. So, here's a chair." She set it down, then pointed at a white table tucked behind a hedge of cactus. "There's some water and other drinks and snacks over there, so help yourself. But please stay seated during filming and silence your phone. Thank you!" Without waiting for a reply, she pranced away.

Pete turned toward me again and gave me a cheerful thumbs-up. Jason Wood strode over to Pete, placed a hand on his shoulder, and began talking to him in an animated, eager sort of way. Pete nodded, listening intently. All traces of Jason's boorish behavior had disappeared. He seemed nearly deferential. Interesting, but not particularly helpful in solving the mystery of the hex.

Jason and Pete finished their conversation, and the crew took their places. I wished I had a nice hot mug of coffee, but then I would have had to pee, and I wasn't supposed to move.

When the cameras rolled, Pete lip-synced and danced in a patch of dirt, kicking up a bunch of dust. The guys dressed as lawmen joined him, and they line danced between two rows of cacti. The back door of the schoolhouse banged open, and Clare appeared, looking disheveled and distressed, in a yellow calico dress. She screamed, "Help! Help!" and the men rushed to her side.

End of scene. People clapped politely.

Whatever terrible thing was happening in the schoolhouse was quickly forgotten, and more dancing followed, including some risky leaps over cacti.

When the crew broke for lunch, Pete came over, apologized for not being able to spend more time with me, and said he was off for a meeting in the commissary, wherever that was. A minute later, Becca escorted me to the building next door, where lunch was being served on an unused soundstage.

People were helping themselves cafeteria style. I thought for a moment there might be burritos, but no. It was make-your-own-rice-bowl day, with grilled meat and tofu options. Clare was already seated at the far end of the room, at a table packed with saloon girls. Theo, bowl in hand, made straight for them and squeezed in next to her. Mia could have won an award for best performance in the Pretending We Didn't Just Hook Up category.

Theo seemed much more interested in talking to Clare than he was in eating his food, and she was hanging on his every word.

Becca stood beside me, watching too. "Oh, brother. Theo the Guru is at it again. I swear, it's his favorite role."

"She's certainly a willing disciple." I picked up a bundle of cutlery and set it on my tray.

"They all are," Becca said dryly.

I watched Clare cover her face with her hands, as if she had just heard something horrifying, and Theo patted her on the back. Clare leaned her head on his shoulder, and he whispered something into her ear. She lifted her head and smiled.

Perhaps I had gotten the wrong end of the stick. He could have just been mentoring the new kid.

"Maybe it's all more innocent than we think," I said, keeping my voice low.

Becca scoffed. "Yeah, right. Don't let him fool you, too."

Clare would soon be eighteen. Her birthday was the next month. If I told Stu or Vicki Wells their daughter was going out with a twenty-four-year-old guy, they might not like the idea, but there wasn't much they could do about it without creating a Romeo and Juliet situation. The last thing we needed was for Clare to set about proving her parents were wrong and Theo was Mr. Wonderful.

Which was what I had done when my mother tried to break up my early romance with an older Mr. Wrong—one of the rare times she had been right about something. Kevin had been good-looking and manipulative, coming on strong and later ghosting me. My mother had said she sensed his "bad energy" the moment she met him. If I hadn't been so quick to dismiss all the red flags she had pointed out, I might have left the relationship with more of my dignity intact.

It was entirely possible I was projecting my bad experience onto Clare. More than possible. Probable.

But it was still pretty clear to me—things weren't going to end well.

Chapter 20

Becca and I found a quiet spot out of Clare's line of sight. I felt a little guilty spying on her, but my gut instinct—which I was getting better at paying attention to—told me to continue. Nothing terribly exciting happened over the next twenty minutes, just more of Theo yakking and Clare looking up at him with wide brown eyes. I was sure I had gazed at Kevin that way too, once upon a time, and shuddered at the memories that came crawling back.

Becca's phone chimed. Across the room, more chimes sounded, and people picked up their cells. Becca stared at her screen and sighed.

"Change of plans. We're back in the cactus garden again after lunch." When she looked up, she said, "That's good news for you. That means we won't be shooting in the saloon until later. Do you want to have a look around before we all cram in there?"

"Hell, yes." I got to my feet. "Do I need to let anyone know?"

Becca shook her head. "Pete knows what you're up to, right? Why raise suspicions? If someone has an issue, I'm sure you can talk your way out of it."

She was right. I *was* a decent liar. But first, I wanted to say hello to Clare. I caught up with her just as she was headed out the door. I tapped on her shoulder, and she swung around, eyes widening in surprise.

"Maddy! What are you doing here?"

I leaned in and said quietly, "Snooping around."

She reared her head back and blinked rapidly. "What?" Clare definitely looked guilty.

Theo, talking to a dancer dressed as a cowboy, spotted us and hurried over.

Clare narrowed her eyes. "Did my dad ask you to spy on me?"

I bopped her nose. "Your father has nothing to do with why I'm here." I lowered my voice and added, "It's that other thing we talked about. The hex." I pressed a finger to my lips.

Clare looked relieved and nodded eagerly. "Sure, yeah. Of course. I won't say anything."

"Say what?" Theo asked, gliding up.

Clare pasted a smile on her face. "Nothing!" Her voice had gone all squeaky.

His eyes flicked between us, and his forehead wrinkled. "Who's this?" he asked lightly, but his expression betrayed his uneasiness. Theo obviously remembered me from the walkway.

Clare smiled. "This is Maddy! I told you about her. She's my dad's girlfriend, and she's the best cook ever." She clapped a hand over her mouth. "Oh my gosh, I haven't even introduced you. Clare, this is Theo. He's been super, super nice to me because I've never done anything like this before and he's been on tons of productions. Right, Theo?"

Theo scraped a hand through his hair. "Wow. Dad's girlfriend, huh?" He forced a smile to his face. "Nice to meet you, Maddy. Clare's a big fan of yours. She's told me all about you."

I nodded. "So, you're a dancer, I hear."

Theo glanced at Clare, eyebrows raised. "Oh, so you told Maddy about me?"

Before Clare could reply, I said, "No. But I work in security, and information just seems to come my way." I gave a little laugh and threw up my hands.

Theo didn't seem to know what to think. All kinds of emotions flitted across his handsome face: confusion, suspicion, and annoyance. Me against Theo wasn't exactly fair—me being forty and his brain under the influence of all that testosterone plus, at his age, an underdeveloped prefrontal cortex.

They exchanged glances, then Theo snapped his fingers and grinned. His teeth were blindingly white. "I'm a dancer, for sure, but I'm hoping to get into acting. Clare here beat me to it. She's totally, one hundred percent amazing. I keep telling her she needs to quit soccer and take a class. And I can help her do it too."

I had to give the guy credit; he was smooth. And quite the actor, pretending I hadn't seen him snogging another girl only a couple of hours earlier.

"Theo's taking acting classes, and I've been really freaking out about my part, even though it's tiny and he's been helping me," Clare said hurriedly. And a little defensively too.

Theo shrugged. "She's a natural. She just needs to get out of her own head." He nudged Clare. "We better get going. They'll need to touch up our makeup before we start up again. Nice to meet you, Maddy. Don't worry. I'll take care of Clare."

Uh huh. Clare pecked my cheek, and they hurried off. Mia was still sitting at the lunch table, watching them go, her chin resting on one palm, eyebrows lowered. Probably pondering her life choices.

Once again, I had been sidetracked by Clare and Theo. The stitches on my scalp had begun to itch, but scratching was a no-no. I found a bathroom and checked the bandage to make sure it was still in place before wandering over to the saloon.

121

The camp chairs were gone, and there was nobody around to stop me from going in. The outside was all rustic weathered wood. I pushed through the swinging doors and saw, with some surprise, that it was very spacious.

There was a long bar lined with stools, the shelves stocked with liquor bottles. Most of them appeared genuinely old, the kind of things you might pick up at antique shops and yard sales. Several were green; a few were a rich ruby. Clear bottles had been filled with colored liquid to make them look more interesting. One bottle, a decanter with a round stopper, was decorated with a hummingbird, flower, and cactus motif.

I turned around, taking in the round tables, the piano in the corner. A cluster of light stands filled one corner, along with a pile of neatly coiled cables. A staircase led to a mezzanine level lined with a bunch of doors. The building, from the outside, didn't seem wide enough for all those rooms. I went upstairs, the wooden steps creaking under my feet, and sure enough, none of the doors opened.

Downstairs, I lifted the piano lid and peered inside. Nothing. The piano bench didn't have storage, so I picked it up and turned it over. Nothing there either. Then I went around the room, searching under all the tables, chairs, and stools and running my hand underneath the edge of the bar. I looked behind framed photos, stood on a chair, and poked my fingers into the red glass sconces—empty except for little electric candles.

Footsteps sounded on the wooden sidewalk outside, and a moment later, the saloon doors creaked open. The production assistant with the bouncy ponytail appeared, clipboard in hand. She was startled when she saw me.

"Oh! I didn't know anyone was in here!"

"Just having a look around," I said.

She gave a little shrug, clutching the clipboard to her chest. "Cool beans. We're shooting in here in about an hour. Are you going to stay and watch?"

Good question. I could have stayed, but unless I were to witness a cast member throwing a hex bag at someone's face, I wasn't sure what that would accomplish.

The saloon was one place the entire cast would have been together, so Pete and Becca could have been exposed to the hex there. Except would Olga have been in the saloon during the shoot? And what about Ben and Julia?

But there was one more place everyone might have been.

"Just curious," I said. "Has lunch been served in the same place since production began?"

She nodded. "Yeah. There's an actual commissary on the other side of the lot, but Jason thought it was too far, so we're having it brought into that old soundstage."

"Does Pete eat there too?"

The production assistant crossed the room and set her clipboard down on the bar. "Normally, for sure. But just not today because he had a meeting with Jason. They went over to the commissary."

I wasn't sure if my team had searched the soundstage. After all, I hadn't told them about it because, honestly, it hadn't occurred to me. But it was the one place everyone had congregated, where Olga Sanchez had served breakfast and lunch, and where Ben and Julia would have eaten while they were working on the sets.

A perfect place to stash a hex bag.

The production assistant moved behind the bar and started poking around under the counter.

"I'll get out of your hair, then," I said.

Her head popped up. "Well, thanks for coming," she said briskly, as if she were a shop clerk and I was a customer who had been browsing too long.

I doubled back to where we'd had lunch. A few people were wiping down tables, so I said I had lost my credit card, which was the only excuse I could think of. They wished me luck and went about their work. I peered under the tables, chairs, and everyplace else that could hide a hex bag, but there was nothing.

When I was just about to leave, I noticed a series of framed black and white photos on a wall and went over for a closer look. It was Western Studios, back when it was just a Western set in the middle of dusty nowhere. I peered behind each one but found nothing.

The photos were interesting, though. Snapshots from another time, taken during the production of one of the most famous Westerns ever made. One of the images, dated June 1950, showed a pretty woman of about thirty sitting in a chair, a costume spread across her lap. She looked vaguely startled, as if caught off guard by whoever was taking her picture while she went about stitching the dress. A caption identified her as Espy Gaitán, a resident of Palo Verde, employed as a seamstress on the movie. Espy had large eyes and dark hair.

A man in a white shirt and a dark jacket hovered nearby, watching her with interest. Correction. Staring at her with barely disguised lechery.

I found him in another photo, standing next to a film camera with his arms folded across his chest, scowling. He seemed vaguely familiar. The caption explained why. He was Mitchell Wood, Jason Wood's famous great-grandfather.

My scalp itched again, only it felt like an early warning system.

I might have been about to fall down a rabbit hole that would lead nowhere, but it was time to learn about the history of Western Studios.

Chapter 21

Unfortunately, digging into the history of Western Studios meant talking to the one person who knew more about the area's past than anyone. Hernan Frias.

I found him in the front yard of his house, fussing over a red rose bush. He was the only man I knew who gardened while wearing a button-down shirt and sweater vest.

"How are you?" I asked politely.

"Alive," he said. "No thanks to those darned gnomes who stole my roses and gave them to those traitors across the street."

I had nearly forgotten about the Mendez ladies and their recall petition.

"How's that going? Did you have a chance to talk it through?"

Hernan waved a pair of clippers in the air. "Talk through what? They're as stubborn as mules, those two. They've done me dirty, is what they did, and they're proud of it. But isn't it interesting how things have turned out? The gnomes are here, and whether or not they followed Malena is immaterial because you've got them well in hand. And I'm hearing people are downright pleased they're here."

"Yes, well...it's early days yet," I warned.

Hernan waved his clippers at me. "Time's running out for me if I want to stay on the board." He lowered his furry eyebrows. "Your mother's not here. Occult Affairs called her in to help with a giant in the Hollywood Hills."

"Well, it's you I came to see."

"Oh?" Hernan replied casually, but his expression said he was both flattered and wary.

"Can we go inside? I could use a cafecito."

Hernan turned and began walking toward the house, gesturing for me to follow. "Me too. Your mother bought one of those fancy espresso machines, and I haven't figured out how to use it yet."

Surprise, surprise. Hernan was one of those men of a certain generation who never lifted a finger inside the house. By all accounts, his first wife had spoiled him rotten, and then after she died, Marta took over. Marta still came every day, and since my mother had moved in, there were *two* women to do his bidding.

"Where's Marta?" I asked.

"Visiting her family in Mexico." Hernan set the clippers down on the tiled floor in the entryway.

I looked around. My mother had been busy in the living room, switching out the summer pillows and throws for fall colors in mustard and gray. Even the altar to Santa Muerte—the cloaked folk saint holding a scythe—had a fall theme going, with gold votive candles, a garland of eucalyptus, and wispy bits of wheat grass. The place smelled vaguely of paint, and I soon saw why. She had painted two walls in the kitchen a lovely shade of sage, which worked well with the Saltillo tile floors. Striped cushions in burnt sienna and cream topped the chairs.

It had never occurred to me to do a little refresh with the change of seasons, probably because Los Angeles seemed to exist in perpetual summer, but it looked nice. I was sure Julia would be more than happy to help out if I asked. It would require a shopping trip, but those were fun with her. And it gave us an excuse to hit Philippe's downtown for French dip sandwiches.

An enormous stainless-steel machine squatted on the kitchen counter. No wonder Hernan was afraid to use it. It was intimidating. I studied it while Hernan rummaged in the cupboards for a bag of ground coffee.

"I could use a little snack with my cafecito," he said. "How about you?" Hernan handed over a silver bag and looked at me hopefully.

I knew what that meant. Fine. Swapping food for information wasn't a bad deal. "I could use a bite," I said, turning my attention to the refrigerator.

My mother had made tomato soup. There was a big glass bowl of it on a shelf. I took it out, along with some corn tortillas and a bag of shredded cheese.

"Quesadillas?" Hernan asked hopefully.

I rolled my eyes but gave him a thumbs-up. After searching the cabinets for a cast iron griddle, I began heating up the tortillas.

Just when I began to sprinkle cheese on the tortilla, Hernan said, "Don't forget to add some oregano and pepper. Your mother does that, and it's delicious."

"I make quesadillas just like she does."

While I finished the coffee, Hernan washed his hands at the sink, then sat at the kitchen table with his hands folded in front of him. He had the expression of a little kid anticipating milk and cookies.

Since I was doing the cooking, I decided it was time for him to do his part.

"Hernan, I need to ask a favor. I'm working on a problem that has all the hallmarks of a hex. And I think it's somehow connected to Western Studios. You're familiar with the history of that place, aren't you?"

He sat up a little straighter and cleared his throat. "I know quite a bit about that place. So many people from these

128

neighborhoods worked there in the old days. But what's this about a hex?"

I gave him a quick rundown of everything, from the strange affliction that had struck some of our most talented residents to the photos at the studios and the creepy director leering at the costume maker.

While I talked, I put a bowl of warm tomato soup in front of Hernan and added a small plate of quesadillas with sliced avocado garnish. Finally, I poured some chili verde salsa into a condiment bowl and added a dollop of crema.

Hernan's dark eyes grew wider while he listened. "A hex! Who would want to hex them? Bad Pete, I can understand. He's very nice but very rich, so he's probably made a few enemies along the way. Olga can be a little moody, from what I hear, but…" His voice trailed off, his eyebrows lowering into a frown. "You know, Maddy…Hexes are deeply personal, so who's to say those people didn't do something to upset someone?"

"Yes, Hernan, I know hexes are personal."

I paused long enough to see if he connected what he had just said with the hex bags he had left under my chair and bed right after I was hired. He kept his eyes on his food, ignoring my gaze.

Yup, he'd made the connection.

"Mmm, this is delicious, Maddy. Thank you."

I lifted a spoonful of soup to my lips and blew to cool it off. It *was* delicious. I had no idea how my mother did it. My tomato soup always came out slightly acidic, but hers was like velvet and butter.

"I've not been able to make a connection between the victims. If they were targeted, there would be something linking them. But this feels random. And why weren't more people affected? If there was something going on at the studio, why were only a few people hexed?"

Hernan sprinkled salt on his tomato soup. The man had survived at least one heart attack and probably didn't need the extra sodium, so I moved the saltshaker to the other side of the table. For a moment, I thought he was going to complain, but his eyes got that look that suggested he was on the verge of a breakthrough.

I sipped my soup and waited, my leg bouncing up and down under the table.

After a few moments, he set down his spoon. "Well, it's possible it's not a hex bag at all. Maybe it's something more serious."

My scalp tingled. "What do you mean, more serious? Like what?"

"Like a cursed object." He picked up a quesadilla triangle and gave a little shudder.

My head began spinning with possibilities. "What's a cursed object look like?"

Hernan dipped the quesadilla in the chili verde salsa. "It can be anything, really."

I sat back in my chair, not sure I had gotten a quesadilla's worth of information out of him.

Chapter 22

I sat in Hernan's kitchen, watching him finish the last of his soup and realizing he probably didn't know how to do dishes. Or so he would claim.

But what he had said about a cursed object was interesting. The curse would only affect people who touched the object, not everyone in the area.

The music video set was filled with all sorts of stuff. If there was a cursed object lying around, it could be anything, like a saltshaker in the dining room or one of the light stands in the saloon.

I pictured the schoolhouse, the dusty street, and the inside of the saloon, trying to remember whether I had felt anything unusual on my visit.

"I'm a bruja, right?" I cleared the dishes. "Wouldn't I have sensed that an object was cursed?"

Hernan gave a dismissive sniff while he sipped his cappuccino. "It doesn't work like that. Being a bruja—and a new one at that—doesn't mean you're a human Geiger counter."

"So, if it *is* a cursed object, how do I find it?"

"I have no idea." Hernan pinched the skin at his throat. "I've only heard about them. I've never dealt with one myself."

I sighed. "All right. If by some miracle I do find it, how do I…uncurse it?"

"It depends on the curse, of course." Hernan tilted his head back and looked upward in a parody of exasperation. "You'd need to know the history of it, the why of it, in order to understand it and figure out what to do. There's no such thing as a generic curse. You ought to know that. These sorts of things are very, very specific."

And very frustrating. I had finally achieved a decent level of magical ability and now it seemed useless. None of my new skills were helping me to solve my current problem. And it had just gotten even more complicated.

It wasn't only a matter of finding a hex bag and whisking it away. I had to identify a cursed object in a sea of items, then undo a curse that could be who knew how old. Plus, I had zeroed in on the music video set, but I could have been wrong. For all I could guess, each of the cursed people had shopped at the Palo Verde Market and touched a cursed bottle of salsa.

Hernan had mentioned something interesting—that I needed to know the history of the curse. Which reminded me why I had come to see him in the first place: to learn about the history of Western Studios.

I ran hot water into the sink and squirted some liquid dish soap into it. Even *that* smelled like autumn. The label read: "Acorn Spice." A little over the top, maybe, but it was nice and soothing.

"There were some photos in the dining hall at Western Studios," I said. "From back in the late nineteen forties and early fifties. Right around the time the eviction notices went out. One of them was a picture of the famous director Mitchell Wood. The fellow who's directing the music video is his great-grandson."

Hernan set down his cup. "Mitchell Wood? Well, he was supposed to be one pinche cabron. He was way before my time, but I heard about him, all right." He frowned. "In fact, he's come up in the oral histories that were done many years ago. One was very interesting, by a lady who used to live in Palo Verde. She was a very talented seamstress, and the studio hired her to work on the costumes. She had a sewing machine at her house, and she did a lot of the alterations and repairs. The lady had some very interesting things to say about that director."

I leaned against the counter, my heart beating faster. "Was her name Espy Gaitán? She was in one of the pictures I saw."

Hernan slapped the table. "That's it! That's the name. Esperanza Gaitán. She met one of the fellows working on the movie, and they ended up getting married. She sold her house to the city and moved in with her new husband. She died before we set up the legacy rules, but she said she always regretted selling."

"And she talked about Mitchell Wood?"

Hernan nodded. "Extensively. That pinche cabron made a very bad impression on her."

"You said they're oral histories? Were they transcribed?"

"Not hers. But you can listen to them if you want. She talks a lot about her work at the studios, if I remember correctly."

"When can I hear them?"

Hernan pushed back his chair and got to his feet. "No time like the present. If we go now, we can pick up the tapes and then stop at Muertos Café for a little pan dulce."

Always with the pan dulce. But it was a small price to pay for getting to hear from the woman who had a ringside seat to the Western that had made movie history.

We had just crossed the little bridge into Palo Verde when Hernan yelled, "Look!" and I hit the brakes. "There!" He pointed at a slope at the far end of one of Chavez Ravine's many small parks.

Gnomes dotted the hillside, busily digging holes and planting away. From the small purple flowers, I guessed they were planting more periwinkle. I spotted Sam's large red form sitting Sphinxlike at the top of the hill, while other cats sauntered among the gnomes.

A crowd of people were gathered at the base of the hill, heads tilted up while they watched the activity. I recognized two of them: Charlie Perez and Eileen Simpson. Very suspicious. Eileen had been a vocal opponent of the gnome strategy and was probably looking for evidence it had gone off the rails.

"That hill's steep," Hernan said. "And look at those gnomes. Now that's really something, isn't it?"

It certainly was. The gnomes clambered around on the steep, uneven terrain like they had been born to do it. And who knew, maybe they were. I'd had a few fleeting psychic glimpses into their home world, but all I had seen was a flying shadow creature chasing them around.

We crossed the park but hung back a bit, watching. Charlie Perez had a large camera hanging from a strap on his neck. Eileen was dressed in her real estate armor: red dress, red heels. Her new, more casual haircut with wispy bangs made her appear younger and less severe than she was. Charlie seemed to be giving her some sort of direction.

"A little more to your left," Charlie said, peering through the viewfinder.

Eileen scooted to her right. "Here?"

"Your other left." Charlie wore an orange polo shirt emblazoned with the Chavez Ravine logo.

Eileen gave a little embarrassed laugh, then took a few steps in the other direction. "How about now?"

"Perfect!"

Why was Charlie Perez, real estate broker and treasurer of the Chavez Ravine Homeowners Association, trying to get a photo of Eileen with the gnomes in the background? What in the world were they up to? Then Ben Tomas walked up to them and said something into Eileen's ear.

The gnomes had stopped working and were staring down at the crowd of humans. Maybe Ben was telling Eileen and Charlie to leave.

Ben pointed up the hill at Sam, who came sauntering down. The head gnome, Beady, was on his heels. Both looked up at Ben. A moment later, Sam began chittering to Beady, who lifted his bushy eyebrows so high they practically disappeared underneath his pointy hat.

Whatever was going on, Beady didn't seem happy about it. With a very human expression of resignation, he trudged toward Eileen, his little hands balled into fists at his side.

"Awww!" Eileen cried, in that tone of voice usually reserved for cute babies or puppies.

Beady winced. The old gnome shot Sam a martyred look while he went to stand next to the real estate agent. Eileen bent at the knees, tilted her head toward Beady, and grinned at the camera.

She was posing with the gnome! Eileen Simpson, who had opposed me every step of the way, had suddenly decided gnomes could be good for business.

Charlie must have snapped a dozen photos before Beady had enough. He stepped out of the frame, turned on his heel, and raced back up the hill. The other gnomes exploded in grumbly laughter. I had never heard them laugh before. It was actually kind of funny.

I couldn't stand it any longer. Leaving Hernan behind and pushing through the small crowd, I walked up to Charlie. "What's going on?" The question came out louder than I intended, tinged with accusation.

Charlie whirled around. "Oh, Maddy! I didn't know you were here." He paused and cleared his throat, looking decidedly sheepish. "You know, just a little marketing."

"A little marketing," I repeated, mystified.

Eileen rushed forward and placed a hand on my arm. "Yes, marketing! People love the gnomes!" She laughed giddily. "Who would have thought it, right? And I have to admit, they're doing an awfully good job." She glanced around and, in a lower voice, continued, "And at no additional expense to the community! Honestly, we've needed some good PR, and this is it!"

The way to Eileen's heart had always been through the HOA's budget. And her own real estate business. Not necessarily in that order.

It was none of my business how the Chavez Ravine Association marketed itself, but I wasn't sure whether using the gnomes for a photo op was the best idea. For one thing, we were just getting started. Nobody knew how long the gnomes would be compliant or if Sam's crew would one day decide to stretch out in the sun rather than work the hillsides. And there was always the risk of looking like we were abusing the gnomes. Entity-rights groups were vocal, and sometimes, they were right. We didn't need protestors at our gates.

So, even though it was none of my business, I couldn't keep my yap shut. "I'm not sure I understand how the gnomes are good PR, to be honest, Eileen."

Charlie's brown skin turned an odd shade of mottled red. "Well, we thought we'd take out some ads with the gnomes. You know. To help advertise the properties we have listed in Chavez Ravine."

"And to update our collateral material," Eileen added eagerly. "There's a lot of public interest in the gnomes. One of the TV stations is coming by later to do a news story. Isn't that terrific?"

This was already spinning out of control. I wondered how much Cora knew about this new marketing plan.

"Mmm," I said in as neutral a tone as I could muster.

Charlie registered my lack of enthusiasm. "There's something on your mind, isn't there, Maddy? Is there anything we should be aware of?" he asked while Hernan sidled up next to us.

Well, the moment the television cameras were recording, the gnomes could decide to stage a revolt. Or whatever was making those large emergence holes could make an appearance in the middle of the crowd. Dark thoughts, but I was head of security, and it was my job to anticipate problems. It was Charlie's job to gloss over them, to project the kind of optimism it took to sell houses.

I forced a smile to my lips. "No. You know everything I do." Which was mostly true.

Eileen had paid no attention to my exchange with Charlie. "And guess what else the gnomes will be doing?"

Wearing frilly aprons and serving canapés at your next open house? "Can't wait to hear it." Another forced smile.

"They'll be planting marigolds along the main streets in Chavez Ravine! You know. In honor of the Day of the Dead! And I'm thinking we should paint their faces like those…what do you call them?" Caliverdes? Wouldn't that be amazing? So cute!"

Hernan turned toward me with a horrified expression before scowling at Eileen. "It's called a *Calavera*. Dia de los Muertos is a deeply symbolic tradition, Eileen, not to be confused with Halloween. You will absolutely not, under any circumstances, dress up gnomes as catrins. I will not allow it."

Eileen reared her head back as if she had been slapped. For a moment, she was speechless.

Charlie pulled the camera strap away from his neck like it was choking him. "Hernan's right, Eileen. In fact, I'm a little uncomfortable with you running the Day of the Dead Festival." He registered the thunderstorm passing over Hernan's features and held up a hand. "As Julia Suarez is the one who proposed the festival, we think it's only right that she organize it too."

"Whose 'we,'" Eileen asked, her eyes narrowing.

Hernan straightened his shoulders. "Me, Cora, and Charlie. We want someone who understands the symbolism and tradition so it doesn't turn into another Cinco de Mayo."

Charlie nodded, his expression unreadable.

I glanced at Hernan, then back at Charlie. Both were locked on Eileen, rigid and silent. I wondered why Hernan hadn't mentioned their plan when we were having lunch. And then I understood.

These two had never discussed taking the festival away from Eileen. They had made it up on the spot. I was impressed Hernan had pulled it off because he was usually a terrible liar. Eileen seemed too stunned to respond.

"That's right, Eileen," Charlie said solemnly. "The Latino board members want to preserve the meaning of this holiday."

Eileen's eyes flicked between Charlie and Hernan, trying to calculate her odds of getting them to change their minds. "Fine. I'm busy with some new clients anyway." Then, as if she needed to reassert herself, she turned to Charlie. "Let's get going, shall we? We have ads to design."

Charlie relaxed, and a slow smile came to his face. He clapped Hernan on the shoulder. "Compadre," then walked with Eileen toward her car.

"Compadre" had a couple of meanings, and I was pretty sure Charlie meant "buddy," but I might have been wrong.

"You're not Charlie's godfather, are you?" I asked.

138

Hernan scowled. "No! His father would never have asked me. We didn't see eye to eye on the legacy rules. Fortunately, Charlie has more sense than his elders, but I still don't see where he gets off calling me 'compadre.'"

I nudged him. "He didn't mean anything by it. He was just being...Charlie."

"I hope so," Hernan said grudgingly. "I'm going to let Cora know that Julia's taking over the festival, just in case Eileen gets up to some of her tricks."

The people who had gathered to watch the gnomes began to wander away. It was a beautiful fall day. Crisp and cool. How long would the cool weather last?

I waved at Sam while he prowled among the gnomes halfway up the steep hill. He pretended not to see me, although I was sure he had. Perhaps it wouldn't have helped his tough-cat reputation if word got out some lady fed him fancy food from a tin.

My phone vibrated. It was a message from Becca Tey.

Look what I saw on the way out of the studios today

A moment later, a few photos appeared. It was Theo and Clare in pretty much the same position he had been in with Mia in the narrow walkway. He appeared to be in the process of devouring her face, with her hands around his neck.

Shit.

Another text from Becca.

Now what are you going to do?

Not sure. But something

Let me know if I can help. Short of castration

Chapter 23

In the community library, Hernan headed straight for a door in the far wall. It opened into a small windowless room lined with steel shelves, with a single table and chair in the center.

Hernan went to a shelf on the right wall, pulled out a box, and set it down on the table. In Hernan's spidery handwriting, the label read: "The Oral History of Esperanza Gaitán Knox."

He lifted the lid with a flourish. I peered inside, my heart sinking.

I wasn't sure what I had been expecting, but definitely something a bit more modern than a half dozen slightly scuffed black cassette tapes.

"How am I supposed to listen to these?"

Hernan turned, frowning. "Your generation is so spoiled. How do you think? With your ears."

I picked up a cassette labeled "Espy Gaitán #1" and held it up to my ear. "Is there a cassette player around, or am I supposed to order one off the internet?"

Hernan stared at me for a moment, uncomprehending, then his eyes widened. "Oh, yes, of course. We've got one of those somewhere."

Hernan rummaged around inside some dusty boxes and, after a couple of minutes, said, "Here it is!" He held up an ancient black Panasonic cassette player with silver trim.

I had not used one since I was a kid. Buttons for Eject, Record, Play, Rewind, Fast Forward, Stop, and Pause. I pushed the Eject button, and the cassette door popped open. I slid the cassette into the door, pushed it closed, and hit Play.

Nothing happened.

"Hernan?"

"Yes?"

"Is there a power cord in that box?"

Hernan peered forward, reached into it with one hand, and triumphantly pulled out a cord.

I plugged the cassette recorder into the nearest electrical outlet and hit Play once again.

A man's deep voice came out of the tiny speaker.

"Thank you for sitting down with me today. We're honored to record your story as part of our community's effort to preserve the history of the old neighborhoods of Chavez Ravine. This recording will be archived for historical and educational purposes. Let's start with your name and how long your family has lived here."

A woman's voice, slightly raspy with age but still warm and gentle, filled the room. *"I'm so glad to do this. Thank you for asking me. My name is Espy Gaitán Knox, but I was just Espy back when I lived in Palo Verde."*

"Is Espy a nickname?"

"It's short for Esperanza, but that's a good question. There were lots of nicknames in the old days." Espy laughed. She had the faintest hint of an accent.

Hernan leaned over me and hit Pause with a sigh. "English probably wasn't her first language. But her voice is beautiful, isn't it?" He sounded wistful.

I twisted in my seat to look at him. He actually had tears in his eyes. I patted his hand. "It is. It is beautiful."

He hit Play again and began pacing around the room.

Espy continued.

"I grew up in Bishop, but when I married for the first time, my husband and I bought a little house in Palo Verde. He died in the Battle of the Bulge. But by that time, I already had a job as a seamstress at a dressmaking shop in the garment district. I was one of the lucky girls. I didn't have to clean houses or work in one of the smelly canneries, and my father had a good job at the railyard, so we were fortunate. Nobody in our family ever had to work in the fields, and we owned our own home."

She paused.

"Is this the sort of thing you're looking for? Do you just want me to keep talking?"

"It's exactly what we're looking for."

"All right, but please let me know if you want to hear anything specific."

"We just want to know about your life, your family…the things you remember about living in Chavez Ravine."

"Well, I'll never forget those terrible murders. They had us scared out of our wits. I knew the victims because we all worked on a movie together."

She might have been scared back then, but there was excitement in her voice while she told the story.

"The killer's victims were all young men. But those poor fellows weren't the only ones who lost their lives. My friend, Catalina Montez, was killed too. By a drunk man. It was an awful, awful thing." Epsy sniffed.

The interviewer gave her a moment, then asked, *"Tell me, how was it you were working on a movie set? It was rare for Mexican Americans to get jobs like that back then, wasn't it?"*

"Oh, yes, it was rare. But I was very, very lucky. I even met my second husband, Bruce, there. He was the prop master."

"It must have been more than luck, no? You must have been very good at your job."

"Well, my boss left to become a costume designer for the movies. It was Beyond the Passage, *a Western, and Westerns had lots and lots of costumes, you see. They were making the movie near Elysian Park. The director built a whole Western set down there, and let me tell you, it was really*

something. I didn't like that man, but he knew what he was doing when he created that set. Anyway, my boss remembered I lived in Palo Verde and asked if I would work for him because there was so much to do and he knew I had a sewing machine at home. So, I said yes. The job paid more money, and I didn't even have to leave my house, except to visit the set when they were shooting so I could hand-sew the repairs. The director made the girls wear their costumes way too tight—he was that kind of man—so it didn't take much for the seams to burst."*

I hit Pause again and sat back in my chair. Though I could have listened to Espy all day, I wasn't sure how that would help me find the cursed object or hex bag or whatever we were dealing with.

And yet, my gut told me the pieces of the puzzle were somewhere in those cassette tapes, waiting to be put together.

Hernan began tapping his fingers on the table. "Have you solved the mystery already? Is that why we're just sitting here in silence?"

"Hernan, this is all very interesting, but I don't even know what I'm looking for. If Espy says something helpful, how will I know? This just feels like a distraction from the job I should be doing, which is figuring out what's causing our residents so much trouble and putting a stop to it."

Hernan shook his head and clucked his teeth. "That's always been your problem, Maddy. You're too darned impatient. You wanted to snap your fingers and become a bruja. You wanted your poor dead great-aunt, God rest her soul, to boost your brujeria because you didn't want to do the work. You wanted Santa Muerte's help without giving her the proper respect she deserves. You even raised the dead without understanding the risks! You want to take shortcuts when the long way is the best." He wagged a finger at me. "Sometimes, the roundabout route is the one that gets you to where you actually need to go."

How long had he been waiting to deliver that speech? Well, I was ready with one of my own.

"May I remind you, Hernan, I have a twenty-four-seven job. Since I got here, there's been one problem after another. Some of them of *your* making. And yes, I've been impatient because we've had chupacabras, vampire birds, and even El Cucuy himself and it's my job to protect our residents from all of them. If I've been in a hurry, it's because I haven't had much choice."

"You didn't even know what a revenant was!" Hernan cried, as if that settled the matter.

I rolled my eyes. "Did too. I was just messing with you."

Hernan pointed at the tape recorder. "You've listened for how long? Five minutes? And you're already wringing your hands?"

"I have a lot of other stuff to do, and people are relying on me to do it quickly!" My voice sounded annoyingly high and slightly shrill.

Hernan threw his hands into the air. "See? See what I mean? This is exactly what I was talking about. You want to snap your fingers and solve the problem. Well, guess what? It's not that kind of problem. You can't throw an amuleto at it…or one of those little pouches filled with magic powder I keep hearing about. There's not a spell in the world that's going to give you the answers you need."

"You have to admit, a spell that would give me the answers I need would be nice."

Hernan came over to the table and thumped his hand against the scuffed wooden surface. The tape recorder jumped. "You worked for the LAPD. You were a cop. You had to solve problems and figure things out like a detective, didn't you? And you did. You figured them out. You just need to put your detective cap on again. That's all."

He made it sound so easy.

"Detectives don't wear caps," I grumbled.

"Detectives don't sit around whining either." Hernan lifted the tape recorder and placed it into the box of tapes.

"What are you doing? I thought you said I shouldn't give up so easily."

Hernan tapped his wristwatch. "You're not giving up. You're taking these home and listening to them there. We need to get to Muertos Café before they run out of pan dulce."

My Lord, that man could focus.

Chapter 24

All that talk about magic had made me feel very far away from mine. I hated to admit it, but Hernan had made some solid points. Nothing in Great-Aunt Lencha's journals would help me restore my friends' skills. It was going to take research and old-fashioned problem solving.

Hernan and I sat down on the patio, where I had a delicious concha and a view of Julia huddled in a corner with Bernie Mora, the restaurant's owner. Julia was a loyal member of Team Olga's Cantina, so I was a little surprised to see her. I left Hernan on the patio with his cafecito and a pumpkin empanada and sauntered over to say a nosy hello.

The two were consulting a stack of menus together. Bernie, a shaggy-haired man with a long face, was tapping away at a calculator.

They glanced up, and Julia's face broke into a smile. She leapt from her chair and threw her arms around me. "Thank you, thank you…for whatever you said about Eileen and the festival," she whispered in my ear.

I squeezed her back. She smelled of lemon verbena. I recognized the delicious scent from one of the lotions she sold at her shop.

"Don't thank me. It was all Hernan's doing."

Julia pulled away, her eyes wide with surprise. "Why would he do that?"

"Because he saw the injustice of it." I smiled at Bernie, who nodded in return.

Julia invited me to sit down. I was curious to see what they were up to, so I happily joined them. Hernan wouldn't mind. He was chatting away with another diner, an older man.

"Whatcha up to?" I asked.

Julia wore a thin brown sweater embroidered with yellow roses. It looked vintage. She beamed. "Planning! Muertos is going to make some special edition Day of the Dead conchas, and they're going to sell them at a stall in the marketplace we're setting up in Palo Verde Plaza. We're talking about Bernie offering a four-course dinner too. But since there's limited seating here, we were thinking about holding a drawing for people who want tickets."

Julia certainly hadn't wasted any time. She must have sprinted over to Muertos as soon as she had gotten the word Eileen was out of the picture. Although, knowing her, she had probably had it all planned out in her head before she pitched her festival idea to the HOA board.

A server appeared at the table, wearing a harried expression. "Sorry to interrupt, Bernie, but a customer has a question about catering. Can you come talk to her?"

Bernie excused himself and hurried away. Julia waited until he was out of earshot, then leaned toward me.

"I feel so bad because I went to Olga first about being one of the sponsors of the festival. The sponsor gets to provide an exclusive festival dinner. I was hoping she'd do it, but she said she didn't dare. Not with the hex. She was so upset about losing out on the opportunity, yeah?"

There was no love lost between Olga and Bernie, so I could only imagine how she was going to react when she found out her nemesis would have his restaurant name splashed everywhere instead of hers.

"That's too bad," I said. And it was. Although festivalgoers would probably be thrilled with either. But the fact that Olga couldn't participate made me feel awful, as if I had failed her by not finding and reversing the hex. The stitches on my scalp started itching again, and I forced myself to resist the urge to scratch them.

Julia nodded sadly. "I know, yeah? Well…Bernie's super excited about the whole thing. And no pressure, but I'm hoping you can figure this out in time for me to make these little Day of the Dead figurines I've got in mind. I was hoping to sell them at the festival." She twirled a strand of auburn hair around a finger, her gaze turning inward.

"I'm working on it," I said. "I promise."

Julia was bothered less about the money than she was about the loss of creative output. My thoughts drifted toward the box of cassette tapes sitting in the cargo area of my Jeep. Each cassette was one hour long, and there were six of them. That meant six hours of listening and not searching for…whatever I needed to find.

Julia lifted one of my hands and pressed it against her cheek. Her skin was soft and warm. She blinked at me with her big brown eyes, her expression grave. "I know you are doing everything you can. I trust you. And Ben does too."

A lump appeared in my throat, and I had to swallow hard to breathe. I could only hope their belief in me wasn't misplaced.

———— ⊱ ⋅ ⊰ · ⛩ · ⊱ ⋅ ⊰ ————

Stu unwrapped white butcher paper from three ribeye steaks. "Clare's joining us for dinner," he said.

We were in Stu's large, functional, boring kitchen, with me sitting at the counter with a glass of Portuguese wine the

148

sommelier at the Palo Verde wine store had recommended. It was smooth and delicious.

"Did she have a change of plans?" The last I had heard, she was going straight from Western Studios to a friend's house in Culver City. Like most teenagers who had grown up in Los Angeles, driving across town in crazy traffic didn't faze her in the least.

Stu was wearing an ancient sweatshirt and shorts. He turned toward me, the crinkles around his blue eyes deepening when he frowned. "Well, I'm not sure what's going on, actually. First, she called me to say she'd had a great time at the music video shoot. As in, the best day ever. And then an hour later she called, and she was upset about something. And I think she was crying, but she wouldn't say what happened. And when I told her you were coming over, she asked if she could come over too. So, of course, I said yes. I think she wants to talk with you."

"Boy trouble?" I recalled the pictures of Clare locking lips with Theo. Which explained why she'd had the best day ever. So, what had happened to wreck it? It wasn't hard to guess.

Stu rinsed his hands and topped off my glass. "Maybe. If so, I'd be the last to know. She doesn't talk about that stuff with me." He sighed. "Or her mother, for that matter. You'll probably have better luck with her than either of us." He grimaced. "I'm sorry. That's a lot to put on you—"

The front door banged open.

"Dad?" Clare shouted. A moment later, she appeared in the kitchen, her face puffy.

She took one look at me and burst into tears.

Chapter 25

Stu wrapped his arms around Clare and said something quietly into her ear. She shook her head.

"I just had a bad day, that's all."

If that bad day had a name, I was sure it was Theo.

"It happens," Stu said, rubbing her back. "But it might help to talk about it."

Clare groaned. "It's too complicated! You won't understand."

"Sweetheart, there probably isn't a problem in the world I haven't experienced."

I had to disagree there. Stu had never been a girl who met a guy like Theo. But I kept quiet, more than happy to let the two have father-daughter time.

Clare raised her head and sniffed. Her eyes were red. She had probably cried all the way from Western Studios.

"It's kind of stupid," she said faintly. "It was just really strange on the set today. Pete was in a really bad mood, which was weird because he's usually so, like, happy and positive, and he's so nice. But he was quiet and wasn't talking much or acting friendly like normal, and then he and the director started arguing. I don't know about what exactly, but they were shouting at each other, and everyone freaked out because they'd never heard Pete shout at anyone before. Becca said Pete was having a bad day because he had to cancel his appearance at the Hollywood Bowl. They're doing this special Halloween concert or something, and

Pete had been really excited about it…Except his voice hasn't come back yet, and the concert people said they needed to replace him soon, and he was really upset about that."

Stu stood up, knitting his brow. "I heard about that. We were supposed to handle Pete's security at the concert, but his agent said Pete had to drop out."

"The whole vibe was bad. Everyone kept making mistakes. The director added a scene with me running through the cactus, like something scary was chasing me, and I did. But it was hard in a long skirt, and I fell down in front of everyone, with the camera rolling. Pete said it was no big deal, but the director was so mean about it." Clare's voice lowered. "It was super embarrassing, and he was such a jerk, and everyone was looking at me. I think that's why they started fighting. Pete told him to stop being mean."

Stu tilted his head. "It sounds like Pete was doing the right thing, sticking up for you. Is there anything else?" Stu's tone suggested he thought she was holding something back.

I thought so too.

Clare wouldn't look at him. "No," she replied in a small voice.

Stu glanced at me, and I shrugged. I didn't know much about teenage girls, except a faint recollection of what it was like to be one, but if Clare didn't want to talk about whatever was bothering her, we weren't going to force it out of her.

Stu kissed the top of her head. "I'm going to go get the grill started." He grabbed his glass of wine and hurried out of the room.

The grill was electric, so getting it started involved turning a knob. I suspected Stu was going to plop himself on a deck chair and sip his wine, purposefully leaving me a few minutes alone with his daughter.

Clare turned in her chair and looked at me with her big, brown eyes. Her lower lip quivered. I had a choice, and I didn't like either option. Either I could keep my mouth shut, pretend I knew nothing, or I could tell Clare what I knew.

Who was I kidding? No way was I going to be able to keep my mouth shut.

Still, I needed to choose my words carefully. "Clare. You're almost an adult, so I'm going to treat you like one. When I walked onto the set yesterday, I saw Theo."

Clare's eyes snapped open, and she straightened. "What do you mean?" Her voice had a sharp edge.

"I mean…I saw Theo on my way to the set. He was with the red-headed dancer named Mia. They were together."

Clare's shoulders slumped, and the rest of her body quickly followed. "Like…together, together?"

"I'm afraid so."

"Oh." Clare's face had gone all pinched. "That explains why he didn't text me back." She shrugged.

I got up, went to the fridge, opened a fancy bottle of sparkling water, and poured out two glasses, setting one in front of her. "I know you're not going to believe this, but it's going to be okay."

Clare gave me a look of utter disbelief. "I just had the worst day. Ever. My life sucks. And why did you even have to tell me you saw Theo with Mia? I could tell you didn't like him."

That was the Clare I remembered from our early days, the bristly girl with sharp edges who didn't want to share her father with some stranger he had just met. I sighed.

"I'm sorry, Clare. I apologize. And what I think of Theo doesn't matter. It's what you think of him that's important."

Clare rolled her eyes. "Is that some sort of reverse psychology or something?"

At that moment, I wished I had gone for Option B and kept my mouth shut. The conversation was slipping away from me faster than a mermaid entity on a boat ramp.

"It's not psychology," I said firmly. "I'm just saying…I understand. You've got every right to have all the feelings you're having. And yes, I did need to tell you I saw Theo and Mia together because I'm on Team Clare."

I crossed my arms in front of my chest, beginning to feel a little testy. Clare was angry at Theo, not me, but there was no reason I couldn't set some boundaries.

To my surprise, she seemed to relax a little, and she nodded. Her phone chirped, then chirped again. Clare snatched it from a pocket, stared at the screen, and gave a little cry. Within seconds, she had undergone a complete transformation. She beamed at me. "It's Theo. He wasn't ignoring me. He said Mia's going through some stuff and she needed to talk."

It seemed like Mia needed more than just Theo's ears, and Theo had only been too happy to oblige. If only there was a spell to get rid of the guy…

Oh, wait. There was.

The palms of my hands felt hot, and when I glanced down at them, they were glowing faintly red. I had seen the spell in one of my great-aunt's journals. It wasn't complicated. It would probably work.

The question was, did I dare try it?

Chapter 26

Maybe I was exhausted by all the teenage angst, or perhaps my wounds were sapping all my energy, but I slept like the dead and awoke unusually refreshed and alert.

I went into the kitchen to make coffee. After I downed two mugs, I powered through a thirty-minute kettlebell workout, mulling over the Clare-Theo situation. I couldn't imagine how Clare would react if she found out I was thinking about using magic to banish her boyfriend.

Would that constitute overstepping? It felt like it might.

Maybe I should talk to Stu about it.

My phone rang. It was Brandon, but he was calling from his personal number. It was a little after seven thirty, and his night shift at the command center had just ended. If there had been an emergency, I would have received an alert, but that didn't stop my pulse from speeding up.

"What's up, Brandon?"

He exhaled loudly. "I've got some bad news, boss. My father had a stroke. A bad one. He lives down in Merida, on the Yucatan Peninsula. He's alone and there's no family nearby, so I need to go down and help him."

Poor Brandon. That was bad news. And if I remembered correctly, Brandon was an only child.

"Of course, Brandon. Take as much time as you need."

A long silence followed. "Thank you, boss. But it's a little more complicated than that. It's not just my dad who needs taking

154

care of. He has a business too. He owns a chain of convenience stores, and he's been after me for years to help him run them." He paused. "I'm sorry, but I need to resign."

It felt like I had been hit in the gut with a baseball bat.

When I first got the job as head of security, Brandon had been working as a guard. Up until then, nothing much exciting happened in Chavez Ravine, so when some scary supernatural dogs surrounded a bunch of kids in a hot tub in the middle of the night, Brandon had faced them down with nothing more than a water hose and a few beer cans.

He had gone on to prove himself in the field time and again, and he was indispensable on the challenging overnight shift, monitoring the heatmap and camera feeds. Plus, Brandon was a great team player. He really fit in with the group, and I had become quite fond of him. His shoes would be tough to fill.

But replacing him was my problem, not his.

"Of course, Brandon. I'm so sorry to lose you. But I'm more sorry to hear about your father. I hope he's okay. I assume this is effective immediately?"

Brandon sighed. "Yeah. I'm getting on a plane this afternoon."

We worked out a few details and hung up. I consulted the work schedule on my laptop. Though I enjoyed scheduling about as much as I enjoyed doing my taxes, it had to be done. I could move people around. There was an older gentleman who had expressed interest in moving to overnights, but I had been reluctant to take shifts away from Brandon. So, I could probably cover that shift, but it still left me down a head. With new types of entity emergence holes popping up, we couldn't afford to be short-staffed for long.

Time to call a meeting with my team.

I tapped out a message, asking everyone to meet me at the command center at ten thirty, then went into the bathroom to change the dressing on my head wound. I could get away with a smaller bandage. That allowed me to wash more of my hair. I was gradually getting back to my old self.

After pouring a mug of coffee, I sat down at the kitchen table to continue Espy's oral history. Rather than plod through all six hours, I decided to fast forward, randomly stopping to determine the subject. About thirty minutes into the third tape, I hit gold.

The interviewer was asking Espy a question.

"You mentioned there was a lot of trouble on the set of Beyond the Passage. *Can you tell us what happened?"*

"Yes, well…the director was Mitchell Wood. That was the first movie I'd ever worked on, so I didn't know anything about him. And I mostly worked out of my house, so I didn't know the girls working on the movie very well, and nobody warned me about him. I learned the hard way he couldn't keep his hands to himself, and after that, whenever I had to go to the set, I made sure I wore pants and a sweater. The way he treated the girls in the movie was terrible. But what he did to my friend Catalina was bad." Her voice dropped to a whisper. *"Real bad."*

"Do you mean Catalina Montez?" The interviewer's voice rose. *"The curandera from Palo Verde?"*

"Yes." Espy's voice was a whisper. *"She was more than a curandera. Much more. She was a bruja. But even she couldn't protect herself from that awful man. He tricked her into going to his trailer, and then he…"* Her voice faded away. She sniffed.

"It's all right," the interviewer said. *"Take your time."*

Espy continued, her voice stronger. *"Oh, who wants to hear about this sort of thing? And it was all so long ago. But it seems so unfair, you know? Catalina told me what he did. He did unspeakable things to her in his trailer, then told her no one would believe a Mexican girl. She never got justice for what happened to her. And then she was accused of doing something she didn't do, and she was killed for it. She was a very strong person, but the last days of her life must have been a misery."*

The interviewer let a moment pass before continuing. *"You said Mitchell Wood never made another successful movie after that. Do you think his behavior on that film had something to do with that?"*

Espy gave a rueful laugh. *"Nobody cared about his behavior. Nobody listened to women back then, especially not Mexican women. Something else happened. I think Catalina did it."*

I could hear the interviewer shuffling papers. *"Are you talking about the stories that Catalina Montez came back as a ghost to haunt Chavez Ravine after her death?"*

"They weren't stories," Espy said primly. *"That's exactly what happened. I saw it with my own eyes. She did come back. I saw her. But that's not what I'm talking about. Catalina was a bruja. When she was a child and someone made her mad, she'd hex them. She knew how to do things like that, even then. I think, before she was killed, she found a way to hex Mitchell Wood."*

I hit Stop, my heart pounding, and jumped to my feet.

I drank a glass of water and checked the time on my phone. Another fifteen minutes, tops, and then I needed to get going. I set an alarm on my phone so I wouldn't lose track of time.

But I was too agitated to sit down, so I hit Play and paced while I listened.

Espy Gaitan continued.

"Catalina was my best friend, but she was secretive. She didn't tell me everything. I'm pretty sure she hexed our neighbor. When I asked her about it, she said the woman had it coming. But after the director did what he did to her, he told her to stay away from the set. I think by that time he suspected she had powers and could be a problem. But she still found a way to get back at him. I think she hexed something and sent it to him."

I stopped the tape. Espy Gaitan thought Catalina had cursed something and managed to get Mitchell Wood to touch it. That

157

was interesting. Hernan had said it was possible I was looking for a cursed object, and that was exactly what Espy had just described.

What if it was still around? What if it had ended up in Pete Drury's production and six people had come into contact with it?

I sat back in my chair. That scenario was downright crazy. The idea that an object cursed by a bruja generations earlier had caused trouble at Western Studios...Could I even explain that theory with a straight face?

But *something* had happened on that set. And besides, Espy's story was the first decent lead I'd had. I needed to focus on a more logical solution, but before I could do that, I felt compelled to rule out Catalina's curse.

Or not.

Chapter 27

I stopped at Muertos Café for some pan dulce and headed to the command center in Palo Verde Plaza. Julia had been a very busy girl. The entire plaza was plastered with colorful posters advertising the Day of the Dead Festival. I wondered how she had been able to produce the artwork for the posters, then recognized the design. It was from a collection of Catrina paintings she had done before she lost her skills.

I couldn't help but admire Julia's talent. The vibrant colors and intricate designs drew me in, making the upcoming festival feel alive even before it had begun. I could almost hear the echo of mariachi music and smell the spicy aroma of marigolds that would soon fill the plaza.

But when I walked through the patio breezeway, I noticed there was something off about one poster just outside Julia's pottery shop. The skull's face was blurry, like it had smudged during printing. Julia would never have hung a damaged poster. I moved in for a closer look.

I touched the Catrina's blurry face and felt a prickling in my fingertips when they grazed the surface of the thick paper. A tingling sensation ran from my fingers up my arm, and I snatched my hand back.

The Catrina smiled back at me. She had long black hair, with red roses woven into an elaborate crown. More roses decorated her frilly white dress. But the colors seemed to shift.

The poster came to life. Vines slithered out from behind the roses and stretched to meet each other, forming a word I couldn't quite decipher. I blinked my eyes hard. Was this the delayed effect of the harpy bite Dr. Chen had been worried about? I took a step back and gingerly touched the wound on my head. It felt fine. The tenderness was nearly gone.

I returned my attention to the poster, and the skull's features shifted. The intricately painted features faded, and a woman's face emerged. She stared at me. It was a beautiful face with high cheekbones, smooth brown skin, and dark, glittering eyes.

A hand rose from the bottom of the poster and tugged one end of the long vine still writhing amid the roses. The green tendril snapped into place, forming a single word: "Catalina."

I reached to caress her cheek, half expecting to feel warm flesh, but the image went blurry again. The woman's face disappeared into the hard edges of a Catrina skull.

I stepped back, breathless. It had to have been Catalina Montez, the bruja Espy Gaitan had talked about. She was trying to send me a message. Not a very clear one. More like a supernatural business card.

But who was I to be so picky? I had no idea what it took to communicate from beyond the grave, and I didn't intend to try it anytime soon. Besides, wasn't a business card an invitation to connect? That was what I needed to do.

I was tempted to find out where Catalina was buried and see if she would be up for a chat. But as I had learned, raising the dead came with pitfalls. Like having to send them back, even though you had taken a liking to them. I could still remember the wistful expressions of my band of street fighters who had risen to fight a flock of vampire birds. It had been an experience I wasn't eager to go through again.

Later, I would try my hand at tarot cards. In the meantime, some good old-fashioned detective work was in order. I called Julia. She picked up immediately.

"Guess what we're doing today!" she said. "Ben's got the gnomes taking the marigolds from the nurseries and planting them by the guard gates, so they'll be the first thing visitors see when they arrive for the festival! And they'll move a bunch to the plazas too. That sounds amazing, yeah?"

"It does. I can't wait to see it. How's Sam?"

Julia laughed. "The gnome boss gatito is fine. I brought him and the other cats some treats from the pet store in Palo Verde, so they had a nice snack. And I saw the cutest ever cat toy—a little mouse on a string. I tried to get Sam to play with me, and you won't believe what he did!"

Sam hated cat toys. They were beneath his dignity. "He didn't choose violence, did he?"

Julia laughed again. "He would never scratch me! But he did break the mouse off the string and bury it. Ben said I'd embarrassed Sam in front of his crew."

"Hey, Julia…I saw your posters. I love them, but I have a question about one. The one with the black hair and the roses."

"Oh, her! She's beautiful, isn't she? She's my favorite, actually. What about her?"

"Well, I could swear she looks familiar. Did you happen to model her after someone?"

A short silence followed. "Oh, that's so interesting. I did, now that you mention it. Sometimes, I go to the library and look through the old pictures of Chavez Ravine. I love doing that. That's how I found the photo of Lencha I used for your figurine. Well, there were some newspaper clippings about a woman who was wrongfully accused of murder, and she was so, so beautiful.

I always thought that Catrina with the roses came out looking like that woman."

My scalp started itching again. I couldn't tell if it was significant or just a sign the stitches were ready to come out. "You wouldn't happen to remember the name of the woman, would you?"

"I do, actually. It was Catalina. It's pretty, isn't it? I don't remember her last name, though. And by the way, I'll be selling tarot cards at the festival, with pictures of the Catrinas. I'm trying to make do with all my old stuff since I can't make anything new. That's cool, yeah?"

More than cool. That could actually be handy. "Can I buy one of those decks from you?"

Julia scoffed. "I won't sell one to you, but I'd be happy to give you one."

We arranged to meet at her shop and said goodbye.

All that remained for me to do was find out where Catalina Montez used to live and pay her a visit.

Chapter 28

Ron Mendez, wearing his usual camo pants, saw me walking into the command center with pan dulce from Muertos Café. He reached out to take the pink boxes from my hands.

"Leave some for the others," I warned.

"I'm just going to take a chocolate concha." He cut through the string on the pastry box with a pair of scissors. "Brandon texted me his news. I can't believe it. This is terrible. He was my wingman, you know. Now what are we going to do?"

I pulled paper plates and napkins from a cupboard. "I'm going to fill his position as soon as possible."

Ron tore off a chunk of pastry and popped it in his mouth. A cascade of chocolate crumbles fell on his shirt, and his eyes rolled back in his head. "Why are the conchas from Muertos so much better than every other place? I saw the new schedule. Looks like we can get by for a little while. I just hope a bunch of entities don't show up."

"You and me both." I started a fresh pot of coffee.

The door banged open, and the rest of my team walked in, dressed for the cooler, breezier weather. Long pants and windbreakers had replaced shorts and polo shirts.

Something was up. Bailey, Justin, and Liam were practically buzzing with excitement, but when they noticed the pink boxes of Mexican pastries, they forgot what they were talking about.

"Oh, thank God. I'm starving." Bailey made straight for the pan dulce. I had known the young woman since we had worked together as officers in Occult Affairs. She was an avid runner, one of those people who could demolish an extra-large burrito and still look like she had just stepped out of a fitness ad.

"She has the worst manners, doesn't she?" Justin said to no one in particular. "Bailey, what do you say when someone is thoughtful enough to bring food?" Justin, father to a baby boy, had taken to good-naturedly reprimanding his coworkers as though they were toddlers at a birthday party.

Bailey had recently trimmed her long copper hair, so now it hung to just above her shoulders. She shot me a dazzling smile. "Sorry! Thank you, Maddy!" she said in a sing-song voice. "And to think I'd never tried pan dulce before getting this job."

"That's just sad," Ron said. "Before Muertos Café, my mom used to get our pan dulce from a panaderia in Boyle Heights. It was good, but not as good as this."

"What's a panaderia?" Bailey asked, peering into a pastry box.

Liam scoffed. "You can't tell what it is by the context? It's a bakery."

"I'm not a big-shot military school graduate like you." Bailey plucked out a sugar-coated pastry resembling an ear of corn. She waved it in the air. "What's this one called again?"

"An elote!" Justin answered with a groan. "We've only told you a dozen times."

After everyone was settled, I began the meeting. They had all heard about the harpy incident, which was inevitable but still awkward. I told them about the supersized pump-action squirt gun, the new entity suppression weapon Steven Zhou had used on me—though I left that part out. They were excited to hear about it but disappointed it would still be a while before the weapons were available for general entity work.

I leaned against a table and brushed a light dusting of sugar from my top. "How did rounds go this morning? Find any more emergence holes?" I steeled myself for the answer.

Bailey, Liam, and Justin exchanged looks. They had worked together as Occult Affairs officers for several years, and their special bond had carried over to their new jobs in Chavez Ravine. They seemed to be deciding who was going to speak.

Liam raised a meaty hand. "Things got a little crazy this morning."

Justin and Bailey nodded and moved closer to the edges of their chairs.

"We were doing a sweep of the gully," Liam continued. "We'd just got to the area near the little dog park next to the bridge in Bishop, and some idiot lets her dogs off leash, and they all come running down, and—"

"She was a dog walker," Bailey interrupted. "She should have known better because not a single one of them had recall. And there were four of them!"

"And she was yelling, 'Here, here,' and they all just ignored her," Justin added, wrinkling his nose.

"One was a Weimaraner and another was an Akita, and those dogs can move. It's a miracle they didn't run all the way to La Loma." Liam crossed his arms in front of his chest. "What were those other two? The brown ones?"

"Pointers," Justin said.

I wondered if the dog breeds were important to the story but decided not to interrupt.

Liam cleared his throat. "Well, as I was saying, the dogs all came running. And you're not going to believe it, but they went straight to a spot we hadn't gotten to yet, and damned if they didn't find a hole. A double-wide, like the one you found up by the construction site."

My heart beat faster in my chest. Dogs never reacted to entity emergence holes. It was a well-known and much-discussed fact among Occult Affairs researchers. They seemed more interested in digging holes.

"So, the dogs found the hole," I said. "And then what?"

Liam's blue eyes widened. "They went crazy."

Justin and Bailey nodded. "Really crazy," they said.

"They stood at the edges and barked and barked," Liam said. "Whatever it was about those holes pissed them off because their hair was standing up. They were growling, and the Akita was practically frothing at the mouth."

Bailey held up her phone. "I've got a video. You can see for yourselves."

She sent the clip to the command center's email. Moments later, Ron pulled it up and played it on the big screen so we could all watch.

The scene played out exactly as they had described. Four large dogs bounded down the side of the steep gully, ignoring a woman's panicked cries begging them to return. Bailey and Justin could be heard yelping in surprise when the dogs rushed past. Liam ran toward the dogs, trying to get the attention of the animals by shouting, *"Here,"* and *"Come,"* but to no effect. The dogs came to an abrupt stop at the edge of an emergence hole, and a moment later, we could hear Bailey yell, *"What the hell?"*

The dogs were in a frenzy. The complete opposite of the way dogs treated every other entity hole.

"I hope it's okay," Bailey said. "But we called it in to Steve Zhou. We figured he'd want to know about this. He's on his way."

"We know you've been busy," Justin said hurriedly.

"Recuperating from that attack and all," Liam added. "Did we overstep?"

So that was what they had been worried about. They thought I'd be angry they had usurped my authority.

"Absolutely not," I said. "You guys did the right thing. Thank you. Hopefully, Steve will learn something interesting that will help us track down those missing entities. How many new holes do we have now?"

"We're up to seventeen, including that one this morning," said Ron. "I've got a spreadsheet going. It's on the shared drive if anyone needs it."

"Good idea. Finally, let's talk about Brandon. I'm sure you all have seen my email about Brandon leaving by now. We're really going to miss him. He was a great guy and a good guard. We're going to need to replace him as soon as possible, and I'd like to ask for your help. If anyone knows a solid candidate who might be interested, please let me know. The job will continue to be a combination of fieldwork and shifts in the command center."

Another exchange of looks passed between Bailey, Justin, and Liam. Liam's hand shot up.

"As a matter of fact, I do know someone. I ran into her at the axe-throwing bar over the weekend, actually. You know her too, I think. Augustina Paz."

I was so surprised I nearly dropped my mug. Of course, I knew Augustina. Who in Occult Affairs hadn't heard of the woman? She was one of the first Occult Affairs cops, a bit of a legend. And the police chief's ex-wife. The one he had banished to a substation far away in the valley.

Chapter 29

I had met Augustina Paz a few times, but only in passing. She was a highly respected officer who'd had the nerve to divorce the chief.

As the story went, she had been on the fast track to detective when the first wave of entities appeared. She was one of the few officers who had faced them head-on, documenting their behavior and helping to contain them. That was in the early days, before they created Occult Affairs and developed all the tools we took for granted.

By all accounts, it had been sheer chaos, but Augustina Paz had been extremely brave and smart. She was one of the founding officers in Occult Affairs, an d she seemed destined for greatness. And then she and the chief split up. The rumor was, her angry ex had derailed her plans to become a detective and had banished her to the far reaches of Los Angeles County.

I called Jo for the inside scoop. "I have a job opening. What's the deal with Augustina Paz?"

"So, what's the deal with you being too busy to visit me and Holly?" she replied. Jo sounded distracted. Probably watching the heatmap in the dimly lit command center.

"It's been a little crazy around here. We're seeing these weird new emergence holes but no sign of what came out of them. It freaks me out, if I'm being honest. And then I got attacked by a harpy and ended up in the hospital."

Jo sighed. "I've heard about all of that, but not from you. Why do I have to find out what's going on with my friend by reading the incident reports?" I could hear her take a deep breath. "I know you're fine. Steve's been keeping me in the loop. So, why are you asking about Gus?"

"Who's Gus?"

"It's Augustina's nickname. Except maybe don't call her that until you've known her for a while. And whatever you do, don't call her Tina because she hates that."

I eyed the scheduling calendar on my desktop. One hiccup and someone would be pulling double shifts. Or I would. "So, what do you think? About Augustina?"

Jo gave a rueful laugh. "If the chief would allow it, I'd transfer her to my group in a minute. She really knows how to read a heatmap, and she's good at juggling crews in the field. She's had a really hard time, you know. The chief's done his best to take credit for everything she's accomplished. If I'd been her, I would have quit."

"So why hasn't she?" Jo had already said enough about Augustina for me to know she would be a great hire—if I could get her—but I was curious about the famous Occult Affairs officer.

"Starting a whole new career isn't exactly easy at her age, I would imagine. She could have applied for jobs in law enforcement out of state, but she has an elderly mother who's not doing so well and needs her help."

I had heard nothing about Augustina that would prevent me from talking to her. But the truth was, I was a little desperate, and considering the challenges we might end up facing, we needed her experience.

After we hung up, I called Augustina's number. She didn't answer, so I left a brief message. Several minutes later, she responded with a text.

Yes! Very interested in the job. What time and where?

We settled on eight o'clock the next morning so she would have plenty of time to make the start of her shift, then I hurried across the plaza to the library.

———⊱·⊰·🏚·⊱·⊰———

The news clippings were exactly where Hernan had said they would be.

I sat down at the wooden desk in the library's archive room and sorted through the brittle, yellow newsprint. The first clipping was easy enough to find. It featured an arresting photo of a beautiful woman with a shocking headline:

SUSPECTED MEXICAN WITCH HELD IN BRUTAL SLAYING OF TWO MEN

Catalina's dark eyes stared at me reproachfully. A tingle raced up my spine. It was the same face that had emerged from the skull on the poster near Julia's shop.

Catalina looked like she was having the worst day of her life, but not even that could diminish her beauty. She had certainly caught the eye of Mitchell Wood and had suffered a terrible fate. In the photo, Catalina seemed more defiant than defeated. If I had to put money on it, I would bet this woman would have done whatever it took to avenge the wrong that had been done to her. If I had any doubt, the third paragraph settled it.

"...some locals claim the 31-year-old woman is not only a folk healer, but a so-called 'bruja,' or Mexican witch."

Catalina had the skills and the motive. Cursing an object and sending it to Mitchell Wood would have been a clever way to get revenge without stepping foot on the set.

Another article a few days later reported she had been killed by the brother of one of the murder victims soon after she was released by the police. Her killer had been arrested. Such a sad end to a difficult life.

I carefully placed the fragile papers back into their box and stashed it where I had found it, doing my part to keep Hernan's archives in order.

I sat back in my chair, thinking. Finding out where Catalina had lived was something I wanted to do, not because I thought her house would still be standing, but because I wanted to get a sense of her. Hernan would probably know.

I called Hernan. "Quick question. Do you have any idea where the bruja from Palo Verde used to live?"

"You mean Catalina?" he asked, his voice rising.

"Yeah. Her."

"No. But I'm sure I could find it. Do you need it right away?"

I thought for a moment. Julia was still expecting me to pick up the tarot cards, and I had promised to have Stu over for dinner. Just the two of us.

"Tomorrow would be great," I said hopefully.

Chapter 30

After a romantic candlelit dinner of chili Colorado, rice, and salad, Stu and I fell into bed with every intention of carefree, wild sex. But we quickly discovered the heavy meal had made us feel about as sexy as wobbly flan, so we fell asleep instead.

Sam woke us up at two o'clock in the morning, scratching at the sliding glass door.

Stu groaned. "Why doesn't he use his litter box like a normal cat?"

"Because he's not a normal cat," I said, pushing back the covers.

"I'll let him out," Stu mumbled gallantly, but he didn't move.

I got up and let Sam out to do his business, shivering in the chilly night air. With any luck, the weather would hold, and we would actually get to enjoy fall vibes for Halloween. It would be nice if kids across Los Angeles didn't melt inside their costumes for once.

Maybe I could even solve the curse problem in time for Pete Drury to appear in the Halloween concert at the Hollywood Bowl.

While Sam scratched around in the dirt, I nervously eyed the trees, hoping nothing scary was hiding in the branches. It had happened before. But nothing came racing down the hillside and within minutes, we were all tucked up in bed again, with Sam curled up against the backs of my knees. Stu snored, but not loud enough to keep me awake.

I tried to sleep but found myself thinking about all the new entities roaming around somewhere, probably in Chavez Ravine. Unless they had moved on. What were they? Were they invisible? What were they up to? Would my team be able to handle them if and when they finally appeared, or would we need the help of Occult Affairs? That would require the emergency approval of the HOA board because Chavez Ravine had a strict no-LAPD policy unless there was a murder.

And on and on.

I swore I fell asleep five minutes before the alarm went off.

Despite my restlessness, in the morning light we were feeling much sexier, so we worked up quite an appetite. I had chorizo from the butcher at the market in Palo Verde, who knew how to make it right, so I cooked it with eggs and diced potatoes with a side of corn tortillas.

"I never thought I'd like spicy food for breakfast, but this is delicious!" Stu wrapped a warm arm around my waist while I spooned more chorizo onto his plate.

I kissed the top of his head. His damp hair smelled like my coconut shampoo. Which reminded me, I had an appointment to have my stitches removed. I couldn't wait to wash my hair in the shower like a normal person.

My abnormal cat swished around my ankles, meowing loudly. I bent to pick him up for a cuddle, but since I wasn't Julia or Leo, he wriggled away and ran off.

"All I do is house and feed you," I called after him. "Don't worry about me." I sighed, then cringed. I sounded just like my mother.

After Stu left and Ben picked up Sam for another day of gnome duty, I carried Julia's Day of the Dead tarot cards into the living room. I set the deck out on the coffee table and began shuffling through them, sipping my coffee.

My mother, the psychic, was the tarot card expert, not me. But with some effort and some help from the saint of death, Santa Muerte, I had been able to use them to bring down the nasty boogeyman known as El Cucuy.

Julia's deck was beautiful. She had done all the illustrations in eye-popping colors. They were strange and whimsical, with skeletons in the familiar roles of characters like The Empress and The Hermit.

I found the Catrinia image inspired by Catalina on The High Priestess card. Julia had chosen well. The High Priestess represented feminine energy, intuition, the past, and very, very interesting secrets. It sounded exactly like the woman Espy had described.

I lit a scented candle and stared at the card, hoping Catalina would come to life again, like she had in the poster at La Loma Plaza. But the beautifully dressed skeleton didn't move, and the black holes for eyes didn't so much as blink.

"Be that way," I muttered, then slipped the card into the outside pocket of my tote bag.

I needed to get to my office to meet Augustina Paz.

When I rounded the corner from the Palo Verde Plaza parking lot, I saw a woman furiously tugging at a scarf around her neck and muttering to herself. The last time I had seen Augustina, her hair had been scraped back into a tight bun, and she had been wearing an Occult Affairs uniform. If I hadn't expected her, I would never have recognized her. This woman had shoulder-length golden curls, a black dress, and a fawn-colored jacket.

"Augustina?"

She quickly turned and pulled again at the scarf, which appeared to be in the process of strangling her. With a cough, she managed to loosen it. Augustina whipped it off and stuffed it into a jacket pocket.

"Yes! And you're Madeline. Nice to meet you. I mean, we've met before, but that was years ago. I think I was working in North Hollywood at the time and…" She paused, blushing. "Oh heck, I'm babbling." She pressed a hand to her chest and took a deep breath. "I hit some bad traffic on the way here, and I was afraid I was going to be late. I hate being late."

I was having a hard time reconciling this jittery woman with the fearless Augustina Paz I had heard so much about, but I gave her my best reassuring smile. "Thank you for coming, especially on such short notice." We walked through the community center lobby and up the stairs to my office. I punched in the code and opened the door.

Augustina looked around with open curiosity. "Wow. They don't spare any expense around here. I'm pretty sure the guardhouse was bigger than my apartment."

We had that in common, then. I had thought the same thing when I first drove into La Loma.

"Where do you live?" I asked.

"Not far. Pasadena. Not a fun commute into the western valley, but Pasadena is close to my mother."

I gestured to a chair and turned to my fancy espresso maker. "I can use another coffee. How about you?"

"After the night I had, I could use a caffeine IV." She smoothed her black skirt over her knees. "Yes, and please. I'd love a coffee. Thank you."

She had a funny, clipped way of speaking, pronouncing each word distinctly.

"Is a latte okay?" I asked.

"Oh, heck no. I'm lactose intolerant. Just a black drip—or whatever you're doing over there—is fine." Her cheeks reddened. "Sorry. TMI."

I made Augustina a black coffee and a cappuccino for myself.

We sat across from each other, sipping our drinks. She had Cupid's bow lips to go along with a heart-shaped face and dark eyes set very wide apart.

"Augustina, thank you for coming in. I hope your drive into Chavez Ravine was pleasant—"

"Whatever job you have, I'm interested," she said hurriedly. "Very interested."

"Well, let's get right to it, shall we? I don't know what you may have heard about this job, but you may be overqualified," I warned her.

She sat up straighter. "I'd rather be overqualified here than in the valley."

I nodded. "Okay. Well, the job's fairly straightforward. I'd describe it as general security with fill-in in the command center. There is the occasional entity, despite what you've probably heard about Chavez Ravine. Our eruptions are infrequent, but they tend to be…dramatic. Your firsthand experience with entities would be very valuable."

Augustina gazed at me steadily for a moment. "Well, I do have a lot of that."

"I put out the schedules two weeks in advance. We're flexible around here, but given your experience, you can have your choice between the day shift or the swing shift."

"The day shift would be fantastic," she replied. "But if something happens, I can do overtime. Not a problem. Not a problem at all."

"As it happens, something might."

No use beating around the bush. Augustina deserved to know what she was signing up for. I pulled out a non-disclosure agreement from a drawer and slid it across the desk.

She leaned closer, and her eyes widened. "An NDA? Oh my."

"I'm about to tell you something we're not ready to make public yet, but in all fairness, it's something you should know so you can make an informed choice about the job."

Her eyebrows shot up, the left one disappearing under a bouncy curl. "I appreciate the honesty. I'm not used to that." She used the tip of her finger to slide the paper closer and studied it for a moment. Without looking up, she held out a hand. "I'll sign it. Do you have a pen?"

Augustina Paz might not have been what I expected, but I liked her. I pulled a pen from the ceramic cactus-shaped holder Julia had made me in her pre-hex days and pushed it across the desk. Like most officers dealing with entities, Augustina's nails were short.

She scribbled her name on the line and sat back in her chair, her coffee forgotten. "All right. Ready."

It didn't take long. I explained the discovery of the extra-large entity holes and that Steve from Occult Affairs and his team were looking into it.

Augustina frowned. "That many holes? And you haven't found the entities?"

I shook my head.

She scratched the side of her face. "So, what do you think? What's your theory?"

"I don't have one. Well, not much of one. But there's a good chance they're the Entities 2.0 the nerds have been warning us about forever."

Augustina gasped. "Oh, that would be terrible. Just terrible. But I don't understand. Los Angeles is four thousand square miles. Why would they emerge here?"

Good question. My thoughts went to the spell I had cast to protect Chavez Ravine from entities. It was still working against normal entities. But it wasn't enough to stop whatever was making those holes. Which suggested we were dealing with something new. Something my spell couldn't prevent.

I shrugged. "I don't know why they'd choose this place."

Augustina leaned forward. "Now that I've signed that NDA, would you mind answering a question for me? But you don't have to if it makes you feel uncomfortable." She paused, her expression turning grave. "Is it true you're a witch?"

I sighed. News did travel fast, but news like that usually did.

"A bruja, yes. It's an inherited kind of thing. I'm relatively new at it, and there are no brooms involved. Well, except to do the occasional limpia."

Augustina frowned at the Spanish words. Paz was a Hispanic surname, but that didn't mean she spoke Spanish.

"Does it matter? That I practice brujería?"

She shook her head, a motion that made her curls dance. "Not at all. Of course not. Not if it helps. And I've heard it does."

That was good enough for me.

I described the team and explained how working for the Chavez Ravine Association meant not only keeping the community safe, but also dealing with the egos and agendas of the board. All the while, she nodded, listening intently.

I wrapped up my speech by asking, "Why do you want to work here?"

Augustina stared at me for a while, as if she couldn't believe the question. "Who wouldn't? You know what it's like out there." She tugged down the sleeve of her jacket and cleared her throat. "Do you have any other questions for me? I'm an open book." She grimaced. "Unless it's about my ex. I would prefer not to talk about him. Ever."

"I'll just scratch these last thirty questions, then." I scraped my pen across a piece of note paper.

Augustina Paz laughed, a pleasant tinkly sound.

I stood up, smiling. "When can you start?"

Chapter 31

Augustina seemed pleased with the salary. She was surprised by the offer of a subsidized one-bedroom condo, though she refused it, saying she needed to remain close to her mother. We agreed she would start in the middle of the following week, which was perfect. That meant she would be on board for the Day of the Dead Festival. It was going to be an all-hands-on-deck event.

Augustina signed the employment contract and left. I guessed she had racked up weeks, if not months, of paid time off, so she could use that for her two weeks of notice.

Technically, I shouldn't have extended the offer without completing a background check, but one couldn't be an active member of Occult Affairs without being a citizen in good standing, so I wasn't worried. And, if there had been anything objectionable in her background, Jo would have flagged it.

The festival was coming up fast, and there was a lot of planning to do, so I dove into my maps and checklists.

My phone rang—a call from the La Loma guardhouse. That was unusual. I accepted the call, my heart beating a little faster.

"Sorry to bother you, boss," the guard said, his voice cracking with unease. "But we've got a bit of a situation."

Behind him, I could hear chanting.

"They dig, they plant, they get no thanks…Gnome labor fills your HOA banks!"

My heart sank so low it felt like it was sitting directly on top of my stomach. "How many are there?"

"Um, a dozen or so? They drove up in two vans." He raised his voice over the increasing volume of the protestors. "The lady in charge says they're not leaving until she's allowed inside to check on the gnomes." He paused. "And there's a TV news crew here too."

I could guess who that lady was. "Is the lady's name Crystal De Lucca?"

"Yeah," Billy replied. "That's what she said. She didn't have a card or anything. What do you want me to do? They're blocking the entrance."

I thought for a moment. Crystal De Lucca was someone I had bumped into a few times when I worked in Occult Affairs. Things had been cordial, but she had a suspicious nature, always trying to prove we were mistreating entities.

Knowing that, I didn't really have any good choices. If I kept De Lucca out, she would claim it was proof we had something to hide. If she came in, there was no telling how she would react to our gnome landscaping crew.

"I'll be there as fast as I can. Tell Crystal I'm coming, and tell her to get her people out of the roadway. They can protest off to the side."

"Got it, boss," Billy said.

After we hung up, I called Cora and quickly explained what was going on. She was babysitting her grandson and sounded relieved I wasn't asking her to join me. My next call was to Ben to give him a heads-up and ask him where he had the gnomes.

"I'm with them now," he said. "We're at the main equipment yard in Palo Verde."

I hopped in my Jeep and drove to gatehouse. Through the wrought iron bars of the gate, I could see Crystal De Lucca pacing back and forth. The chants of the protestors drifted through the open window.

"You sip champagne, they trim your hedge—gnomes are done with your pri-vi-lege!"

Lame rhyme, but it got the point across. I only *wished* I had time to sit around and sip champagne.

I walked through the guardhouse and strode toward Crystal De Lucca.

"We demand to see the gnomes," she said without preamble.

"Hi, Crystal. It's nice to see you again." I smiled my biggest, fakest smile.

Crystal had short dark hair with a side part, bangs sweeping across her forehead. Wire-rimmed glasses. An earnest round face. She was a social worker with a soft spot for entities. A burly man rushed forward with a TV camera on his shoulder.

I kept my expression neutral and my voice pleasant. "I'll be happy to escort you inside." I put out my hand. "We've met. I'm Maddy Madrigal."

Crystal pushed her glasses up on her nose. "I know who you are. You were the OA officer who knocked a sprite to the ground at a water park. I saw the video. I can only imagine how the gnomes are being treated."

More like wrestled the sprite to the ground after she scraped her hair comb across my face. But I wasn't about to let Crystal bait me while the camera was rolling.

"The gnomes are fine, as you'll see."

Crystal stepped forward, brandishing a piece of paper in the air. "So, you think exploiting gnomes for financial gain is fine? We're here to tell you we're not about to stand by and allow you to abuse them. We know all about you using them as a free source of landscaping labor." Her face had turned an alarming shade of red.

I plucked the paper from her hand and studied it, careful not to let my face register a reaction. It was a brochure. Eileen

Simpson's smiling face stared back at me. Next to her, Beady didn't exactly look abused, but he didn't appear happy either.

Crystal threw up her hands in a theatrical gesture. She turned toward the cameraman and said, "Well, Ms. Madrigal…Did the gnome receive financial compensation for appearing in that advertisement? Did the gnome receive financial compensation for its labor performed in your exclusive, gated community?"

"Entities do not have bank accounts, as far as I know," I said in a quiet voice.

Crystal's face got a little redder. "Can you say that a little louder for the benefit of the public?"

The TV station hadn't bothered to send a reporter, just a harried-looking photographer. If I could keep things from escalating, the guy would grab some video and a sound bite and be on his way. But if things got heated, he would call a reporter, and we would end up as the lead story.

I turned to Crystal. "Are you coming in?"

Crystal looked torn between accepting my invitation and continuing to make a fuss for the camera. She bit her lip and then gave a curt nod. "The TV crew is coming too. You better not try to keep them out."

The cameraman quickly glanced over his shoulder at his van.

"I think she means you," I said. "The guard will keep an eye on your vehicle."

The cameraman's mouth twitched. "Thanks, Ms. Madrigal. Let me grab my sticks, and I'll be right there." He headed toward his van. When he returned, he had a tripod on his shoulder. "I'm Mike Malone."

"Nice to meet you, Mike. If you don't mind, it'll be much easier if I drive you both in. You can stash your gear in the back of my Jeep."

He nodded. "Yeah, great, thanks."

Crystal did not look pleased.

"Fair pay for a gnome workday!" a protestor shouted in the distance.

After we were all settled into my Jeep, Mike shotgun, Crystal in the backseat, she said, "I would have thought you'd be driving some ridiculous gas-guzzling SUV."

"Oh my, no," I said mildly, deciding to score a couple of points while Mike was listening. "In fact, most of our patrols are on e-bikes these days."

Mike rolled down the window and pointed his camera out. "This is some place," he said.

I glanced at Crystal in the back. Her arms were crossed, her lips pursed in disapproval. The tension in the Jeep was palpable.

When we pulled up to the equipment yard, I turned off the engine. "All right. Before we go in, some ground rules," I said firmly. "You're here to see the gnomes. You're free to ask them questions, but no disruptions. No provocations. And whatever you do, do not antagonize the cats."

Mike swiveled in his seat to stare at me. "Cats? Why are you talking about cats?"

"Because she's abusing them too," Crystal snapped. "Forcing them to guard the poor gnomes."

I sighed. "Do you know any cats? It's impossible to force them to do anything."

"This I gotta see," Mike said brightly. "Sounds like a regular circus. I should get some good video out of this at least."

If everyone cooperated, he would. If the gnomes and cats misbehaved, he would get spectacular footage and it would go viral.

I went through the gate first, not quite knowing what to expect. Crystal followed so close behind me I could hear her breathing.

The equipment yard was a riot of orange marigolds. The gnomes appeared to be in the process of transferring flowers into large, decorative pots. Sam and a dozen cats lounged under the shade of a green canvas awning.

Ben came rushing over.

"We're getting ready for the Day of the Dead Festival," he said.

"You mean, the gnomes are," Crystal said sourly.

Ben gave a little shrug. "They love to plant. That's what they do."

Mike swung the camera onto his shoulder and hit a button.

"It's what you're *making* them do," Crystal snapped. "Entities are not here to be the slaves of mankind."

Ben shrugged again. "No, but the gnomes are different. They have a powerful need to garden, and I get it because I do too. I'm Ben Tomas, the head landscaper. We're not forcing them to do this. They *want* to do it. I think that's why they just…showed up here one day and didn't want to leave. So, we had to make some sort of arrangement. Give them something productive to do. Otherwise, people would be resentful and might try to hurt them, like happens in Beverly Hills sometimes."

I hadn't asked Ben to act as spokesperson, but he was doing an awfully good job. His calm, serious demeanor took Crystal off guard.

Her eyes flicked from Ben to the cats. "Then why the feline force? They're like prison guards."

Ben scoffed. "They *are* entities, after all. Someone needs to watch them, make sure everything is going well. And the gnomes seemed to prefer their company over humans, so it works out."

"So you say." Crystal scowled. "They don't look too happy to me." She pointed at Beady, who had paused working to glare at us.

"They don't like being stared at," I warned.

Ben cleared his throat. "Look, if you don't believe me. You can ask them yourself."

"I don't speak *gnome*," Crystal sputtered.

Ben smiled. "You don't have to. We've worked out a nice system of communication. Haven't we, Maddy?"

I nodded. Things were going much better than I could have hoped.

Ben beckoned to Beady. "Would you mind joining us for a second?" He pointed at Sam, who was now sitting at attention, ears perked, tail flicking back and forth. "And you too, Sam."

Crystal, uneasy at the sudden proximity of a glowering gnome and an oversized Bengal, took a hasty step back. "He won't understand me!" Her voice had gone high and squeaky.

"He will," Ben said. "Just tell the cat what you want to ask, and he'll translate."

The other gnomes gathered around, arms crossed over their barrel chests.

Crystal's mouth fell open. "You've got to be kidding me?"

"I'm not," Ben replied. "Just try it."

Crystal pushed her bangs from one side of her forehead to the other. "All right. But this is ridiculous." She leaned forward and inhaled loudly. "Mr. Gnome, are you here of your own free will? Are you working here of your own free will? Because if you are being coerced in any way, I want you to know that help is available to you. Just say the word, and I will do everything in my power to get you out of here as fast as humanly possible."

Beady listened with an intensity I had never seen before. With green, unblinking eyes, Sam gazed at the young woman, as if he couldn't believe his pointy cat ears. Then, turning to Beady, he began chittering away.

186

When he was done, Beady gave a long, gravelly laugh, flapped a dismissive hand at Crystal, turned on his heel, and marched back to a low bench. He muttered to himself while he resumed potting a marigold bush. The other gnomes went back to work too.

If Beady hadn't been so creepy, I would have kissed him.

Mike stopped looking through the viewfinder long enough to say, "Now, that was really something."

I couldn't agree more. PR crisis averted, at least for now. I drove Mike and a silent Crystal back to the gate, but not before stopping to buy them some pan dulce from Muertos Café, just to show there were no hard feelings.

At the guardhouse, Crystal turned to me and exhaled loudly. Up close, I could see the crow's feet at the outer corners of her eyes. She was older than I thought. Late thirties, maybe.

"Well, I'm glad I was able to see for myself the gnomes aren't being abused," she said without much enthusiasm. "I wish that were the case everywhere."

Mike lifted the camera to his shoulder. "Hey, Crystal…Can you give me a quick soundbite repeating what you just said?"

———→·→· ⛩ ·←·←———

After lunch, I remembered my stitches and drove straight to the clinic. Dr. Chen wasn't available, but a physician's assistant happily removed them, talking all the while about scoring tickets to the Halloween concert at the Hollywood Bowl.

My mind bounced from one thought to another. Poor Pete Drury. He'd had to pull out of the concert, which made me think about the music video shoot. Stu had mentioned that Clare had to take another day off school because they were running behind schedule. During the conversation, I had to bite my tongue to keep from telling him about Theo.

I felt a slight tugging on my scalp and the occasional pinch, and then it was over and I was on my way back to Chavez Ravine. When I passed the guard gate in La Loma, I spotted Ben's white truck, but no sign of Sam or the gnomes. I pulled over, hoping nothing was wrong.

Ben stood in a small parklet next to a massive Spanish-style house. He appeared to be in the middle of putting together some sort of wooden structure, hammering nails into place.

"What's up, Ben?"

He whipped around. "Oh, hey, Maddy. This? Another project for the festival. We're putting together altars for the residents to decorate. Julia's idea. Back in the old days, people used to build shrines all over the place to the Virgin of Guadalupe. Things even got a little competitive, with people trying to outdo each other. Julia thought we could do something like that for Dia de los Muertos. See if we can revive the tradition."

"That sounds great," I said. And I meant it. "Do people have to sign up or something?"

Ben nodded. "Yeah. She started sign-up sheets online, but if it's something you'd like to do, I can build one outside your house. We're doing one for Charlie. And Cora. And probably Hernan, him being the professor and all."

"I'd love that, if it wouldn't be too much trouble." And I knew just whose pictures I would put on the altar.

"Okay, but you owe me a beer," he said with a wink.

"Deal."

I was just getting back in my Jeep when a nondescript silver car pulled over and came to an abrupt stop. A well-dressed man with floppy hair got out. It was Steve Zhou, wearing a rust knit polo with orange geometric designs. Very retro. Very hip. Especially for the OA nerd who not long ago had worn only khaki pants and thick Oxford shirts.

"I was just coming to see you." His voice was louder than usual, and his eyes sparkled.

Behind him, the silver car seemed to rock back and forth. I looked past Steve, squinting, trying to make out what was going on. The unmistakable sound of barking reached my ears.

"Is that a dog in your car?"

Steve thrust out his chest. "It is. I borrowed one from the canine unit. It's a Belgian Malinois."

The barking grew more frantic.

"I heard they're crazy."

Steve rolled his eyes. "They are a much-maligned breed. This one is very well trained. He was also very helpful. We just came from that new hole in the gully. And Sarge went just as crazy as those dogs in the video your team sent me earlier."

"Does that tell you anything?" I asked.

Steve frowned. "You just yucked on my yum, didn't you?"

"I have no idea what that means," I said, even though I did.

"Sarge's reaction didn't really tell me anything new. But he's highly trained and should have been calmer. So, he did confirm that something about these holes bothers dogs to an extreme degree. I also did some additional testing, of course, and *that* did yield some really interesting new data. I've already sent it back to the farm for further analysis."

That was another thing about nerds. They loved their drama. They couldn't just tell you what they discovered. They spooled it out slowly and ended on a cliffhanger. If someone wanted more, they had to ask for it.

I knew how to play the nerd game. "And what did you find out?"

Steve grinned and ran a hand through his hair, making it stand straight up. I wondered how much product he had put in it to achieve that effect.

189

"I used one of the new audio probes. It comes with a really cool extender, so it was able to go pretty deep." He raised his arched eyebrows. "And guess what? It detected a high-frequency buzz, which could have explained the dogs' reactions. It's the first time we've recorded anything like it." Steve looked even more pleased with himself than he had after subduing the harpy.

It was my turn again, apparently. "What do you think it means?"

"At the very least, it's not like any entity hole we've ever seen before."

I began to feel a knot in my stomach. "Are you saying what I think you're saying?"

All sorts of emotions flickered across Steve's face, and a faraway look came to his eyes. "Yeah." His shoulders slumped. "Entities two-point-oh. Because if it's not that, what else can it be?"

Just the thought of Entities 2.0 gave me a headache. I popped two ibuprofen and headed to my office to message my team a summary of Steve's findings. And I reminded them, though it wasn't really necessary, to be on high alert for anything unusual.

These new holes had popped up in several places. There was no pattern, so they could appear anywhere in Chavez Ravine. That was a lot of ground for my people to patrol.

I was making myself an espresso when Becca Tey called. I put her on speaker.

"Everything okay?" I asked.

"I'm fine, but Clare's having a bit of a meltdown. We're on break, and she's in the bathroom, having a cry. She won't talk to me, but I can guess what's going on. I saw her talking to Theo this morning before we started shooting, and things looked pretty intense. I was doing a scene with the saloon girls, so I lost track of them for a while, and now she seems pretty upset. I just wanted you to know."

I jammed the key in the ignition and thought for a moment, my head throbbing. Clare had made it perfectly clear she didn't welcome my input when it came to Theo. But I had seen how he operated, and I didn't like it one bit. If he was out of her life, she would forget about him soon enough. If he stayed and she discovered the extent of his betrayal, it might send her back to the dark place she had been after her mother had blown up her marriage to Stu by cheating.

Clare deserved better for her first real relationship than what Theo had to offer.

"Maddy?" Becca said. "Are you still there?" The familiar chords of Bad Pete's music blared in the background.

"Yeah, sorry. Thanks for letting me know, Becca. I'll see what I can do."

Until that moment, I hadn't decided whether to use magic to split up Clare and Theo. Becca's call had made things a little clearer. Technically, I would be meddling, but I could live with that if it meant sparing Clare from a lying, cheating guy who was using his age and life experience to take advantage of her.

I sent a message to my team, letting them know I would be working remotely for the rest of the day, then drove home, eager to get started.

It had been a long time since I used my magic, and by the time I had gathered all the ingredients I could remember for the banishment retiro, my hands were warm, and the tips of my fingers were glowing red. That was a good omen. It told me my brujería skills had kicked in. I had made the right choice.

I liked the idea of a spell because, if it worked, nothing bad would befall Theo. He would just lose interest in Clare.

191

Something that would eventually happen anyway. The spell just sped things up, before he did too much damage to her confidence and self-esteem.

I dug out Lencha's journals, double-checked her instructions for the retiro, and saw with a sinking heart that I was missing an essential ingredient, one that would require a trip outside of Chavez Ravine.

To a cemetery, no less.

Chapter 32

It seemed a bit excessive to drive all the way to the cemetery for some dried flowers when I had a cute little bunch hanging from a nail above my workbench. But the instructions did say the dried flowers had to come from a grave.

It didn't specify whose grave, so I decided to visit Evergreen Cemetery. It was where I had brought some old-school street fighters back from the dead so they could help me kill vampire birds invading Chavez Ravine.

My time with the revenants had been short—just one night—but the truth was, it had been just long enough to make me genuinely like them, and it broke my heart a little when they began to fade away. Especially Ripper and Junie.

If I was going to the cemetery, I might as well pay my proper respects, so I brought a bucket and some cleaning supplies, then stopped at a small shop in Boyle Heights and purchased fresh flowers. Unlike the last time I had visited Evergreen, I didn't have to sneak around, and since it was daylight, I could see where I was going. I found Junie's grave first and set to work, washing his gravestone and setting out the flowers.

With all the decrepit tombstones and grass that was more brown than green, Evergreen Cemetery wasn't exactly the prettiest graveyard in Los Angeles, but on that brisk fall day, the wind rustled through the trees and made it a quiet, peaceful place among all the gritty bustle of the city. And because it was a cemetery, I was confident entities wouldn't show up because, for some unknown reason, they never did.

I left Ripper's grave for last. After plucking dead flowers from the in-ground vase and slipping them into a paper bag, I sat there for a while, remembering the man's shocked reaction at how much Chavez Ravine had changed since he had last seen it. I hoped, wherever he was, he had forgiven me for disturbing his peace.

During the drive home, I thought about my plan and decided a little modification was in order. I had a strong suspicion that Theo was a player and Clare was his next mark. But I had also been around long enough to know things weren't always what they seemed.

So, rather than perform a brute-force, come-hell-or-high-water banishment, I decided to incorporate a little insurance policy. As long as Theo behaved himself, everything would be fine. But at the first sign the little jerk had ill intent, the banishment would come down on his pretty little head like a ton of magical bricks.

I was pretty sure I could modify Lencha's spell to make that happen.

At home, I got out my molcajete. Just like many brujas before me, I ground the dried flowers against the volcanic rock and added the other ingredients.

Lencha's directions called for a tin medal of a saint I had never heard of. But that was where my modification came in. I substituted a medal of El Santo Nino de Atocha. Granted, he wasn't an official saint, but a patron saint known for his miraculous deeds and role as a protector. A protector would know when Clare needed help and could trigger the banishment.

I placed the medal in the molcajete and covered it with the herb mixture, then lowered my head and said a few quiet words that included repeating Theo's name numerous times. That was it. And if I had any doubt that what I had just done had worked, my hands glowed bright red.

I cleaned up my workbench, wondering how the retiro spell might actually work. When triggered, it was supposed to banish Theo from Clare's life, but exactly what would happen was a mystery.

Whatever. It felt good to have done some magic, and for a good cause.

The fall air streaming in through the windows filled me with energy. I felt a strange and rare need to clean, so I decided to give the house a quick scour instead of waiting for Saturday, like I usually did.

After changing into sweats, I poured Fabulosa into a bucket and added hot water. The strong scent of lavender and pine filled the room. I started in the kitchen, mopping the floor and wiping down the counters. Next came the bathroom and all the hardwood in the rest of the house. I followed up with a dust rag. My weird midweek cleaning left the house refreshed and me feeling satisfied.

I had just finished wringing out my old-fashioned mop when the phone rang. While I followed the sound to find my cell, I wondered if it was Steve with more information about our new entities. Or Augustina calling to say she had changed her mind. I grabbed the phone and checked the screen. It was Hernan.

"I have that address you asked for," he said. "For Catalina's old place."

———≻·→· ▥ ·◅·↤———

I had learned the hard way that people sometimes freaked out when they saw me on their street. While I wasn't crazy about being thought of as an entity harbinger, I understood where the sentiment came from. So, I waited until after dark to check out the address Hernan had given me.

Stu was out for the evening at a business dinner. Sam was home, grooming himself on his favorite ottoman. I had texted Clare to say hello but hadn't heard back. Becca messaged, saying Clare had finally come out of the bathroom and had fun shooting her scenes. No mention of Theo.

I parked on a quiet side street in Palo Verde and walked toward the address. Catalina's old house was long gone, replaced by a large craftsman with a small park next to it. Hernan told me, once upon a time, the park had been an empty lot Catalina rented to grow roses, which she sold at the flower market downtown for extra income.

Lights blazed from every room of the craftsman. The shutters were open in the living room, and a couple was moving around. No use bothering them. They wouldn't know anything about Catalina anyway. But it was a stroke of luck that part of her property had become public space. There wasn't anything to keep me from checking out the park.

The wind picked up, lifting my hair from my neck, and I shivered. I wished I had worn something heavier than a hoodie. Up the street, toward the nearby T-intersection, must have been where Espy had lived. The two friends had lived close enough to pop in and out of each other's houses.

Like Lencha, the beautiful bruja from Palo Verde had worked out of a shed where she had dispensed cures and spells. Not many people who lived in Chavez Ravine had been able to afford cars when Catalina was alive, so one of the brujas was walking distance from just about everyone in the three old neighborhoods.

After Catalina died, the people of Palo Verde had to travel to Lencha's place in La Loma. My grandmother Liliana moved in with Lencha and became her apprentice to help with the workload. Later, Liliana had dispensed remedies from the back of the house I owned, using the workbench to mix her cures and potions.

The landscaping in Chavez Ravine was one of the attractions of living there. Ben Tomas had turned the dusty hills and washes into lush, native gardens that thrived in the dry climate. Residents especially loved the cacti, colorful wildflowers, and ornamental grasses.

But this small park was different. It had rows of red roses with heads the size of dinner plates. They were strange and beautiful. Also, not quite normal. I was no expert, but Hernan fussed over his roses endlessly, and they weren't half the size of the red blooms in Catalina's old garden.

While I walked through the opening in the split-rail fence, a hundred tiny spiders crawled up my spine. It wasn't exactly a pleasant feeling, but it confirmed I was where I needed to be. I knew not to ignore my intuition. Catalina might have been gone, but she had made contact with me through the poster, and I needed her to answer my questions.

There was no one around to see or hear me. I slipped out the tarot card with the Catrina in her image and held it out in front of me.

"Catalina…It's me, Maddy Madrigal. I'm a bruja too. Maybe not as powerful as you were, but I'm learning."

I was beginning to feel a bit foolish, but I continued anyway.

"I could use your help. I think you cursed something and gave it to Mitchell Wood. I know what he did to you. I would have done the same thing. And it worked. Did you know that? It did. It ruined him, just like you wanted. And I'm glad. He got what he deserved, and I'm sure you kept him from doing the same terrible things to other women. But that object you cursed? It's still out here. And now other people are coming across it, and they're being cursed too. But they don't deserve to be cursed. They're my friends. And I need to find the object and end the curse. Can you help me? Please? Tell me what I'm looking for."

At the edge of my peripheral vision, roses twisted on their thick stalks to stare at me. Like I was being watched by a hundred round, red faces, and they were judging me…hard. It was very creepy. Also, possibly, totally in my head.

"Catalina?" Her name came out of my mouth like a croak.

I started to wish I had asked my mother to conduct a séance, where we could be nice and cozy in my living room, with flickering candles and snacks. All the spirit of Catalina would have had to do was write the answer on a chalkboard or something.

But no. I was alone in the middle of a park at night, surrounded by weird roses, with a cold wind picking up.

Chapter 33

Something touched my ankle, and I jumped. It slithered under the leg of my jeans. I lurched to the side, trying to yank my leg free, but it tightened around my calf, and I toppled sideways.

In the dim light of the streetlamps, roses lowered their blooms and swiveled on their stems.

Roots broke through the ground and crawled toward me. I scrambled away, my heart pounding so hard all I could hear was blood roaring in my ears, but the tendrils were too fast. The wind was gusting now, almost as strong as the storm winds of the harpies. A whirlwind of dirt and dried leaves came at me from one side; a towering rose bush bent toward me from the other.

"Catalina!" I cried.

I was in trouble, and I needed to call the command center and let someone know. I fumbled for my phone, but my jeans were tight and twisted, and I couldn't pull it out. At least, not in that position. I scuttled backward like a crab.

Another knot of roots lifted out of the ground, the earth widening around it, forming a deep hole, dirt pouring in from all sides. A vine shot out from somewhere, encircled my right leg, and began pulling me toward the hole. I screamed. Was Catalina doing all this, or had I accidentally summoned someone or something else?

I scrabbled to my feet. The thorny vines clawed at my pants, and I lost my balance and lurched sideways into the hole.

I kept falling, dropping into blackness, surrounded by the smell of wet earth and decaying leaves. A sinkhole. I had to be falling into a sinkhole. I braced myself, certain I would hit bottom and shatter every bone. But I landed painlessly, sprawled, coughing in the heavy, thick air. How was I still breathing? I blinked and let my eyes adjust to the gloom.

A cramped room came into focus. Four wooden walls tilted toward me, earth visible through the boards that strained to contain it.

I sat up. By some miracle, I had landed on a pile of burlap bags. Along one wall was a cluttered workbench crowded with glass jars, mortars and pestles, and bundles of dried herbs. Every shelf overflowed with candle stubs and tin prints of familiar faces: El Santo Nino de Atocha, the Virgin of Guadalupe, and Santa Muerte.

I was in Catalina's shed. Every hair on my body was standing on end. I got up and looked around. A dirt floor, broom marks etched on the ground where it had been swept clean. A chair in a corner, with a blanket thrown over one arm. A newspaper atop a small table against a wall, the pages folded back to reveal an article about "The Mexican Witch" arrested on suspicion of murder. This article had a photo I had never seen before. Catalina was getting out of the back of a police car, a shapely leg outstretched, eyes staring reproachfully at the camera.

The air grew colder. A candle flickered, casting a faint glow pulsing with an eerie light. The glow expanded outward, took shape, and morphed into a figure. A woman with smooth, long black hair.

"Catalina," I whispered, wondering if this were all some sort of hallucination.

The figure floated closer. Not a revenant, I thought with relief, but a ghost. Hands reached out, coming to rest on both sides of my face. Her dark eyes seemed to burn into mine. I felt overwhelmed with emotions. Sadness that her life had been cut short. Fury that she had been accused of a murder she did not commit. Powerlessness, unable to defend herself.

I saw an expanse of garden filled with beautiful red roses, with Catalina walking among them, a pair of clippers in one hand. The earth seemed to hum beneath her feet, and there was magic in the soil. The same magic fueling the red clay in Lencha's yard. That was why Catalina had been able to grow such extraordinary flowers and sell them to help support herself.

The spirit raised her hand and pointed at a wall. Words appeared. *The Night Lady.*

I turned back to those dark eyes. They were angry but determined.

"Were you the Night Lady?" I asked.

Catalina nodded. Her anger blossomed in my chest. I understood what she knew. Some of the people who lived in Chavez Ravine had sold their properties to the city after receiving the eviction notices, and that had infuriated Catalina. She thought they were traitors. After her death, the magic in the soil had been restless. It called to her, and she had risen. Catalina had haunted the vacant properties and used her magic to send vines and thorns to fight the crews demolishing the houses.

It had worked. Workers had refused to show up for their shifts, and I felt her victory.

In life, Catalina had been a healer. In death, she had become something else. Vengeful. Her anger was a palpable thing, a bitter storm crashing through me. I wanted to look away, to break the connection, but I didn't dare. The sheer force of Catalina's will locked me in place.

The room tilted and darkened, and my vision faded. When I could see again, I was in another room. I looked down. I was wearing a dress. Red. With flounces. My hands were different, smaller and browner. I tried to move, to speak, but my body was not my own. I was trapped inside it.

A bald man with broad shoulders moved toward me, his pupils dilated, lips parted. His face was flushed. I could feel his hot breath on my face while he moved closer, hands fumbling with his belt. He smelled of whiskey. Despite my rising terror, I couldn't move. Was Catalina about to make me experience one of the worst moments of her life?

I understand! I screamed inside my head. *You don't have to do this!*

And then I was in a jail cell, hands wrapped around the bars. A baby-faced officer strode past, his eyes flicking over me. He licked his lips, then laughed.

The next moment, I was running down a dirt path surrounded by roses, the sun warming the top of my head. I was home. Free.

In the distance, a man shouted, "Catalina!" His voice carried his anger, his rage. He was coming for me.

I ran, fell, got up. Had to keep moving. Had to get away from this man. Roses whipped past me, thorns tearing at my skin. And then, a pain seared my back. I stumbled, pitched forward into the dirt.

I didn't do it. I didn't kill your brother! Please.

The man wouldn't listen. My garden shears were in his hand, raised over his head. My hands flew in front of my face while I begged for my life.

A blast of icy air swept over me, and when I managed to open my eyes again, the man was gone, and I was back in the hole. I rose to my feet and clawed at the dirt, hauled myself up and over the side. There I collapsed, staring up into the night sky, breathless. I had experienced Catalina's final days, but mine had ended differently. I was alive.

An enormous velvety bloom appeared above. It tilted to the side, as if studying me.

My heart went still. Not again. "Catalina?"

A woman's face appeared in the middle of the bloom. It was Catalina, still beautiful but with a hard edge. We stared at each other for a long time. I was completely at her mercy.

"Please," I said. "I understand. I know what you went through. I understand the injustice."

The petals around her head fluttered. The blossom gave a curt nod, and a cloud formed in the air above my head. An image began to form—a shimmering, not quite real. Some kind of projection.

Suspended in the cloud was a bottle, colorfully painted with a desert scene. I had seen it before. It was the decanter I had spotted behind the bar at the saloon in Western Studios.

The visage of Catalina gave me one long, sad, and penetrating look, went blurry, and vanished.

At home, I needed something stronger than wine. I poured myself two inches of whiskey and drank it down before collapsing onto the couch.

It was obvious I had missed something. I had expected Catalina to be like Lencha, supportive and helpful, but Catalina's life had been very different from Lencha's. Her final days had been terrifying, and she had died alone, angry at her fate and the forces that had ended her life so early. The *men* who ended her life so early.

I should have continued to listen to Espy's tapes. Though I had found the information I thought I needed, I had missed the context, the rest of Catalina's story. Maybe if I had been patient enough to listen to all of Espy's interview, I would have understood what Catalina had become. Perhaps I would have been able to comfort her rather than simply expecting her to help me.

Maybe Hernan was right.

I took too many shortcuts, and this one had nearly cost me my life.

Chapter 34

Espy had been right about one thing: Catalina Montez had had a mean streak.

Some things didn't change, even after death. Catalina had given me what I had asked for, but not without first trying to scare me. Or impress me. Or just prove she was still the top bruja in Chavez Ravine. The fact was, she could have killed me, and I had been an idiot not to have taken more precautions.

Whatever. I had too many other things to worry about. It made no sense wasting time trying to psychoanalyze a ghost. I knew what I needed to do, though not exactly how to do it, and I needed to move fast.

The Halloween concert at the Hollywood Bowl was two days away, and if I hurried, I could reverse the curse, and Bad Pete would regain his voice and sing as planned. Clare could get back on the soccer field, and Olga could take her place in the kitchen in time to give Bernie Moura some competition during the Day of the Dead Festival. Julia and Ben could go back to creating beautiful artwork and landscaping and would fully enjoy the Day of the Dead Festival they had worked so hard on. And Becca Tey would be able to remember her lines and guest star on the series she had helped make famous.

When I got home, interrupting Sam's nap on the ottoman, I headed for the bathroom. I needed some serious scrubbing after getting dragged through the dirt. While I stood in the shower, brown water swirled around the drain. When it finally ran clear, I washed my hair with my favorite coconut shampoo and rubbed my skin with vanilla-scented sugar scrub. I was too tired to blow-dry my hair, so I rubbed it with a towel and crawled into bed. Sam soon joined me and curled up, pressed into my side, while I stared up at the ceiling, thinking.

I needed to get my hands on the cursed bottle sitting on the shelf in the saloon at the music video set.

Correction, I absolutely did *not* want to get my hands on it. I couldn't touch it at all unless I wanted the cursed object to take *my* skills. If I lost my magic, it would be disastrous, not only for me, but for the entire community of Chavez. Then the curse would never be undone, at least not until another bruja came along.

I couldn't ask my staff to risk touching the bottle either. Only someone already cursed could handle the bottle safely. But it also needed to be someone who knew about the curse and my bruja skills.

Becca and Clare were the only options. Both had been cursed. Both worked on the set. Both had access to the saloon.

But Becca had lost her ability to act. If she got caught with the bottle, would she be able to remember her cover story? This plan could not fail. The stakes were too high.

I picked up my phone. Ten o'clock. Late for oldsters like me, but not for a teenage girl. I tapped out a text.

Are you up?

Yeah of course.

Call me?

The phone rang a moment later.

"Wazzup?" Clare sounded wary, probably suspicious I was going to bring up Theo again.

Of course, I was dying to ask about him and find out if my retiro spell was working, but I didn't dare.

"I figured out the curse," I explained. "I know what's causing it. It's something on the set."

"It is?" Clare gasped. "What is it?"

"It's a painted liquor bottle in the saloon. It has a round stopper, and it's pretty vintage. Does that sound familiar?"

A short silence followed. "Yeah. Julia found it in a warehouse where they keep old props. That's where the wagon wheel on the building came from too…and a bunch of other stuff. She said she thought it might be really valuable. That was the day we were doing the first run-through in our costumes. That's when I was still a saloon girl, before they made me the schoolmarm. The director wasn't there, but Pete was. He asked to see it, and then we passed it around. Becca was there too…and Ben Tomas because he'd brought Julia a coffee."

"What about Olga? Was she there?"

"She was. She was handing out breakfast burritos from a little cart outside the saloon, and she came in to see what all the fuss was about. She recognized the style of the bottle. Said it was an old tequila bottle from Mexico. Hand-painted."

"And did she touch it?"

"For sure. Apparently, she's into stuff like that, so she was telling Pete and Julia all about it. She said it was an amazing example of folk art."

Sam swatted my side, a none-too-gentle reminder I was talking too loudly and disturbing his sleep.

I lowered my voice. "Clare, I need your help. No one can touch it without getting cursed, but it can't curse you twice. You can safely touch it, so I need to ask if you can bring it to me?"

"You mean, you want me to steal it?" Clare gasped.

I sighed. "Sort of. More like borrowing. Think of it this way: at any moment, someone else could touch it, and they'll be cursed too. It could end up cursing tons of people if we don't put a stop to it."

"Oh," Clare said in a small voice. "Okay. We're shooting again tomorrow. It's my last day, so I can get there early, before everyone else. The saloon isn't locked or anything, so that's not a problem. I'll take it, then bring it to you. Does that work?"

"Perfect," I said. "How about you text me when you leave?"

"Sure."

A plan began to form in my head. "But, Clare, don't bring it to my house. I'll text you another address in La Loma. I'm going to try and reverse the curse there."

She agreed, and we hung up.

I collapsed onto the bed, feeling very tired. It had been a good day. I had discovered the cursed object, and I had a good idea of how I could reverse the curse. It would give me another chance to put all that beautiful, magical red clay I had inherited from my great-aunt Lencha to the test.

I just hoped it would work.

Chapter 35

I woke at dawn. My usual habit was to roll around in bed, wishing I could sleep for another hour, but instead, I hopped out, anxious to start my day. Sam, on the other hand, slumbered on. He had spent the night prowling around the house and dodging the pillows I threw at him to get him to stop, so he needed his rest.

"Lazy cat." I tiptoed out of the room, feeling just a little bit sorry for him. He was nocturnal by nature but had to spend his days keeping the gnomes in line.

I started a pot of French Roast, paced the kitchen, waiting for it to brew, and then took my mug into the sunroom and parked myself on a stool at my workbench. There I made a mental note to buy a better stool with a padded seat and a backrest.

I took out a sheet of nice, thick drawing paper and, in my best penmanship, wrote the names of the six people cursed by the antique tequila bottle, the decanter that had wrecked Mitchell Wood's directing career and had very nearly done the same to some of my closest friends. I left plenty of space between the names.

When I was done, I lit a bundle of sage and ran the paper through the smoke, saying a few heartfelt words of hope. With my iron scissors, I cut out each name, rolled up the six rectangles, and dropped them into a small glass jar. I didn't want to risk creasing them on the way over to Lencha's house.

Correction. *My* house. It still didn't feel real.

At seven thirty, my phone chimed. Clare was on her way. That kid was an early riser. Most people her age slept until noon if they could, but not Clare. It probably had something to do with all those years of soccer practice. Or she had taken after her dad.

Regardless, the timing worked out perfectly.

I was pacing on the sidewalk in front of the gate when Clare pulled up in her SUV, a canvas bag decorated with soccer balls over her shoulder. My heart twinged at the sight of it. She had lost her ability to play the sport that brought her so much joy. I really wanted to help her get back to the game she loved. And, to be honest, back to the rigorous schedule that came with playing on a competitive team so she would have less time for Theo. Who—so far, anyway—had not been banished. Had my spell fizzled? Maybe I shouldn't have messed with Lencha's original formula. Perhaps I had ruined the whole thing.

Or maybe I was putting too much pressure on myself. But it did feel like the stakes were very high.

I really, really needed this morning's magic to work. For Clare's sake, and for everyone else's.

Clare was wearing a dark green tracksuit. She appeared pale and tired while she took in the gate with its keypad, scrunching her eyebrows together. "Why didn't you want me to come to your house? What is this place?"

"I'll show you." I punched in the code and pushed open the gate, then stepped aside to let her pass.

She took a few tentative steps and stopped. "I don't understand. Why are we here?"

I threw my arms wide. "This is my garden. It used to belong to my great-aunt Lencha."

Clare's mouth fell open. "This is yours?"

I nodded. The long yard looked emptier without all the colorful marigolds, but it was still pretty, with the palm trees and begonia bushes. And, of course, there was the shed, with its funny little gothic roof.

"My aunt used to work in there. Ben Tomas fixed it up. Including the new roof."

"It's so cute," Clare said in a wondering voice. "Are you going to work in it?"

I shrugged. "Maybe. I haven't quite figured it all out yet."

"Tell my dad he should sell his house and you can build one here. Together. That would be cool, right?"

Maybe. I was a little surprised Clare wanted us to move in together. It seemed a little soon for that.

I was trying to figure out how best to respond when Clare asked, "What are we going to do?"

"We're going to bury the bottle," I replied, relieved she had moved on so quickly.

"That's it? That'll work? Burying it will lift the curse?" She sounded doubtful.

"There's more to it than that." A defensive note had crept into my voice. "Can you take out the bottle, please?"

I waited while Clare shifted from foot to foot, frowning at the clay, and pulled a cloth bundle from her bag. She was a clever girl. Clare had done her best to make sure the bottle arrived in one piece, wrapping a T-shirt around the bottle and securing it with some blue electrical tape.

A moment later, I was staring at the colorful bottle.

It really was beautiful. The colors had faded over the years, but it was still possible to make out the hand-painted hummingbirds and cactus. It must have been a family heirloom, filled and refilled by a couple of generations, at least.

She thrust the bottle toward me, and I jumped back. "I can't touch it," I reminded her.

Clare gave a little yelp. "I'm sorry, I'm sorry. Of course. I forgot. What do you want me to do with it?"

I slipped the glass jar from the pocket of my field jacket and set it down on a nearby bench. "I need you to take out those bits of paper and put them into the bottle. They should fit through the opening."

They did. Quite easily. I watched, holding my breath, while she slipped them into the bottle one by one.

"Now what?"

"Put the stopper in, and I'll dig the hole." I grabbed the shovel and got to work. It didn't take long. The clay was soft, and the tip of the shovel moved through it easily.

Clare knelt next to the hole and looked up at me, blinking. "Do I just...put it in? Or do you need to do something first?"

"Go ahead and put it in," I said. "I'll do a few things later. After you go." I was still too self-conscious to practice brujería in front of other people unless it was an emergency and I didn't have any other choice.

Clare lowered the bottle into the hole, straightened, and took a giant step back. "That's done. I guess I should get back to the studios."

She sounded about as excited as if she were off to clean her room. Clare had many qualities, but keeping a tidy room was not one of them.

"Is everything okay?" I asked, keeping my voice light.

She stared at me for a long time, blinking as if she were trying to decide something. "Not really, no. It's kind of weird, though. Like, super awkward, but Iris said I should talk to you about it. That you could help me figure out what to do."

Iris was Clare's best friend and, apparently, dispenser of good advice.

"I'd be glad to help if I can."

212

Clare went over to the bench, sat down, and drew her knees up to her chest. It was one of those positions that only skinny teenagers seemed to find comfortable.

"What's going on?" I asked.

She looked away, biting her lip. When Clare turned back toward me, her eyes were moist. "Uh, this is so embarrassing. And if my dad finds out, he's going to have a fit, and it's going to turn into this huge drama. You have to promise you won't tell him. Nothing really happened, I swear. It's just weird, that's all."

There it was. The moment I had known would eventually come. She was finally on to Theo. But I couldn't imagine why her father would have a fit if nothing really happened.

I took her hand and squeezed it. "I can't make you any promises without knowing more. And I don't want to lie to you."

Clare swiped at her eyes with the back of her hand. "Uh, I hate this. It's so stupid." She squared her shoulders and placed both feet on the ground. "All right. It's the director. Jason Wood. He's been totally weird since we met. He keeps telling me I can become an actress. That he can help me. And then a few days ago he invited me to his house to talk about it, and I thought his wife was going to be there, except she wasn't. And then he wanted to go swimming. They have this massive house with a pool, and I was like, 'I don't have a bathing suit,' and he said, 'No problem.' They have extra bathing suits in the cabana because they have people over all the time. So, I went into the cabana, and I was about to change when he walked in, and he was being totally, totally creepy." She stopped, grimacing at the memory.

I was so shocked I could hardly get the words out. "Oh my God, Clare. What did you do?"

She pressed the heel of her hand between her eyes. "I grabbed my stuff and left. I just left. And then he freaked out. He ran after me, and he was yelling and pounding on the car

213

windows. He made it seem like he had done Pete a big favor by having me in the video, and he complained that I kept making stupid mistakes. Iris says that's because he was afraid I was going to tell someone and he'd get in trouble. I just drove away. Iris told me to tell Pete, but he and Jason aren't getting along as it is, and I didn't want to make things worse. So, I told Theo. He's been super nice about it. He told me I could make an anonymous complaint about Jason, and he'd help me to do it, but I didn't want to."

Her face was flushed as she continued. "I think that's why Jason gave me the schoolmarm role instead of having me be one of the bar girls. It was like some kind of bribe. So I wouldn't tell anyone. Except I don't care about acting. I just wanted to be in Pete's video because I'm a huge fan."

Talk about a plot twist. I had pegged Theo as the villain in Clare's story when it had been Jason Wood all along. The apple hadn't fallen far from that tree.

To think what might have happened if she hadn't bolted out of there...

"Clare," I said sternly. "You were very smart and very brave. I'm so sorry you had to experience that. That man is a—"

"Predator," Clare finished. "That's what Theo says. He's friends with the other dancers, the girls, and they all call him Mr. Misconduct. Theo says one of these days, someone is going to come forward and he's going to get in big trouble and get canceled. But like I said, nothing actually happened, so I'm not the one who's going to do it. No way. Not me."

Which explained why Becca Tey had warned Clare about him and, while on set, had watched him too. She obviously hadn't known that Jason had invited Clare to his house. If she had, I was sure she would have put a stop to it before it happened. I wondered how many women Jason had harassed over the years. And how bad it might have been for Clare.

"So, how about you and Theo? Are you a thing? Or not?"

Clare rolled her eyes. "Not really. I mean, he's hot. He's been really nice to me, and yeah, we've kissed and stuff, but nothing *serious*. He's a total man whore. Plus, he's weirdly intense. It was just a bit of fun."

I snorted. I had been such an idiot. *Just a bit of fun.* Hah! If I had known Clare was capable of such ruthless objectification, I would never have gone to the trouble of banishing Theo. But no harm done. At least, I didn't think so.

"Are you going to tell my dad?" Clare eyed me nervously. "About Jason?"

I got to my feet with a sigh. "No. *You* need to tell him, Clare. He needs to know about this. And I know you're embarrassed, but there's no reason for you to feel that way. You didn't do anything wrong. And think of Pete. If this gets out, Pete's reputation could take a hit too."

Clare's eyes went as big as saucers. "Oh my God. I hadn't thought about that."

"It's not your fault. You shouldn't *have* to think about things like that. But before you tell your dad, give me a day. There's something I need to do."

"What do you mean?"

I looked toward the expanse of red clay. There was a teeny tiny chance my spell would break Catalina's curse on the bottle, but I didn't think so. I was pretty sure it would only lift the curse from the six people who had touched it, and even then, I would have to wait and see if it actually worked.

But before I got rid of the damn thing, I had one more victim in mind. One who deserved a little bit of Catalina's brand of justice.

Chapter 36

I didn't want to take any chances, so the next morning, I explained everything to Ben Tomas and asked him to dig up the tequila bottle. "But, Ben, wear gloves. Just in case."

He was so accustomed to my weird requests that he did it without asking any questions, but I could tell, by the enthusiastic way he pulled on his thick leather gloves and dug into the clay, he was excited his days of being a cursed man were nearly over.

In fact, they might have been over already. We were about to find out.

Ben gently brushed the dirt off the bottle and turned to me. "Now what?"

"Now we put my bruja skills to the test." I pointed to the nearest begonia bush. "Let's see what happens when you touch that."

Ben set the bottle down on a bench and strode over to the begonias. He glanced over his shoulder and took off his gloves. "Okay, here goes."

The moment deserved a drum roll, but a crow did the honors, cawing a few times from high in a tree. It was another gloriously cool autumn morning. It felt more like Northern California than Southern California.

I held my breath when Ben touched a bright purple blossom. Nothing happened. The flower swayed gently in the breeze. It didn't droop. It didn't turn black, wither, and fall to the ground.

Ben let out a whoop. The crow joined in and cawed some more. Ben ran from palm tree to shrub to bush, brushing his hands against trunks and foliage.

"You did it," he cried. "You did it!"

"Let's see if it worked for the others before we get too excited," I said cautiously.

Ben called Julia at her studio. Within seconds, we had our answer. He held out the phone while Julia's excited shouts came over the speaker.

"I just did a little sketch of a Catrina, and it came out great! This is wonderful, yeah? Just wonderful! I'm going to get started on my little Catrina figurines right now."

Ben was grinning when he ended the call. "It's great to hear her so happy again."

It took less than an hour to confirm the others were back to normal too. Pete was apparently running around the music video set, belting out songs from his latest album. He couldn't wait to tell his agent and said he was going to rock the Hollywood Bowl hard.

When I called Clare, she ran to her SUV, grabbed a soccer ball from the cargo hold, and kicked it all the way down the dusty main street at Western Studios.

"I'm back!" she yelled into the phone. "I can play again!"

Becca Tey reported the script from the audition she had blown had come rushing back to her. "I'm calling my agent to see if I can get a do-over. I think I can!"

Olga Sanchez was also thrilled, in her own way. "I made scrambled eggs, and they came out perfectly! I can't wait to come up with a special Dia de los Muertos menu!"

I felt a bit like a fairy godmother who had just granted a bunch of wishes.

My phone chimed with a message from Stu.

Heard the news from Clare. You are one hot bruja.

The guy had a way with words. My cheeks felt warm.

I turned back to Ben, who had found some clippers and was busily trimming an overgrown bush. He probably had more important things to do, but I guessed he had a lot of pent-up foliage-related energy to release.

"Um, Ben. I need your help again."

He stopped clipping and frowned. "Oh?"

"Yeah. We need to do a little experiment. Can you pick up that bottle without the gloves and see if it curses you again? If not, it means you're immune."

His dark eyes opened wider. "Are you kidding me? What if it curses me again? Then what happens?"

"Then I put your name back in the bottle, bury it overnight…and you're free and clear by morning. I know it's annoying, but it's not that long."

"Says you," Ben muttered. "You're not the one who's cursed."

"I know. But I wouldn't ask if it wasn't important. Please?"

Ben dropped the clippers with a martyred sigh, marched over to the bench, and snatched up the bottle. He rubbed it against the front of his shirt, for dramatic purposes, no doubt. Then, with a dark look in my direction, he crossed over to the begonia bush and cupped his hand around a dangling bloom. When he withdrew his hand, the flower swayed slightly on its stem but remained perfectly normal and perfectly beautiful.

Ben exhaled loudly. "I guess that means I'm immune."

It certainly did. Which meant I could proceed with my plan. "Would you mind going with me to Western Studios? I need you to hand that bottle to Becca Tey for me."

Ben narrowed his eyes. "What for? That thing's dangerous."

"That's why I can't touch it. It's for a good cause. Honest."

—→·→·||||||·←·←—

Ben and I took his truck to Western Studios.

"I need to chat with Becca for a few minutes before we hand her the bottle. So let me call you in a few minutes, and we can meet up, okay?"

He gave me a skeptical look. "Okay, I need to check the plants on the set anyway. But I hope you know what you're doing."

After I found Becca, we grabbed a coffee from the cart. I told her what Clare had said about Jason Wood.

Becca looked horrified. "You're kidding? He tried *that*? With Clare? He must be out of his mind. She's a minor! And he has to know who her father is."

"I'm sure he does. But I believe her."

"Oh, I believe her too. No question. I know enough about Jason that as soon as she appeared on set and I saw the way he looked at her, I told her to steer clear and if he ever tried anything to let me know. Jason's pretty sneaky. He always seems to go after the women who are just starting out, who need to keep their jobs and are afraid to speak out. I've been hearing rumors about him for years. But you know how it is. He's a big-time director, and he's connected, plus his dad's a famous producer." She paused. "I think Pete's noticed something is off about him."

It sounded like a lot of people, mostly vulnerable women, would be relieved if Jason wasn't around. But coming into contact with a cursed object would ruin his career, and that might claim other victims.

"Is Jason married?" I asked. "Kids?"

"No kids, but yes, he's married," Becca said. "For now. They've separated because Nicole—that's his wife—walked in on him and his assistant. The assistant quit right after that whole episode. I'd bet my last dollar he was coercing that poor girl too.

Anyway, Nicole doesn't have much to worry about. She comes from Hollywood royalty herself, and she's a power broker, putting together financing deals for movies. Jason's loss, if you ask me."

That made my decision much easier. But it wasn't my decision alone. I couldn't trick Becca into helping me curse Jason. She needed to know the truth so she could make her own decision. If she didn't want to do it, I would walk away. Maybe some brave woman would step forward, blow the whistle on him, and let the wheels of justice crush him.

I told Becca my plan. With her Botox-frozen forehead, it was hard to gauge her reaction. When she didn't say anything, I asked, "Well?"

She took my elbow. "What are we waiting for? That's a fabulous idea. Let's go find Ben."

———·⊱·⊱·🏛·⊰·⊰·———

I was at Julia's studio, nervously watching her sculpt skeletal figurines and sipping red wine, when Becca called.

"Reporting in to my local witch," she whispered.

Pulling Becca into my plan had meant revealing the full extent of my brujería, and she couldn't have been more delighted. "I'd heard, of course, that Chavez Ravine used to have a few witches. I always thought it would be nice to bring that back. And now we have you!"

I just hoped Becca would keep my confidence. Too many people already knew my not-so-secret. If it became general knowledge, it could make my job as head of security much harder. Sky-high expectations, suspicions whenever things didn't go perfectly, requests for magical favors…I had played out the whole nightmare scenario in my head.

But Becca was a professional, and I was confident she would keep things under wraps.

"How did it go?" I asked, nervous.

"Like a scene in a movie," she said. I could hear the smile in her voice. "We were reshooting a scene in the saloon for the hundredth time, and when Jason popped out to the bathroom, I swept by his director's chair and took out the bottle from my voluminous skirts and placed it on top of the clipboard he'd left behind. God, he loves that fucking clipboard. Everyone was too busy arguing about something to notice me. And then a few minutes later, I'm inside the saloon, and I hear him shouting, 'Who left this damn bottle here?' And so I peeked outside, and there he was, waving it around over his head."

"Thank you. Sounds like you played your part perfectly." The tone of my voice didn't match my words. "I just hope I did the right thing."

Becca *tsked* in disapproval. "Do not second-guess yourself. That's not like you. We did the right thing. He's earned what's coming to him. Trust me. And I grabbed the bottle before anyone else touched it, just as we planned."

I felt slightly better after the call. When I looked up, Julia was posing a little Catrina statuette wearing, of all things, a trench coat instead of a frilly dress. The skull face looked slightly familiar. I gazed at it, frowning.

"It's you, silly!" Julia cried.

I wasn't sure how I felt about being used as a model for a Dia de los Muertos figurine. But when I saw Julia's expression, as bright as a sunbeam, I forced a smile to my face.

"I love it. I absolutely love it." And the thing was, I kind of did.

Chapter 37

Bright and early the next morning, Steve Zhou called to say the nerds at Occult Affairs had a plan to learn more about the mysterious eruption holes, but they required my permission. Specifically, they needed me to allow more nerds to come into Chavez Ravine.

I was drinking my coffee in the kitchen, staring out the window while Ben Tomas put together my wooden altar, my ofrenda. It was about three feet high and a couple of feet wide.

The HOA board had sent a note to the community outlining the Day of the Dead Festival events. It mentioned that altars would be going up all around Chavez Ravine for families who wanted to remember their loved ones. And of course, the HOA was suspending rules regarding decorations for the duration of the festival.

"How many researchers are we talking?" I asked.

"Seventeen. One for each new hole."

"Make that eighteen because my team found another one near Phantom's Pass. Why do you need so many people?"

"Because we're going to try something new." Steve could barely contain his excitement. "We're going to monitor the relative strength of the sound at each hole so we can triangulate and possibly detect subterranean movement. It's possible we can predict where the next hole will appear."

I nearly dropped my mug. Coffee sloshed over the sides. "Are you telling me…if this works, we can actually witness a hole in the making?"

"Bingo," Steve said smugly. "We'll make a nerd out of you yet."

I grabbed a dish towel and mopped up the coffee. "The way you're describing this, it sounds like you think entities are moving around underground. If that's true, it would be brand-new entity behavior, right?"

"Right." Steve sounded grim.

Cold morning air poured through the open window, and I shivered. Steve, like most nerds, hated to speculate about where his findings might lead, but I had to ask. "What does all this tell you?"

Steve exhaled loudly. "It's impossible to say. But theoretically, it could mean these entities are searching for something, or—worst case—it could mean they're communicating." He cleared his throat. "Or coordinating."

I went cold all over.

That word suggested all sorts of bad things. Strategy. Attacks.

At the very least, it suggested these entities weren't going to emerge disoriented and easily rounded up. They were already here, they were acclimated, and they might be making plans.

"Let's not get ahead of ourselves." It was like Steve could read my mind. "It's all guesswork at this point."

I thought back to what Augustina had asked. Something I had been wondering about myself.

"Why are we only seeing these new holes in Chavez Ravine?"

"You got me." Steve sighed. "But the area has a long history with the supernatural, so that might be one reason. I've collected samples from all three neighborhoods, and I can't find any significant differences between the soil in Chavez Ravine and other hilly parts of the city. But who knows? There may be supernatural signatures we can't detect with the tools we have."

I felt lightheaded. Hopefully, that "supernatural signature" wasn't me and my brujería. That would have been the ultimate nightmare. The woman hired to protect the residents of Chavez Ravine was a giant magnet for the worst entities Los Angeles had ever seen.

Steve brought me back to reality. "So, can I do it? Bring in some extra people to help me out?"

I shook my head to force my spiraling thoughts back in line. This couldn't have been happening at a worse time. The Day of the Dead Festival was just two days away. I would need to tell Cora and the board what Steven Zhou suspected and that he needed more personnel. Of course, they were going to freak out.

I could predict how Eileen Simpson was going to react. She would want to do whatever it took to maintain the illusion everything was fine, which would mean no OA nerds anywhere. Dan Berman would probably agree with her. I thought Cora would take my side, but Charlie was a wild card, and Hernan would do whatever he thought would protect his board seat in the recall election.

But if Steve and his team discovered something that would help keep the Day of the Dead Festival safe or if they helped us to prepare for whatever might be coming our way, we would be much better off if his team had access.

But I would have to call Cora.

"Okay, Steven, yes," I said. "Yes, you can do it. Send me the list of names, and I'll get them to the guards. But here's the deal: they are not Occult Affairs researchers. They are with the U.S. Geological Survey, and they're working on new maps. I repeat,

Debra Castaneda

they are *not* from Occult Affairs, and if anyone asks, that's what they need to stay. Got it?"

"Got it," Steve said. "I'll get you that list ASAP."

When we finally ended the call, my hands were trembling slightly. I called Cora Bernal to give her the bad news.

225

Chapter 38

I needed to tell my team about Steven Zhou's plan, so I called an emergency meeting for late morning, after everyone had done their morning rounds looking for new entity emergence holes.

It would also give me an opportunity to introduce Augustina Paz, who showed up carrying a covered container and wearing a white sweater, black jeans, and sturdy black boots. She looked much younger than she had in a dress and jacket. The jeans showed off her figure to its best advantage. It was obvious the woman took her workouts seriously. And from the pumpkins dangling from her ears, she took Halloween seriously, too.

Augustina walked into the command center, nodding hello to the new faces and smiling nervously.

She set down the container on a table and lifted the lid. "I hope you all don't mind, but I brought cupcakes. They're German chocolate."

From the number of people who charged the table, no one minded.

"I love German chocolate," Bailey cried. "Did you make these?" She lifted a cupcake, eyeing it with admiration.

It was so perfect it looked like it could have won an award on one of those TV baking shows.

Augustina nodded, gold curls bouncing. "I did. I love baking. And I'm so happy to be here." She turned to me and continued. "When I was driving in, I pulled up next to a large van. I recognized Steve Zhou and some of the other researchers from OA, so you can imagine my surprise when they followed me through the La Loma gate." She lifted her eyebrows. "I thought OA wasn't allowed in here. Is there something going on?"

What a way to start a meeting. Everyone who needed to be in the room had arrived, so I introduced Augustina.

"Everyone, I'd like you to meet Augustina Paz. She's joining the team effective today. Those of you who came from Occult Affairs will recognize her name. For the rest of you, she is a highly regarded officer. She was one of the first to deal with entities when they originally appeared, and she was instrumental in establishing the Occult Affairs division. I'm very excited she is joining us, and I think you'll all enjoy working with her."

There was a polite round of applause while Augustina gave a little wave.

"Now, as to your question, Augustina…There *is* something going on. And remember, everybody, as usual, what we talk about in these meetings stays here. We'll be doing some sensitive research, and we don't need people jumping to conclusions before we have all the facts."

I then recounted what Steve had told me and watched the reactions roll across the faces of my team. Only Augustina appeared composed. When I was done, the room exploded with questions, and I spent the next ten minutes answering them as well as I could.

Bailey's hand shot up. "What are we going to do about the Day of the Dead Festival? Are we going to cancel it?"

"No!" Justin cried. "We can't do that! My wife's family is coming from all over. My in-laws got tickets to that dinner they're having at Muertos Café and everything."

Bailey snorted. "Perfect. Maybe some more ghouls will show up at La Loma Plaza and give them a show. That'll be fun."

"I hate to think what a next-level ghoul is like," Liam said with a shudder. "We had a hell of a time with the last one, even with those pouches you made us."

"Speaking of pouches, boss," Ron said. "Is there something you can make? To help us deal with whatever might be coming?"

Augustina's eyes flicked from Ron to me. "I heard about those pouches. Some sort of magic-infused stuff?"

I bit my lip so hard it hurt. Even though everyone knew I practiced brujería—although not all the details—I still felt awkward discussing it in meetings. It seemed wrong somehow. A weird blending of my official and unofficial lives.

"Yes," I said quickly, eager to move on. "Ron, pouches may be a possibility at some point, but I have to know exactly what I'm dealing with to produce anything that's effective, and even then, there's a bit of trial and error. We'll just have to wait. Unfortunately."

I cleared my throat.

"So, here's the plan. I'd like everyone to continue looking for new holes. If you find any, let me and Steve know. Immediately. He'll rush someone over to the location. They're not here for very long, so I don't have to tell you how important it is for them to gather as much data as possible. When we're done here, I'm sending out a message letting residents know about the 'surveyors.' Cora is in the loop, so you shouldn't have to worry about the board for the moment."

Since I had the team together, we went over the security plans for the festival before I ended the meeting.

"What would you like me to do?" Augustina asked.

"Why don't I take you for a quick lunch, and we can talk about a few things? Then you can join Bailey and Justin. They're going on patrol in Phantom's Pass. It would be good for you to get familiar with that area. It's got quite a history."

"Sounds good. Let me hit the ladies first." She crossed the room toward the door.

Ron stared after her, frowning. "How old is she, anyway? Is she going to be able to keep up?"

Augustina had just turned forty-nine, but it was none of Ron's business. Before I could scold him, Liam laughed and clapped him on the back, maybe a little too hard.

"She could kick your ass in the field, dude. Last week, I heard she bench-pressed two trolls."

Ron blinked. "Wait, like, literally?"

"No, you idiot," Liam said. "But she is into CrossFit, and I have seen her in the field. I've also seen *you* in the field, and I know who I'd bet on."

Ron reared his head back. "I'm not that bad."

"No," Liam said, patting his shoulder. "You're not. But, dude, you gotta watch your mouth. That's not how we talk about our teammates."

Ouch. But Ron deserved it. That message coming from a peer meant more than if it had come from me.

Ron looked properly chastised. Those remaining in the room trooped out, and Augustina and I headed off for lunch and a chat.

——❖·❖· ⧊⧊⧊ ·❖·❖——

Stu and Clare were coming over for pizza night, so after a long, busy, and worrisome day, I stopped at Agostino's, picked up a couple of pies, and stashed them in the oven to keep warm.

Pizza night was usually at Stu's, but I had been feeling guilty for leaving Sam alone so much. I figured he deserved a little company. Not that he would notice.

I fed him his favorite treats while I tidied up the house and set out fresh hand towels in the bathroom. Sam wasn't the only one I had been neglecting lately. I went into the sunroom, dusted my workbench, and updated Little Lencha about everything going on in Chavez Ravine. Her clay eyes seemed to watch me warily, as if suspecting I was about to ask for her help again. The figurine didn't light up like she used to do, and I found I missed it. I missed her. Her constant presence.

But maybe I didn't need her quite as much anymore. I told her about the Dia de los Muertos altars going up, and I could have sworn she perked up at that.

Just when I was walking out of the room, she glowed orange—the same bright shade as the marigolds Ben and the gnomes had planted all over Chavez Ravine.

Stu arrived first, still wearing a sharp gray suit and red tie. He looked delicious.

Thirty seconds into a hot kiss that turned my insides into a velvety lava flow, Stu pulled away with a yelp. "Ow!"

Something big, red, and furry darted away.

Stu bent over and rubbed his ankle. "He hasn't done that for a while. I wonder what got into him."

I pulled Stu into the light of the living room and inspected his pants. No rips or tears. Sam must have aimed for the sock. "I think he likes to remind us he's the alpha male asshole of the house."

Stu started walking toward the bedroom. "Maybe if we move to neutral territory, he'll calm down. You know. A new place together."

I leaned against the door frame, arms crossed, watching Stu change into joggers. "Did you just ask me to move in with you?"

Stu continued dressing, avoiding eye contact. "I guess I did. It's something I've been thinking about for a while."

"Have you, now?"

Stu walked toward me and put his hands on my shoulders. "I think I just screwed that up. Let me try again." He looked me in the eye and took a deep breath.

"Maddy, I love every minute I spend with you, and I'd like to experience as many of those minutes as possible. I think we should move in together, and I really hope you agree."

The truth was I'd thought about moving in together too, but I'd been so distracted I'd pushed the thought to the back of my mind. Hearing Stu's words, it came rushing right back up to the front.

"You really should work on your presentation, but I like the way you think, Mr. Wells."

Stu's eyebrows twitched. "Does that mean you agree?"

I put my hands on his hips and pulled him closer.

"I agree."

I lifted my face to meet his and we kissed again. The lava flowed once more, and it was even hotter than before.

I started calculating how long those pizzas would keep in the oven, when something struck me and I pulled away.

"Wait, when you say 'neutral territory,' are you talking about moving to my new property?"

He winked. "Yeah. It's a great location. I sell my house, and we use the money for a custom build. You can ask your construction buddy Rory Tuck if he wants to take it on."

"You've really given this a lot of thought."

Stu went back to the closet and pulled an ancient T-shirt over his head. "I have, actually. My house is too big and not your style. This place is too small. We can hire Julia to help with the decorating."

I was a bit stunned. "What about this house?"

"You can't sell it. It wouldn't be right. It belonged to your grandmother." Stu nudged his work shoes against the wall where we wouldn't trip over them.

My house was small and cozy. The right size for me, but it felt a bit crowded when Stu stayed over.

Stu took my elbow and guided me back into the living room, where he headed straight for the wine cabinet. He grabbed a nice bottle and uncorked it.

"Here's what I'm thinking. I don't see any reason to wait. I'll put my house on the market. It'll go quick, I'm sure. Everything does around here. That'll free up the money for us to start work on our new place. We can live here during the construction. Clare will be off at college next year, and as long as we promise her a bedroom at the new place, she won't mind. What do you think? Too much too soon?" He poured out the wine.

It all seemed to make the most perfect sense in the world. But it had come out of the blue.

"I think I like it," I said slowly. "I just need a bit more time to process it."

Stu went into the kitchen and came back with a dish towel. He polished two glasses until they sparkled in the lamplight. "Take as much time as you need," he said gently.

The front door flew open, and the moment was over. Clare came stomping in and flopped on the couch. She threw an arm over her forehead like a fainting Victorian maiden.

"What a day! You won't *believe* what happened!" She paused, then sat up and threw her arms wide. "Isn't anyone going to ask me what happened?"

Stu and I exchanged looks. He shrugged and nodded at me.

"Okay, what happened?" I asked.

Clare folded herself into a sitting position, back straight. Her dark eyes glittered with excitement. "Jason Wood is out. *Out!* As in, fired!"

Whatever I had been expecting, it wasn't that. With everything going on, I had completely forgotten to follow up with Becca. "Really? What happened?" My voice was faint.

"We're not totally sure, but Theo told me it had to do with Mia, the dancer. Apparently, Jason had been harassing her, and Theo had been telling her to make a complaint. Jason had sent her a bunch of creepy text messages and pictures and stuff, so she had evidence. Theo thinks she must have done it because neither of them showed up today. And then the assistant director made an announcement that Jason was off the music video and that he was taking over. It was absolutely insane."

"That'll make Pete happy," Stu said. "He really soured on Jason. Said he was nuts."

Clare clutched a pillow to her stomach. "And mean. *Really* mean. They finished shooting my scenes, so I'm all done. I don't have to go back unless the new guy decides he wants to reshoot something I'm in. But it better not be tomorrow because tomorrow is the Halloween soccer tournament and I'm sure they'll let me play 'cause I've got my mojo back. Thanks to Maddy."

She blew me a kiss. I pretended to catch it.

I gave Stu a little push toward the kitchen. "Let's eat our pizza, and we'll get caught up on everything. There's some stuff happening with those new entity holes, too."

Clare jumped up from the couch and twirled past us. "And I'll tell you all about the new guy I met on a group chat college thing. He's so unbelievably hot, and he plays soccer too."

So much for Theo. Turned out Clare had been completely in charge the entire time.

Chapter 39

On Dia de los Muertos, Sam and the gnomes had the day off. Ben and I decided it was best for them to stay out of sight with so many visitors coming in from the outside. The gnomes didn't seem to mind the break, and Sam enjoyed taking flying leaps at the tissue paper banners I had hung around the house. The fluttering of the papel picado symbolized the fragility of life. That was never truer than when Sam was attacking them.

My mother and Hernan stopped by to deliver things for my altar. Hernan seemed genuinely concerned about my ability to pull off an authentic ofrenda. I didn't mind the help. It was nice, and I practically cried when my mother presented me with several framed black and white photographs Hernan had dug up from the archives.

There was one of my grandmother, Liliana Bantacorte, and another of Lencha that I had never seen before. She was staring straight at the camera, a defiant expression on her lined face, her single, long braid pulled forward onto her blouse.

The third photo took my breath away. A rugged, handsome face stared at me, with a scar running down his cheek and a thin pencil mustache above his lips.

"Ripper," I whispered.

My mother tapped the frame. "He was a handsome devil, wasn't he?"

I sighed. "He was. And a good man too."

"Did he look like that?" Hernan asked, patting my arm. "When he came back?"

He had been even more handsome, but it would have felt weird to say that aloud. "Yes. Yes, he looked just like that." My mouth had gone dry. "Thank you," I croaked. "Thank you so much." When I turned around and hugged them, my eyes were wet with tears.

In the driveway, a car horn blasted. Sam raced into the kitchen, and a moment later, we could hear his clawed feet scrabble across the countertops.

"That cat has no business on the counters, where all the food is. It's unhygienic!" my mother snapped.

"Who's out there?" I asked. "Did you leave someone in the car?"

"It's the Mendez ladies. We're all going to Muertos Café. They were booked up for dinner, but your mother got us reservations for lunch in exchange for doing some readings on the patio."

I was doubly shocked. First, that my mother had agreed to barter her valuable services, and second, that Ron's mother and grandmother were part of the lunch group.

"I thought you were sworn enemies with those ladies?"

My mother threw back her head and laughed. "Oh, Maddy, don't exaggerate. They're old friends. Even friends can have their differences, can't they, Hernie?"

I stifled a snicker. *Hernie* had the grace to blush.

"Ay, yes, they can. All has been forgiven."

"Forgiven!" I echoed. "They were trying to boot your nalgas off the board. What happened to the recall petition?"

My mother tittered at the mention of "nalgas." It was one of few things we had in common. The Spanish word for "butt" turned us into eleven-year-old boys.

Hernan smoothed the front of his black sweater vest. I wondered how many of those he owned.

"They finally saw reason and changed their minds about the petition. After all, the gnomes turned out to be just fine."

"Can they withdraw it like that?" I asked. "After getting all the signatures and sending it to the board?"

Hernan nodded. "Cora hadn't issued the recall notice yet, so the Mendez ladies were able to send in a formal withdrawal." He winked and pretended to wipe sweat from his brow.

It was hard to imagine the two ladies I had met changing their minds about anything, but that was none of my business. I was just glad Hernan would stay on in his role. He could be just as annoying inside the boardroom as he was outside of it, but I had come to appreciate his support.

"Well," I said. "I'm glad that's over."

When they left, I swept up the shredded bits of colorful tissue paper and hung two more banners with a strict warning to Sam to leave them alone. I dressed in gray pants and a dark green trench coat and headed out to see how the festival was progressing.

It had already been a long day. I had spent the morning watching Steven Zhou and his nerd colleagues poke long sticks into holes and holler numbers while someone jotted down notes on a clipboard. It all looked very scientific and quite mysterious.

I was really looking forward to enjoying the festival. After the curses, questions, and accomplishments of the past few weeks, I needed some downtime with friends.

Though the puzzle of the new emergence holes hung over my head, those were, for the moment, Steven Zhou's problem. Clare had survived not only the imaginary threat posed by Theo, but also the very real one from Jason Wood. My friends who had lost their talents to an old curse were back at full capacity, turning out music, food, artwork, performances, and top-notch landscape design once again. And Clare was back to her old self, scoring three goals in her Halloween soccer tournament.

By the time I pulled into my parking space at Palo Verde Plaza, the festival was in full swing. It was early November but still unseasonably cool, a chilly-for-Los-Angeles fifty-two degrees.

I walked through the stalls on the plaza, slowly moving through the hordes of visitors. Julia was swamped at her booth. She had sold out of her Catrina figurines in two hours, and her signed prints were going fast. People were crowded around her, asking if she took orders.

She looked joyful in her bright pink sweater and a long, swirling black skirt with red roses. Her auburn hair was swept up into a messy bun, and tiny skeletons dangled from her ears. Julia spotted me and blew a kiss, then bent her head over her clipboard. I left her alone to tend to her customers.

All the booths were doing a booming business, especially those selling pan de muerto, or bread of the dead—a light, sweet yeast bread. Strips of dough formed a skull and crossbones.

The stalls seemed to be selling a little bit of everything: incense burners in the shape of skulls, skull masks, champurrado, dancing figurines with wide-brimmed hats, and lots of jewelry.

The shops in the plaza had gotten into the spirit by decorating their windows with skeletons of clay, paper mâché, and wood. Life-sized skeletons flanked the main entrances to the plazas.

Later in the afternoon, I found Hernan in his element, giving hourly talks about Day of the Dead in the community library.

He was standing next to a large screen, clicking through slides. "The dead are not forgotten. They are not separate from the living, and woe is the family who does not care for their departed ones."

That sounded a bit dramatic, but his audience was eating it up.

"Dia de los Muertos is a beautiful tradition, and at the heart is the ofrenda, an altar for the dead. Most people create their ofrendas inside, but with the festival, we also wanted to build public ofrendas outside so everyone can enjoy them. So today, you'll see the altars all around Chavez Ravine."

And that they would. In fact, the ofrendas had turned out so beautifully that Eileen Simpson arranged for a fleet of golf carts to take visitors around to see them. Which helped reduce traffic and made it easier for my security team to patrol the streets on their e-bikes. Eileen had even ordered festival-branded decals that everyone could add to their orange Chavez Ravine polo shirts.

I was tempted to ask if she'd had Julia's buy-in before she ordered them, but I decided I could forego the jab in honor of the holiday.

Augustina had been assigned to the command center, and I moved Ron to field duty. Both seemed pleased with the change. Ron because it let him experience the hustle and bustle of the festival and the food stalls, and Augustina because she was eager to run things. I was glad to have her there; I was confident Augustina could handle the command center with minimal fuss.

When the sun began to go down, I met Stu and Clare, and we stood in line for a golf cart tour. I laughed when Charlie Perez pulled up. Stu and I climbed into the back while Clare sat in front, clutching a paper mâché skeleton she had picked up after long deliberation at one of the stalls. Stu's arm went around my shoulders when the cart lurched forward, and we all laughed.

Charlie was a good tour guide. The altars were everywhere. People emerged from their houses, lighting candles in tall glasses and flicking on twinkly lights. Beautiful fabrics covered the wooden structures. Reds, gold, purples. One altar was covered in gold brocade. Some had awnings. Others had arbors of greenery topped with marigolds. There were vases of fresh flowers and piles of pan de muerto.

When we rolled past another altar, Clare pointed. "Look, someone left out chocolate!"

Charlie made a sharp right, and we all listed to the side and laughed again. It was a bit like being on an amusement park ride. "You gotta see this one," he said, pulling up to a large altar in front of a massive home.

A half dozen male skeletons, each about four feet high, wearing white suits and red sombreros, danced around a skeleton woman in a floral dress, with a crown of flowers on her head.

"Is that Frida Khalo?" Stu asked.

"It is," Charlie said. "And look. They even included her dogs. I can never remember what they're called."

"Mexican Hairless describes them pretty well," I replied. The dogs were dark gray and regal, and their eyes sparkled at us from under the spotlights.

When we drove along the street where Ripper and his crew of street fighters had helped to battle the vampire birds, I thought of them and felt a lump rise in my throat. If I could choose anyone to visit me from the land of the dead, it would have been those guys. But they deserved to rest in peace, and I wasn't sure my heart could take watching them fade away again.

It was almost as if Charlie knew what I was thinking. He drove to my house and stopped the cart. "How about I leave you off here? You're going to Olga's, right? It's an easier walk from here."

Clare jumped out of the cart and clapped her hands. "Oh my god, Maddy! Your altar looks so pretty. And who's this guy?" She lifted a photo from the altar and whirled around. "Is he your grandfather or something? He's, like, practically hot."

Stu laughed. "That doesn't sound very respectful, Clare."

Charlie beckoned me over and leaned toward me. "So far so good, right? It's been a great festival. Good food, great music, no chupacabras…"

I smiled. "Yeah, this time, everything went our way."

I gave Sam his dinner, kissed him on his big head, and sprinkled some fish-flavored treats on his food. Then Stu, Clare, and I walked to La Loma Plaza, admiring the altars while I told them what little I knew about the life of Ripper Cuevas. Clare was enthralled.

"It sounds like a movie," Clare said dreamily.

We met Julia and Ben outside Olga's Cantina. Olga herself came out of the kitchen when she saw me at the host station and walked us to a candlelit table on the patio. A few propane heaters kept the chill at bay. A server quickly came by with a stack of colorful blankets and handed them around.

"Street tacos or regular tacos?" Ben asked, tapping his chin as if posing a very important question.

"Street tacos!" Julia and I said.

We ordered mezcal flights with some appetizers, and within a few minutes, I was feeling a little tipsy. The stuff was stronger than I had remembered, and I vowed to switch to red wine.

So, when I heard a buzzing sound, I assumed it was the mezcal at work. But the sound began to rise around us—a sharp hum coming from the edges of the patio, where the Saltillo tiles gave way to a garden bordering three sides.

I turned in my chair toward the source of the noise. Stu looked around, his mouth opening slightly. Julia stared at her empty mezcal glasses as if they were responsible for the racket. Clare was peering into the dark corners of the garden. Ben appeared frozen.

Other people on the patio had noticed too and were looking around, as if expecting to be attacked by a swarm of bees.

"Does everyone hear that?" I tried to keep my voice calm, but I sounded panicked.

Then another buzzing sound—my phone vibrating on the white tablecloth. When I reached for it, an alert blasted from the tiny speaker. One long, awful note. I picked up the call. It was Augustina.

"I'm so sorry to bother you, Maddy, but we have a problem," she said. "It's the heatmap. It's blowing up."

The feelings of joy and peace I had felt at the beginning of the festival were gone. I didn't know what was causing the terrible sound, but I had never heard anything like it, and I was certain it wasn't from our world.

Whatever data Steve Zhou and his team had gathered, it was too late to help us now. We were past analysis, beyond investigation. My protection spell had failed. My glowing hands told me we were under attack.

"Maddy?" Augustina asked, her voice rising. "Can you hear me?"

Ice ran through my veins. I wasn't sure what was happening, but I wasn't about to wait.

"Everyone inside," I shouted. "Inside! Now!"

Author's note

Thank you so much for joining me on Maddy Madrigal's journey through book five! I'm already deep into writing the sixth installment, so you won't have to wait long to see what happens after that cliffhanger.

If you'd like to be the first to hear about release dates (and get a peek behind the scenes), I'd love for you to join my newsletter at debracastaneda.com. It's also one of my favorite ways to stay connected with readers.

And if social media is more your style, you can find me on Facebook at Castanedawrites—come say hello!

Debra Castaneda

Keep reading for a preview of

A CHAVEZ RAVINE STORY

THE NIGHT LADY

DEBRA CASTANEDA

The Night Lady
Chapter 1

Los Angeles, July 1950

Jane Acevedo, on the lookout for the boogeyman, crept along the fence of her front yard, using the vines as cover. It was getting dark, and her mother had said she couldn't play with the other kids down the street. Not unless she wanted El Cucuy to snatch her away and drink her blood.

So far, all she'd seen with her pretend binoculars were her neighbors coming and going, but then she spotted Catalina Montez, the beautiful lady who lived down the road. Jane got to see her plenty at the empty lot across the street where Catalina grew plants for her cures. Her remedies were famous—even better than Vick's VapoRub.

Jane stood on an overturned washtub so she could get a better view. Blood dripped down Catalina's face. It made Jane feel all wobbly, but she couldn't stop watching, like a scary movie at The Brooklyn—she had to know what happened next. Besides, she'd been so bored having to stay in the front yard with nobody to talk to, and nothing much ever happened in Palo Verde.

And just like a movie, the door of the house next to the garden banged open, and Espy Gaten gave a dramatic cry, then ran down the steps. Espy, with her hair tied up in a scarf, didn't resemble a movie star like Catalina, but she was pretty too, just taller and skinnier. Espy helped Catalina into the house.

Jane would have loved to find out what was going on, but her mother didn't allow her to step foot past the gate. Not unless Jane wanted a swat on the *nalgas*. But Catalina with blood all over her face was even better than the gorilla girl matinee she'd seen. And besides, she was only going across the street. Jane checked for her mother to make sure she was still hanging laundry in the backyard, and she was.

Jane dashed across the dirt road and around the side of Espy's house, skirted the wild roses and thorns, then flattened herself against the fence so the *nopales* cactus wouldn't scratch her. Luckily, the kitchen window was open, and that's where the two women were, huddled together. She could hear Catalina crying, and when she managed a peek inside, standing on her tiptoes, she saw Catalina's torn dress, busted lip, and blood coming from an ugly cut above her eyebrow.

Jane couldn't picture Catalina getting into a fight like Uncle Beto. Maybe she'd fallen, or maybe someone got mad at her for one of her cures going wrong. But that was also hard to imagine— Catalina Montez was the most famous *curandera* around.

Keeping one eye on the front door of her house to make sure her mother didn't appear—in which case she planned to make straight for the back alley, jump a fence or two, and end up in her own backyard—Jane peered through the window again. Espy was walking back and forth in front of the stove as Catalina sat, looking as miserable as a kid on the first day of school.

"We should call the police," Espy said, in the same tone of voice Jane's mother used to threaten Uncle Beto.

"No, no, no," Catalina moaned.

The healer muttered something Jane couldn't hear, then the two women switched to Spanish, which Jane understood well enough to know they were having a secret conversation. Espy asked if Catalina couldn't hex the man who had done that to her, and Catalina said he deserved the worst magic she could summon, even if it meant she had to call on Santa Muerte herself. At this, Jane shivered because her mother would not even allow her to mention the saint of death with the face of a skeleton. But Jane's thoughts were spinning elsewhere.

Magic. *Magia*.

The two women talked about magic as if it were real, and Jane remembered something her mother had said about Catalina, that she wasn't just a healer but a *bruja*, a witch. Jane's father said there was no such thing, which had surprised Jane because if he believed in *El Cucuy* and *La Llorona*—and he did because he always said if Jane didn't behave, they'd get her—then how could he not believe in brujas?

"But we can't just let him get away with it," Espy said in a loud voice.

Catalina stood, slowly enough for Jane to hunker down so they wouldn't see her. "I'll figure out a way, Espy, and he'll be sorry he ever touched me. Can you help me home?"

"Why don't you stay here? You shouldn't be alone. Not after everything you've been through."

"I just want to take a bath. In my own place."

"Then I'll go with you," Espy said firmly.

A chair scraped against wood, and Jane knew it was time to get going. By the time the two ladies left the little house, Jane was standing on her own front porch. She watched them walk down the street.

When they disappeared from view, Jane put on her pretend binoculars, searching for the bad man who hurt Catalina.

Books by Debra Castaneda

Maddy Madrigal Mysteries
Monsters, mayhem, and Mexican food

Barely Magic
Maddy lands a cushy security job in a gated community but must confront a supernatural threat and come to terms with her magical heritage.

Somewhat Magic
In the heart of Los Angeles, Maddy Madrigal battles legendary creatures and unscrupulous developers as an old protective spell begins to fail.

Desperate Magic
Maddy Madrigal must unravel a web of supernatural clues and confront ancient predators to stop a string of brutal murders.

Mortal Magic
Something ancient and deadly is roosting outside Chavez Ravine, and Maddy's weapons, magic, and extremely agitated cat aren't enough to fight it off.

Tangled Magic
Maddy must combine her magic and detective skills to put an end to a dangerous and powerful legacy. But HOA politics and a dangerous romance get in the way.

Dark Earth Rising
Themed novels that can be read in any order

A Dark and Rising Tide
When a massive storm surge hits the central coast of California, the ferocious surf destroys buildings, floods streets, and washes up something sinister from the depths of the Monterey Bay.

The Devil's Shallows
Eight miles of mystery. One night of terror. Residents trapped in a remote neighborhood confront the unimaginable.

The Copper Man
Haunted tunnels. Unexplained deaths. Eerie sightings. Decades after The Copper Man killed her brother, Leah Shaw returns to the remote mining town of Tribulation Gulch where a lethal mystery awaits.

The Root Witch
A beautiful forest. A terrifying legend. It's 1986. Two strangers, hundreds of miles apart, grapple with disturbing incidents in a one-of-a-kind quaking aspen forest.

Circus at Devil's Landing
Creatures that howl in the night, a mysterious circus, and a clash between a ringmaster and a woman determined to rescue her captured lover.

The Spore Queen

A charming reporter, an ailing tech mogul, and two strangers hiding secrets are brought together by a mysterious fungus, one that will either save them or destroy them.

Chavez Ravine Novels

Stand-alone novels set in Chavez Ravine, Los Angeles during turbulent times

The Monsters of Chavez Ravine

A 2021 International Latino Book Awards Gold Medal Winner! Before Dodger Stadium, dark forces terrorized Chavez Ravine.

The Night Lady

A rebel curandera, a plucky seamstress, and a young reporter are pulled into the investigation of a killer terrorizing Chavez Ravine.

The Haunting of Chavez Ravine

La Llorona is terrorizing people in the hills of Chavez Ravine, and a sassy curandera and her clever young niece must stop her.

The Christmas Cucuy

It's Christmas Eve, 1949, and Kiki's dreams are about to come true: she'll be singing at Palladium with her old bandmates. But when she threatens her rambunctious son with El Cucuy, her plans change.